THE CENTENARY CORBIÈRE

THE CENTENARY CORBIÈRE

Poems and Prose of Tristan Corbière

Translated and with an Introduction
by Val Warner

A CARCANET NEW PRESS PUBLICATION

First published 1974
by Carcanet New Press Limited
266 Councillor Lane
Cheadle Hulme, Cheadle
Cheshire SK8 5PN

Acknowledgements are due to the editors of the following magazines, in which some of these translations, or earlier versions, have appeared: *The Anglo-Welsh Review*, *The Dublin Magazine*, *The Honest Ulsterman*, *Ostrich*, *Poetry Nation*, *Poetry Review* and *Samphire*.

The translator acknowledges assistance from the Arts Council of Great Britain.

Printed in Great Britain
by W & J Mackay Limited, Chatham

CONTENTS

Introduction

That winter night of 1883, during which we read in turn, Trézenik
and I, the precious volume, from the first to the last page, to the
master of *Sagesse*[. . . .]
    Unforgettable hours! [. . .] Verlaine laughed continuously, and,
in the most moving, the most poignant passages, his laughter inter-
rupted us: laughter that held tears.*

This picture of Verlaine's introduction to *Les Amours jaunes*,
published ten years earlier without any success, recalls Villon's
'je ris en pleurs'. Tristan Corbière (1845–75) who, apart from this
book wrote only a handful of other poems and several prose pieces,
died quite unknown. Verlaine subsequently publicized Corbière
as one of his 'poètes maudits', but he characterized him primarily
as a Breton poet, and at least in France, this misleading description has died hard.† As Pound wrote, denying that Corbière lost
force 'on leaving the sea-board': 'His language does not need any
particular subject matter, or prefer one to another.'[1] There seem
fewer grounds for any modification of the anti-religious attitude
attributed to Corbière by Verlaine, and for the attempt to
synthesize into a polarized 'moral structure'[2] the Parisian and
Breton sections of the book. Even so, underestimating Corbière's
technique, Verlaine did not recognize the pragmatic unity in
which the voices of 'Breton bretonnant' and 'poète maudit' have
been combined.

    It is partly as a result of this belittling of Corbière's technique
even by his admirers, such as Huysmans, Laforgue and de
Gourmont, that 'Corbière has remained a curiosity.'[3] Although
in France Corbière's work influenced the later symbolists and
subsequent writers, like Villon's, it is particularly sympathetic to
English-speaking readers. Interest in the influence he exerted on

    * 'Cette nuit de l'hiver de 1883, durant laquelle nous lûmes, Trézenik et
moi, tour à tour, le précieux volume, de sa première à sa dernière page, au
maître de *Sagesse* [. . . .]
    Inoubliables heures![. . .] Verlaine ne cessa de rire, et, aux passages les plus
émouvants, les plus poignants, son rire nous interrompait: du rire où il y avait
des larmes.' Charles Morice, *Tristan Corbière*, Paris, 1912, p. 22.
    † Jean Rousselot and Henri Thomas are outstanding exceptions to this
generalization.

Pound and Eliot has focused attention on Corbière in his own right. A strong line of Anglo-American criticism has emerged: the best general study of Corbière remains Albert Sonnenfeld's (despite his highly questionable conclusions), and Francis Burch and Marshall Lindsay have followed his example in publishing their books in French.

Yet the biography of Corbière remains to be written, and it will be weakened by the loss of correspondence, especially with his aunt, Mme Le Bris, and with Marcelle. Only one letter of Corbière's adult life has survived. Ida Levi has investigated the disappearance of the rest:

> I have ascertained from his relatives that they were destroyed by Corbière's father and by his sister Lucie who were anxious not to let details of the private life of the family become public. It is interesting to notice that they took care only to preserve a large number of letters belonging to the period 1860–62 (when Corbière was at school at Saint-Brieuc and at Nantes), which show a morbid attachment to the family and particularly to his father.[4]

It was felt necessary to insert a note[5] in the 1912 edition of *Les Amours jaunes* to the effect that the poet's sister and brother-in-law disassociated themselves from 'the legend of ugliness and misanthropy' that had grown up around Corbière. More recently, the rehabilitation by the nephew, Jean Vacher-Corbière, in *Tristan Corbière, portrait de famille* (1955) may be contrasted with Rousselot's *Tristan Corbière* (1951), with its hints of transvestism and stories of brothels. Even posthumously, Corbière seems unable to escape from his Charleville.

At one time, the bourgeois of Morlaix, in Brittany, accused even Corbière's father, the novelist, Édouard Corbière (1793–1875), of undue 'originality' in his varied occupations,[6] but he had a substantial position in the town, becoming President of the Chamber of Commerce there in 1842. Once called the French Fenimore Cooper, Édouard Corbière had a remarkable career for a man who left school at fourteen, basing his novels on his experiences at sea, where he rose from cabin-boy to captain. His sickly eldest son could not hope to emulate the active side of his father's success story.

It has been suggested that Corbière's illness stemmed from the discrepancy in his parents' age: his father was thirty-two years

senior to his mother, Marie-Angélique-Aspasie Puyo,* whom he married late in life in 1844. Whatever its cause, the first great crisis of sickness came when Corbière was sixteen, leading to the premature termination of his school studies, and thereafter he was deformed by arthritis, later exacerbated by the first symptoms of TB, which finally killed him. His younger brother, Edmond, also turned out unsatisfactorily, becoming a dipsomaniac.[7] All his life Corbière depended on subsidies from his father, who also defrayed half the expenses of printing *Les Amours jaunes*.

From Laforgue on, critics have underestimated Corbière's curtailed education, but it is clear he had a good grounding, with a heavy emphasis on Latin.[8] *Les Amours jaunes* abounds in references to 'the great poets whom I've read',† often unacknowledged or parodied. He made use of classical allusions only after his trip to Italy 1869–70 had apparently brought them to life.[9] The dominant literary influence was his father, to whom, as 'l'auteur du *Négrier*', he was later to dedicate *Les Amours jaunes*. In 1860, Corbière wrote to his father, 'Also (with no less modesty) I have an idea that one day I'll be a great man, that I'll write a *Négrier*[. . .]'.‡ At an even younger age, Corbière seems to have totally identified Captain Léonard, the hero of *Le Négrier*, with his father, who had based the character on himself. Alexandre Arnoux imaginatively reconstructs a scene with the young Corbière reading the proofs of a later edition of this book over his father's shoulder, spellbound.[10]

As the letters translated here indicate, Corbière's father expected much of his son, who in turn was at pains to please him. The fifty letters that have survived from his schooldays show his fear of losing his parents' affection by low marks. This fear was worsened by his intense loneliness at school: 'Here I have no one who likes

---

* In the light of the first line of the first sonnet in the 'Paris' sequence in 'Ça', 'Bâtard de Créole et Breton', there has been speculation that Corbière's mother, whose name is not known in Brittany and about whom very little is known, could have been of West Indian descent, encountered on one of Édouard Corbière's voyages.

† '[. . .] Des grands poètes que j'ai lus!', from 'Un jeune qui s'en va', *Œuvres complètes de Tristan Corbière*, ed. P.-O. Walzer, 'Bibliothèque de la Pléiade', Paris, 1970, p. 730.

‡ 'J'ai aussi (avec non moins de modestie) dans la tête que je serai un jour un grand homme, que je ferai un *Négrier*[. . .]', quoted from Henri Matarasso, 'Tristan Corbière: Lettres à son père', *Les Lettres nouvelles*, 19 (Sept. 1954), pp. 426–7.

me and who means anything to me to encourage me or make me patient.'* This outburst was provoked by the persecution of an usher, who even taunted the boy with his appearance. Soon, illness and the resulting ugliness, which in any càse Corbière exaggerated, combined to produce a complex of pariah, leading Pol Kalig† to call him 'a repressed soft heart'.‡

Acutely as Corbière missed his home, he seems to have been especially attached to Le Launay, the home of his aunt, Mme Le Bris (*née* Puyo). Corbière later brought her§ a sheep's heart, saying, 'Here is my heart!'‖ Pol Kalig wrote: 'Two people have known him, his aunt Mme X . . . and me. . .'.¶ Of Corbière's correspondence with his aunt, a little of which he had read, Pol Kalig wrote: 'Corbière has poured all his soul and spirit into these letters in the nicest prose it has been my lot to enjoy.'**

Nevertheless, Corbière's mother, at least in later life, came to regard him as an ugly duckling.[11] What we know of Corbière's attitude to his mother merely reflects the dominant role of his father in his life. He made a practice of referring to his mother as his wife, and to his brother-in-law as his son-in-law.[12] The latter's copy of *Les Amours jaunes* has survived, inscribed in this way. Very significant in this context is the poem 'Le mousse' (p. 110), describing how, 'I'm her husband on this shore'.

* 'Ici je n'ai personne qui m'aime et qui me dise quelque chose pour m'encourager ou me faire prendre patience.' Quoted by Albert Sonnenfeld, in *L'Œuvre poétique de Tristan Corbière*, Paris, 1960, p. 20, from *Le Goéland*, Autumn 1950, p. 3.

† Pseudonym of Dr Jules Chenantais, Corbière's cousin and friend. He played a major role in publicizing the *Amours jaunes*, lending a copy to Trézenik, who with Morice took it to Verlaine.

‡ 'un tendre comprimé', in an unpublished letter from Pol Kalig to René Martineau, quoted by Micha Grin in *Tristan Corbière, Poète maudit*, Évian, 1972, p. 55.

§ Jean Rousselot states that the recipient was a local prostitute. *Tristan Corbière*, Paris, 1951, p. 70.

‖ ' [. . .] "Tiens, voilà mon cœur!" ' René Martineau, *Tristan Corbière*, Paris, 1904, p. 51.

¶ 'Deux personnes l'ont connu, sa tante Mme X . . . et moi . . .', quoted by René Martineau, in *Tristan Corbière*, Paris, 1904, p. 65.

** 'Correspondance où Corbière a versé toute son âme et son esprit dans la plus jolie prose qu'il m'a été donnée de savourer', from an unpublished letter from Pol Kalig to René Martineau, quoted by Micha Grin in *Tristan Corbière, Poète maudit*, Évian, 1972, p. 55.

Some reaction against his father[13] may be inferred from 1863, when Corbière was medically advised to live at Roscoff; by that time his poor health had imposed an abnormal pattern on his life. It was then that Corbière jettisoned his baptismal name of Édouard, which applied to his father connoted so much glory, and of which he had once been so proud, as a letter included here reveals (p. 168). He had already begun to call himself Tristan, saying of the name, 'Je l'ai pris à mon frère', Tristan of Lyonesse,[14] who must have had an ironic appeal for him as a romantic figure and a sailor. In *La Vie parisienne*, he several times signed his work 'Trist', punning on 'sad'. Typical of the way he turned his life to an endless bitter joke against himself, he called his spaniel Tristan too.

At Roscoff, about twenty miles from Morlaix, his father had a house where the family stayed during the summer, when Corbière retreated to a fisherman's cottage. In winter he returned to the house, sleeping in a boat. His love for the place itself comes out in his poem 'Au vieux Roscoff' (p. 110), where the town is compared to a boat.

> –Sleep, old hull, with a firm painter;
> The ember-goose and the cormorant
> Your great poets of wild weather
> To the tide will descant . . .

But he must have been in an anomalous social position, as the eccentric, apparently idle, son of the substantial fishing magnate of Morlaix. His elaborate practical jokes, in which an antecedent for Dada has been discerned,[15] made him unpopular with the villagers. One of these, who as a child had known Tristan, later recalled him:

'We followed him', said Lédan, 'shouting *An Ankou!* (image of death, the phantom). He continually invented practical jokes in doubtful taste, like making his dog swallow meat balls into which he'd ostentatiously slipped a small gold coin. The local beggars followed the animal until she returned the coin.'*

* ' "Nous le suivions", disait Lédan, "en criant *An Ankou!* (image de la mort, le revenant). Il inventait sans cesse des farces d'un goût douteux, comme de faire avaler à son chien des boulettes où il avait ostensiblement glissé une piécette d'or. Les guenilleux du pays suivaient la bête jusqu'à ce qu'elle

Like his other caricatures of himself, the self-portrait inscribed
with the first four stanzas of the poem 'Sous un portrait de
Corbière', exaggerated his ugliness, as well as mocking his temperament: 'Above the poet's head is a large spider.'*

René Martineau went on to compare this painting to Daumier's
work, to which Corbière's Parisian poems, particularly 'Idylle
coupée', have often been likened. Corbière at first wanted to be a
painter, and there is a tradition in the Vacher-Corbière family of
his skill as a caricaturist, although most of his work has failed to
survive. The etching in the first edition of *Les Amours jaunes* was by
the author himself. At Roscoff, Corbière was the friend of a colony
of artists, including Michel Bouquet, Gaston Lafenestre, Jean-
Louis Hamon, Louis Noir, Dufour, Besnard and Drouet, who
stayed there during the summer.

As a schoolboy Corbière wrote satirical verses, clearly influenced by his father's own early satirical verses, but it must have
been at Roscoff that he began to write seriously, composing the
Breton sections of *Les Amours jaunes* and some of the poems placed
in other sections. Unfortunately, the chronology of the book cannot
be determined with any certainty. Just as Corbière indicated
'Bohème de chic' was written at Jerusalem, when he almost
certainly never travelled beyond Italy, and arranged the locations
of the poems in the section 'Matelots' to suggest a long voyage,
which he could not have taken, the dates scattered through the
book are also often misleading. Only occasionally can a poem be
dated by some contemporary reference, and the date, for instance,
of 'Le convoi du pauvre' could well be correct since Corbière was
in Paris at that period.

Francis Burch suggests that it was Corbière's visit to Italy in 1869
with Hamon that provoked him into writing seriously, since *en
route* they stopped at Florence to see a self-portrait by Hamon
which had recently been publicly hung there. Burch contends that
this made a profound impression on Corbière, since 'at Florence,
for the first time, he had really been struck by Hamon's success'.†

restitue la pièce." ' Charles Lédan, the librarian at Morlaix, quoted by Jean de
Trigon in *Tristan Corbière*, Paris, 1950, pp. 52–3.

* 'Au-dessus de la tête du poète il y a une grosse araignée.' René Martineau,
Tristan Corbière, Paris, 1904, p. 57.

† '[. . .] à Florence il avait été, pour la première fois, pénétré de la réussite
d'Hamon', Francis Burch, *Tristan Corbière*, Paris, 1970, p. 145.

Even if this particular incident were less crucial, the combination of Corbière's literary background and artist friends with his own weak position, debilitated by sickness and financially dependent, must have provoked him into artistic achievement, as at least one avenue open to him.

This motivation of hurt pride must have been sadly enhanced by his love for the 'Marcelle' of *Les Amours jaunes*, the actress Armida Cuchiani, mistress of Count Rodolphe de Battine. The couple arrived in Roscoff in the spring of 1871, and Corbière at once secured an introduction by his usual method of drawing a caricature on the table-cloth. Le Gad, the proprietor of the *pension* where they stayed and where Corbière ate, recalled this conversation that evening: ' "I want to know that woman", he said to me.[. . .] "Yes, I know", he went on, "You think I'm ugly; I want to know her and I'll manage to make her love me." '*

In fact Marcelle was attracted to Tristan. The poem 'À mon cotre *Le Négrier*' marks the sale of *Le Négrier* and the purchase instead of a yacht *Le Tristan*, in which he took Marcelle sailing. But in October 1871 she accompanied Battine back to Paris, where in the spring of 1872, Tristan followed her, for his only long period of residence away from Brittany. 'Le poète contumace' (p. 28), that 'masterpiece of despair',[16] must surely have been written during the previous lonely winter. The 'idylle atroce'[17] continued for the rest of Corbière's life.

Although Corbière published a little in *La Vie parisienne*, in Paris he seems to have mixed only with the painters he had known at Roscoff, and his cousin, Le Bris. His incomplete prose piece, 'L'Atelier', parodying Murger, sketches his life in the capital, which many of the poems, for instance 'L'Idylle coupée', also depict with keen observation. Under Battine's influence he dressed as a dandy, though in his room he still dressed as a Breton sailor. His saddest eccentricity was spending hours making exquisite miniature boats, which he then stamped on. When he was dying, his mother took him back to Brittany, where his father's death followed only a few months after his own.

* ' "Je veux connaître cette femme", me dit-il.[. . .] "Oui, je sais," reprit-il "vous me trouvez laid; je veux la connaître et j'arriverai à me faire aimer d'elle." ' Quoted from Charles Chassé, 'Souvenirs inédits sur Tristan Corbière', *Paris-Journal*, 21 March 1912, by Micha Grin, *Tristan Corbière, Poète maudit*, Évian, 1972, p. 36.

Especially in the light of Marcelle's devoted behaviour at Tristan's sickbed, there has been much controversy about whether she 'really loved' him. In view of her constant association with Battine, this question might have seemed a little precious to Corbière, condemned at best to the weakest position in a trio. Yet it had been almost out of bravado that he had wanted to 'make her love me', but she responded more than he expected. Pol Kalig wrote that 'when he became aware of his own feelings, he was as astonished as he was frightened: the ideas of suicide which often preyed on him became very frequent at that time.'* There is no gentle moment in *Les Amours jaunes*, since life did not vouchsafe one to Corbière. In the prose piece 'L'Américaine', Corbière seems to catch 'a kind of breath of beauty' (p. 154), which another, less disturbed by his own ugliness and consequently driven always to reject, might have termed happiness. But Corbière proudly identified himself with the toad† nailed above his mantelpiece in Paris,[18] insisting, 'My self-love doesn't like being liked'.‡

*

For a few months, Corbière became temporarily deaf. This was sated *en passant* by René Martineau in the first book devoted to Corbière,[19] although no medical documentation has ever come to light. 'Rapsodie du sourd' (p. 46), which describes this experience, also symbolizes 'the spiritual and mental exile of the poet'.§ It is the only individually dedicated poem in the collection, though in view of its subject, the dedication could well be ironic. Henri Thomas has recently made this poem pivotal in his reading of *Les Amours jaunes*, in which he traces Corbière's recession into a Beckettian inability to communicate.

* '[. . .] lorsqu'il s'aperçut du sentiment qu'il éprouvait lui-même, il en fut aussi étonné qu'épouvanté: les idées de suicide qui le hantèrent si souvent furent à ce moment-là fréquentes', from an unpublished letter from Pol Kalig to René Martineau, quoted by Micha Grin in *Tristan Corbière, Poète maudit*, Évian, 1972, p. 36.

† See 'Le crapaud', p. 18.

‡ 'Mon amour, à moi, n'aime pas qu'on l'aime', from 'À une camarade', *Œuvres complètes de Tristan Corbière*, ed. P.-O. Walzer, 'Bibliothèque de la Pléiade', Paris, 1970, p. 728.

§ '[. . .] l'exil moral et mental du poète', Jean Rousselot, *Tristan Corbière*, Paris, 1951, p. 52.

We are very far, here, from the single circle where the lonely spirit rejoined the vortex of Being in the prose of the *Epitaphe*. The dispossession sung, with a kind of Byronic joy, in *Paria*, is also revealed to be an illusion, or was at least only a stage, whereas it seemed the end finally attained. In the *Rhapsodie du sourd*, an end is no longer conceivable.*

Even if the extreme emphasis placed on this poem is not justified, M. Thomas' stress elsewhere in his book on Corbière's pragmatic approach, turning to good artistic account whatever life chose to present him with, is exemplified in this poem's combination of the experiential and the metaphorical.

There has been much controversy about the significance of the placing of the later, 'Parisian' poems before the earlier 'Breton' ones in *Les Amours jaunes*. But there is no reason to think that Corbière necessarily had any plan in the arrangement of the book, other than the desire to present the different themes of his poetry effectively. Concern with effective organization is a large qualification, and seems sufficient motivation for an artist like Corbière who not only never wrote any *ars poetica*, but was always content to let any statement in his poems be implicit. Within the sections, as well as the groups within groups, such as the Italian poems in 'Raccrocs', certain poems are interrelated, for instance, the trilogy (pp. 24–8) formed by 'Pauvre garçon', 'Déclin' and 'Bonsoir', and the pair (pp. 22–4) 'Duel aux camélias' and 'Fleur d'art', but Corbière indicates this only by juxtaposition. In 'Sérénade des sérénades', by means of repeated imagery, Corbière constructs the frame of reference of a troubadour singing beneath his lady's window: 'The poet's suit of his lady is concretized in the window, or glass, figure, and his song is visualized as literally wearing down the window by abrasive action.'[20] In this closely organized section, many of the poems answer and continue each other. A chronological arrangement of the poems in *Les Amours jaunes* would have unduly heightened their autobiographical tone, and perhaps over-

---

* 'Nous sommes très loin, ici, de la ronde unique où l'esprit seul rejoignait le tourbillon de l'Etre dans la prose d'*Epitaphe*. La dépossession chantée, avec une sorte de joie byronienne, dans *Paria*, se révèle illusion elle aussi, ou du moins n'était qu'une étape, alors qu'elle semblait le but enfin atteint. Dans la *Rhapsodie du sourd*, aucun but n'est plus concevable.' Henri Thomas, *Tristan le Dépossédé*, Paris, 1972, p. 115.

emphasized a familiar theme of the experiences of the provincial drawn to the metropolis.

The theme of death is recurrent in *Les Amours jaunes*, culminating, in 'Rondels pour après' (pp. 118–20), in the cradle which is the grave. 'Of all the Celtic peoples, none have preserved as have the Bretons that ancient preoccupation with the problem of Death and the Beyond.'[21] Brittany is 'the land of death' not only in a religious and mythological sense, but also on account of the sea, killing men who elsewhere would survive. The arrangement of *Les Amours jaunes* illustrates the assertion in the prose epigraph to the 'Épitaphe', itself placed at the *beginning* of the book:

> [. . .] no more distinguishing when the end begins from when the beginning ends which is every end of every beginning equal to every final beginning of the infinite defined by the indefinite–This equals an epitaph which equals a preface and conversely[.] [p. 3]

By ending with 'Rondels pour après', a group of lullabies for a dead child, Corbière reintroduces the theme of the contemporaneity of the beginning and end of life. Whether the reader begins at the first page or the last, he arrives at the same point. *Les Amours jaunes* is a statement of suffering ironically formulated not only in its component poems but also in their interacting arrangement.

Though linked with compassion in the Breton sections, irony runs through *Les Amours jaunes*. As the Parisian sections are more subjective, their irony is more astringent. Corbière never loses his detachment, which stemmed partly from his feeling of being a stranger in both Paris and Brittany. 'Le poète contumace' (p. 28), which despite its setting on the Breton coast belongs in the section 'Les Amours jaunes', shows Tristan's alienation by conventional provincialism; another barrier in Brittany might have been his attitude towards religion.

The irony of the title applies to the whole book. 'Jaune' has many implications: yellow, the colour of treason, also suggests 'rire jaune' (to give a sickly smile),[22] as used in 'À l'Etna' (p. 70). The title may also imply an ironical analogy with 'fièvre jaune' (yellow fever), and with Saint-Beuve's 'Les Rayons jaunes', where yellow is also the colour of death. The heaviest irony, however, lies in the double meaning that Pol Kalig asserted Corbière particularly intended, suggesting a pornographic book. Gladys

Frères, his publishers, were in any case notorious in that field, and it must have appealed to Tristan to exploit bitterly this fact. Pol Kalig's statement also presupposes a pragmatic organization of *Les Amours jaunes*, whose various sections of betrayed loves for the devouring sea as well as for Marcelle, and for art itself, were drawn together with unifying irony by Corbière when he thought of publication.

Although *Les Amours jaunes* was published in August 1873, there is no indication what form subsequent work by Corbière would have taken, had he not died at thirty. Martineau asserted that he was working on another book, *Mirlitons*,[23] but no manuscripts have survived to substantiate this,[24] and the disappointing reception of *Les Amours jaunes* might have convinced the poet that, like everything else in life, art had failed him – or that he had failed art – and Corbière's counter to failure was to reject what he had failed in. Described by Laforgue as 'the most delicate, the subtlest, and the purest section artistically: *Rondels pour après*; pure mauves with a pale admixture of irony filigreed on to a posthumous tone',* critics have often seen in the breath-taking technique of the 'Rondels pour après' a new lightness, despite their preoccupation with death. However, their chronological placing does not necessarily correspond to their culminating position in *Les Amours jaunes*, which offsets the eight opening sonnets entitled 'Paris'.

The poignant charm of the 'Rondels pour après' comes from the dark undertones below the gossamery images, typical of Celtic folklore. Fanch' Gourvil considered that 'Paysage mauvais' (p. 74) reveals Corbière's familiarity with this folklore. 'Death s wheelbarrow' in 'Nature morte' (p. 76) is Breton, but, although birds, especially the owl, are believed to have an instinct for *l'Ankou*,† the Breton personification of death,[25] the cuckoo, crow and owl are birds of ill omen throughout European folklore. Corbière's atmospheric descriptions of Brittany rarely depend on precise knowledge of Celtic folklore.

Despite Corbière's love for Brittany, he owed little to the principal Breton writers. He didn't know Breton. This 'Breton

---

* 'La plus fine, la plus ténue, la plus pure partie comme art: *Rondels pour après*; de fines mauves pâle filigranées d'ironie sur un ton posthume.' 'Une Étude sur Corbière', in *Mélanges posthumes, Œuvres complètes de Jules Laforgue*, Paris, 1903, p. 128.

† Corbière's nickname. See above, p. xv.

bretonnant' took no part in the Breton literary renaissance, led by
Brizeux, Le Godinec and Proux. Perhaps the chief value of his
Breton heritage was his involvement in a society older than the
rapidly expanding urban one. Corbière's poetry shows an attraction to imagery drawn from the natural human functions of birth,
reproduction and death, which accorded well with his basically
plain diction, though he embellished this even in the Breton poems
with a variety of word-play.

Corbière, who played the hurdy-gurdy,[26] also made use of Breton
folk-songs in his poetry. He revealed the depth of his attachment to
these at Paris, where he missed Brittany bitterly, just as he had at
school.

> With tousled hair, his forehead smeared with soot, Corbière, disguised
> as a beggar, stretching out his stiff leg on the floor and with only one
> arm, held out his begging bowl till dawn, singing Breton laments,
> canticles of Saint Anne of the Marsh.*

Later than in Germany and England, it was not until the post-
Parnassian period that French poets began to turn to the folk song.
Influenced by Villon and attracted to Béranger and Breton folk
songs, Corbière reintroduced the 'chanson des rues' and the 'complainte populaire'. 'À mon cotre Le Négrier' is based on the tune
'Adieu, mon beau navire!', and the third stanza of 'Le mousse'
(p. 110) echoes the song 'Trois Matelots de Groix':

> On n'a trouvé que son chapeau,
> Sa boîte à chique et son couteau.[27]

In 'Cris d'aveugle' (p. 94), based on an old Breton song often
hummed by Corbière in Paris, the character of 'complainte' comes
partly from the then new device of omitting punctuation.[28]

Brittany had been the stronghold of religion in France against
laicization. But Breton religion mingled potently with superstition,
as Corbière brings out ironically in the prose epigraph to 'Saint-
Tupetu de Tu-pe-tu', written in the style of a folklore study.

---

* 'Les cheveux en broussaille, le front barbouillé de suie, Corbière déguisé
en mendiant, allongé sur le parquet la jambe tendue, n'ayant qu'un bras,
tendit la sébile jusqu'à l'aube en chantant des complaintes bretonnes, des
cantiques de Sainte-Anne de la Palud', quoted by Sonnenfeld, p. 42, from Léon
Durocher, 'Tristan Corbière à Paris', *Le Fureteur breton*, April–May 1912, p. 133.

In the district of Léon.–A little chapel to Saint Tupetu. (In Breton: *One side or the other*.)[. . .]

The oracle functions during high mass: for each of them, the officiant arranges a go on the *Wheel-of-chance*, a big wooden hoop fixed to the vault and manoeuvred by a long rope that Tupetu himself holds in his granite hand. The wheel, hung with bells, chimes as it turns; where it stops betokens the judgement of fate:–*One side or the other*.

And everyone goes away as he has come, ready to return next year . . . . In the end *Tu-pe-tu* inevitably has his effect.*

Corbière here ironically elaborates on Saint Tu-pe-tu, who was popularly believed to relieve the agony of the dying,[29] but he was only following Breton tradition. Other exclusively Breton saints, unknown to the Church, are revered in the region.

Corbière's schoolboy letters show his child's acceptance of the Catholic practice in which his mother brought up her family. But as he grew older, he would have felt the influence of his Voltairian father, whose letters to his son at school, though often exhortatory, never referred to religion. Édouard Corbière had polemicized against Church and State until given a prison sentence in 1823 for his attacks on the regime. Possibly age modified his views, and Corbière l'Ancien died a Catholic, unlike his son who did not receive the last sacrament.

'His experience of physical suffering has admirably prepared him for moral suffering.'† Corbière's attitude to religion must also have been moulded by his physical suffering, which at least in the

* 'C'est au pays de Léon.–Est une petite chapelle à saint Tupetu. (En breton: *D'un côté ou de l'autre*.) [. . .]

L'oracle fonctionne pendant la grand'messe: l'officiant fait faire, pour chacun, un tour à la *Roulette-de-chance*, grand cercle en bois fixé à la voûte et manœuvré par une longue corde que Tupetu tient lui-même dans sa main de granit. La roue, garnie de clochettes, tourne en carillonnant; son point d'arrêt présage l'arrêt du destin:–*D'un côté ou de l'autre*.

Et chacun s'en va comme il est venu, quitte à revenir l'an prochain . . . *Tu-pe-tu* finit fatalement par avoir son effet.'

Œuvres complètes de Tristan Corbière, ed. P.-O. Walzer, 'Bibliothèque de la Pléiade', Paris, 1970, p. 797.

† 'Il a connu la souffrance physique qui l'a admirablement préparé à la souffrance morale.' Quoted by René Martineau in *Promenades biographiques*, Paris, 1920, p. 44, from a letter from Pol Kalig published in *Marches de Provence*, Aug.–Sept. 1912, pp. 26-7.

earlier, Breton poems he was able to objectify. These poems include 'La pastorale de Conlie', socially Corbière's most significant poem: it is a plain indictment put into the mouth of one of the 20,000 Breton volunteers in the Franco-Prussian War left to rot in camp by Gambetta, who feared a Breton anti-Republic insurrection. Even if the horrifying scenes Corbière describes in 'La Rapsode foraine' (p. 78) were out of date by his day,[30] he realistically pictures extreme physical suffering momentarily highlighted by wan hope.

In *Les Amours jaunes* Corbière's attitude towards religion is not explicit, and what is implicit is the subject of controversy, centring round 'La Rapsode foraine'. In this long, descriptive, narrative poem, Corbière shows imaginative understanding of religious attitudes. But it is difficult to see how *Les Amours jaunes* can be made to sustain the positive attitude to religion, which some of Corbière's commentators have seen. If 'La Rapsode foraine' ends with a positive statement, it is by *human* agency that the old woman has a 'good moment', and the previous verses have already indicated her closeness to death, with no hint that this will be anything but the ultimate end.

Compassionate irony underpins Corbière's appalling description in 'La Rapsode foraine':

> – Alms in their platters! . . .
> Together, our ancestors have carried
> These fleur-de-lis of scrofula
> Which these *chosen ones* have inherited. [p. 89]

Just as juxtaposition often gives an ironic function to Corbière's classical allusions, in 'Cris d'aveugle' the poet uses liturgical formulas to produce religious irony:

> A tear that mists
> Wherein is paradise I notice
> *Miserere, De profundis*[. . . .] [p. 97]

It is by excepting the Breton sections from the pervasive irony of *Les Amours jaunes* that Albert Sonnenfeld is able to insist on the book's 'moral structure',[31] in terms of a symbolic return to Brittany in reaction against Parisian evil. Certainly 'Un riche en Bretagne'

reveals a very different attitude to ugliness and poverty in Brittany than in Paris, but this poem, too, has its ironic undertone:

> In passing, the huge farm dog gives him a caress . . .
> – Is that a way of doing without a mistress? . . .*

Brittany also offered Corbière the frustration and satisfaction of the sea, although his love of the sea was complicated by his father's achievements as a sailor, in a career including a spell as prisoner-of-war in England. 'La fin' (p. 114), 'in which is all the sea',† may be read as glorifying the active life, by contrast with the emphasis on death in Hugo's 'Oceano nox'[32] which it parodies. Charles Le Goffic saw the sea as the means whereby Corbière was freed from the physical handicaps afflicting him on land.[33] Nevertheless, he was still debarred from membership of the crew, or the captain's role of his father. Despite the realism of Corbière's sea poems, an element of personal fantasy appears in this section with the arrangement of the poems to suggest a long sea voyage, which in fact he never made. Corbière seems to have sought compensation for his deprivation in reckless sailing in the worst weather: even Verlaine, who clearly knew very little of Corbière's biography, mentions these audacious exploits at sea.[34]

If the American girl of the prose piece so titled is identified with Marcelle, the sea becomes the scenario for Corbière's assertion of superiority over her; yet, as he himself says, his real mistress is the sea.

> . . . Love? . . . Come on then! love for me? . . . She's up there, my sweetheart! . . . Do you hear her howling after her lover, battering the sides, shaking the masts, slashing the sails . . . We'll sleep together this evening perhaps . . . and the little one also, in that case. [p. 151]

Corbière's skill as a sailor meant he could stand up to the sea as well as a man could, though, typically, in the solitary role that circumstances had imposed.

---

* 'Le gros chien de la cour en passant le caresse . . . /–Avec ça, peut-on pas se passer de maîtresse? . . .' *Œuvres complètes de Tristan Corbière*, ed. P.-O. Walzer, 'Bibliothèque de la Pléiade', Paris, 1970, p. 796.

† '[. . .] où est toute la mer', Paul Verlaine, *Les Poètes maudits*, Paris, 1888, p. 11.

In the section 'Gens de mer', Corbière comes closest to his father's work, realistically portraying sailors in verse as his father had done in prose. In the original preface to *Le Négrier*, Édouard Corbière had asked rhetorically: 'Should I describe sailors as I've seen them, or should I present them once more to the public as they're used to seeing them?'* Édouard Corbière reacted against the picturesqueness of Eugène Sue's ' "mateloteries" échevelées', and Tristan against the sentimentality of 'Oceano nox'. Verlaine admired Corbière's sea poems so much that he advised the publisher Vanier to issue a separate edition of this section, which appeared in 1891, and Laforgue praised Tristan's handling of sailors, especially in 'Le bossu Bitor'.[35] Martineau states that 'Gens de mer' was the one section of *Les Amours jaunes* that the father appreciated.[36]

Yet Corbière l'Ancien was the chief literary influence on *Les Amours jaunes*, notions of whose primarily Breton character his own work helped to foster, since the heroes of his novels were Breton sailors. Predictably, Corbière's school compositions, some of which may be related to poems in the Breton sections, show a strong paternal influence, no doubt from his father's reminiscences of his exploits. In *Les Amours jaunes* there are numerous references to Édouard Corbière's novels. For instance, in *Les Pilotes de l'Iroise*, Édouard Corbière described a sailor after the battle in these terms: 'There, he's got one eye the less—And you others, do you have an extra one?'† In 'Matelots' Tristan wrote:

Still you see some come back: shipwrecks' debris, [. . .]
—One eye the less.—And do you have one extra, you?
—Yellow fever.—What about you, do you have the blue?
[p. 103]

Among several other references to Édouard Corbière's work in the same poem, Tristan includes the song chorus '*Un curé dans ton lit, un' fill' dans mon hamac!*' already used in a slightly different form by his father in *Le Négrier*.[37] The poem opens with the bitter lines,

---

* 'Dois-je peindre les marins tels que je les ai vus, ou dois-je plutôt les livrer encore une fois au public, tels qu'il est accoutumé à les voir?' *Le Négrier*, I, Paris, 1832, p. ii.

† 'Tiens, il a un œil en moins—Et vous autres, en avez-vous de plus?' quoted by Sonnenfeld, p. 122, from a citation in Léon Durocher, 'Le Père de Tristan', *Le Fureteur breton*, August–Sept. 1912, p. 109.

Your sailors of the Opera footlights . . . the comic opera,
In sky-blue frock-coats swear 'A thousand portholes!' [p. 99]

echoing Édouard Corbière's essay 'Des emprunts libres faits à la
littérature maritime': 'These passengers have only seen sailors at
the comic opera!'*

The influence of Corbière l'Ancien extends beyond the content
and style of the nautical poems in *Les Amours jaunes*. The Breton
sections 'Armor' and 'Gens de mer' are arranged in the pattern
of the short prose pieces in the father's *La Mer et les marins*.[38] Even
Corbière's great poem 'La Rapsode foraine' owed much to
Édouard Corbière's *Cric-Crac*, which contains this description of a
gift of tobacco:

> On the path taking me straight to Saint-Pol-de-Léon, I en-
> countered not a druids' monument but a colossal woman who was
> smoking[. . . .] This rustic beauty, having accepted the stuff with an
> appearance of great satisfaction, made the sign of the cross with her
> pipe.†

Here is not only the subject of 'La Rapsode foraine', but also a
description closely echoed in the last two verses of the poem:

> –Poet, if you cross her track,
> With her old soldier's knapsack:
> It's our sister . . . give her–it's a festivity–
> For her pipe, a little baccy! . . .
>
> You will see in her hollow face,
> As in wood, hollowing itself anew
> A smile; and her scabby hand trace
> A true sign of the cross for you. [p. 93]

Sonnenfeld, who cites this parallel,[39] goes on to compare the irony
in Édouard Corbière's description with the 'respect for the old
Breton religious tradition' attributed to Tristan, but in the context

---

* 'Ces passagers qui n'ont vu des marins qu'à l'Opéra Comique!', quoted by
Sonnenfeld, p. 125, from Ida Levi's 'Tristan Corbière, a Biographical and
Critical Study', unpublished thesis, (MS. D. Phil. d. 1019), Oxford, 1951.

† 'J'ai rencontré sur le chemin qui me conduisait tout droit à Saint-Pol-de-
Léon non un monument druide mais une femme colossale qui fumait [. . . .]
Cette rustique beauté, après avoir accepté le toc avec de grandes marques de
satisfaction, a fait avec sa pipe le signe de la croix.' *Cric-Crac*, Paris, 1846, p. 75.

of the poem this final humanistic gesture is ironical at the expense of religion.

Jean de Trigon has demonstrated a second strong literary influence in 'La Rapsode foraine', that of the Breton poet, Gabriel La Landelle, whom Tristan and his father knew.[40] Corbière adapted the rhythm of La Landelle's poem 'Le Pardon de Sainte-Anne' for 'La Rapsode foraine'. La Landelle's sea poems in *Chants marins* (1861) and *Le Gaillard d'avant* (1865) also influenced him; here Corbière innovated by interpolating phrases from sailors' songs.

Édouard Corbière's literary attitudes were partially absorbed by his son. In the Introduction to his translation of Tibullus (1829), Édouard Corbière outlined the classical theory, with no trace of Romanticism. But Corbière l'Ancien's most important work was his novels; he soon abandoned both his own poetry and translation. In fact there was a divergence between the rules he had followed in his poems and those he rejected for prose. Francis Burch has modified the traditional view of Édouard Corbière as an intractable anti-Romantic, who later became converted to the new movement.[41] His criticism of Romanticism was mainly confined to its lack of realism. Burch concludes from *Les Amours jaunes* that, 'Tristan did not remain insensible to his father's later affirmations of the writer's right to innovate.'*

There was also a certain temperamental affinity between the two Corbières as writers. 'The preface of this novel [*Le Négrier*] reveals a very proud spirit, very contemptuous of the public: the same spirit with talent and a more acute sensibility–you have Tristan Corbière.'† Tristan's natural gift for parody, the twin of his talent for drawing caricatures, was more effective than his father's pen. He applied it with particular deadliness to Lamartine, 'Inventor of the *written tear*,/Subscribers' lachrymatory',‡ especially

---

* '[. . .] Tristan n'est pas resté insensible aux affirmations plus tardives de son père, sur le droit de l'écrivain à innover.' Francis Burch, *Tristan Corbière*, Paris, 1970, p. 58.

† 'La préface de ce roman [*Le Négrier*] décèle un esprit très hautaine et très dédaigneux du public: le même esprit avec du talent et une nervosité plus aiguë,–vous avez Tristan Corbière.' Rémy de Gourmont, *Le Livre des masques*, I, Paris, 1914, pp. 157-8.

‡ 'Inventeur de la *larme écrite*,/Lacrymatoire d'abonnés! . . .', from 'Un jeune qui s'en va', *Œuvres complètes de Tristan Corbière*, ed. P.-O. Walzer, 'Bibliothèque de la Pléiade', Paris, 1970, p. 731.

in 'Le Fils de Lamartine et de Graziella', also attacking com-
mercialization in Italy, where he encountered the man claiming,
paternity from Lamartine, the subject of this poem.

Despite his abuse of Hugo as 'the apocalyptic Man,/[. . .] epic
national guardsman',* and his parody of him in 'La fin', Corbière
reflects his influence in other poems. Rhymes from 'Les Djinns' are
echoed throughout *Les Amours jaunes*, and not only in parody. For
instance, 'Le poète contumace' has: '[. . .] celle après qui tu
brames, / [. . .] Mais ton front est sans flammes. . .'. The striking
ending of this poem is probably a memory of the closing lines of
'Vere novo'.[42] There is a distinct resemblance between Hugo's
'Le crapaud', and Corbière's poem of the same name, though
Hugo's toad is a universal symbol of suffering humanity, whereas
Corbière's is a subjective symbol of his own solitude.

Corbière's motivation in attacking the Romantic poets, certainly
not associated with the academic admiration of the eighteenth century and only partially accounted for by his father's attitude, was
a defensive reaction against his 'spiritual brothers' induced by his
own basic romanticism. 'He's a modernist, but also a counter-
romantic, and that means an exasperated romantic.'† This basic
romanticism may be defined even more loosely as an overriding
concern with the expression of emotion, untrammelled by intellectual constructs, which many critics have seen as the prime concern
in Corbière's work. Tristan Tzara relates this motivation very
closely to the career of Édouard Corbière, who in 1842 gave up
writing novels, apart from a collection of short pieces published in
1846, though this so-called 'betrayal' was scarcely to 'enrich himself', as Tzara suggests, since his novels were very profitable:

> Even Tristan Corbière's sincerity, that is to say the resolution to
> write about only that which he himself has seen, known or felt is a
> protest against the *imposture* of his father for whom talent and
> fantasy are the attributes of the art of writing and not the basic
> identification with life's depths, the lived adventure, which the poet
> advocates.‡

* '–Hugo: l'Homme apocalyptique, /[. . .] gardenational épique', ibid.
† 'C'est un moderniste, mais c'est aussi un contre-romantique, et par là
même un romantique exaspéré.' Gustave Kahn, 'Tristan Corbière', *La Nouvelle
Revue*, Nouvelle série, XXIX (14 July 1904), p. 272.
‡ 'La sincérité même de Tristan Corbière, c'est-à-dire la résolution de
n'écrire que ce qu'il a vu, connu ou senti par lui-même est une protestation

It seems more likely though that Tristan arrived pragmatically at poetry at 'les limites du cri', through the irresistible fascination of extremity for a frustrated and therefore defiant nature, rather than from Rimbaudian *a priori* ideas about the role of the poet, at which he would surely have poked fun.

Corbière's appreciation of Musset supports this analysis of his complex attitude to Romanticism. Without succumbing to any of Musset's romantic excesses, Corbière drew on his irony. It was probably Musset's 'Spanish' poetry, (such as 'Madrid' and 'L'Andalouse') that inspired 'Sérénade des sérénades', Corbière's section of pseudo-Spanish satirical poems. In 'Après la pluie', Corbière mentions the Marchioness of Amaëgui, heroine of 'L'Andalouse', and in 'Portes et fenêtres' and 'Grand Opéra', in the 'Sérénade', he quotes the closing lines of this poem. Corbière's borrowing of expressions and images from Musset, as from Villon and Baudelaire, without subjecting them to his usual parodying, reveals his admiration for these poets.

Verlaine was the first to compare Corbière with Villon.[43] Pound, who considered him 'perhaps the most poignant poet since Villon',[44] declared: 'If Corbière invented no process he at any rate restored French verse to the vigour of Villon and to any intensity that no Frenchman had touched during the intervening four centuries.'[45] Corbière often applied his 'hard-bit lines' to subjects similar to Villon's. Fear of imminent death prompted Corbière, too, to produce a series of 'testaments': 'Ça?', 'Épitaphe', 'Une mort trop travaillée', 'Sous un portrait de Corbière', 'Décourageux', 'Paria', and 'Laisser-courre', which strikingly recalls Villon's *Grand Testament*. Yet antithesis, a technical device in Villon's 'Ballade des Contraires', is used in Corbière's 'Épitaphe' in a more modern way to express mental complexity.

'Épitaphe' contains one of the only two close textual echoes of Villon in *Les Amours jaunes*. Corbière's

> Coloriste enragé,–mais blême;
> Incompris . . .–surtout de lui-même [p. 4]

contre l'*imposture* du père pour qui le talent et la fantaisie sont les attributs de l'art d'écrire et non pas l'identification substantielle que le poète préconise avec les profondeurs de la vie: l'aventure vécue.' Tristan Tzara, 'Tristan Corbière et les Limites du Cri', *Europe*, 60 (Dec. 1950), p. 90.

echoes these lines from the 'Ballade des Menus Propos':

> Je connais coulourés et blèmes, [. . .]
> Je connais tout fors que moi-même.[46]

However, the 'Villonesque' character of Corbière's poetry derives from its shared realistic subject matter, especially descriptions of down-and-outs, including prostitutes, with the same techniques, such as the use of slang. Both poets also had a stance of self-disparagement. The attitude to religion of the medieval and the modern poet contrasts: 'The wretchedness of man's fate and of his daily occupations is clearly in evidence in Villon and Corbière, but such disaster in Villon is never considered without its relationship to the poet's religious faith and hope.'[47]

Realism and pessimism were characteristics which also attracted Corbière to Baudelaire. Laforgue declared that *Les Amours jaunes* was not at all Baudelairean,[48] but the book abounds in textual and thematic echoes of *Les Fleurs du mal* (1857). In his Parisian poems, Corbière followed the path pioneered by Baudelaire in his elevation of city imagery 'to the *first intensity*',[49] and Corbière's portrayal of woman, though stamped by his own masochistic psychology, owes much to *Les Fleurs du mal* and to the vision of woman derived from it which became fashionable after Baudelaire's death. Corbière also took over 'Baudelairean dandyism',[50] though both his realism and his extremism subverted it; he mocked the cult of spleen.

Imagery is often paralleled in the two poets. 'Paris diurne' and 'Paris nocturne' (pp. 122–4) relate to Baudelaire's pair, 'Le Crépuscule du matin' and 'Le Crépuscule du soir'. Similarly, while 'La pipe au poète (p. 16) was obviously inspired by Baudelaire's 'La Pipe', Corbière is also able to establish his own tone. Echoes of Baudelaire are not confined to Corbière's 'Parisian' poems; Corbière's description of sailors in 'Matelots',

> À terre–oiseaux palmés–ils sont gauches et veules.
> Ils sont mal culottés comme leurs brûle-gueules [. . .] [p. 98]

recalls Baudelaire's 'Albatros':

> Ce voyageur ailé, comme il est gauche et veule!
> Lui, naguère si beau, qu'il est comique et laid!
> L'un agace son bec avec un brûle-gueule[. . . .][51]

Corbière absorbed Baudelaire's taste for the macabre and the satanic, as instanced in the last verse of 'Paysage mauvais' (p. 76), which echoes these lines from 'Sépulture':

> Et des sorcières faméliques,
> Les ébats des vieillards lubriques
> Et les complots des noirs filous.[52]

In 'La Litanie du sommeil' (p. 50), Corbière uses the formula of 'Toi qui . . .' from Baudelaire's 'Les Litanies de Satan'. This poem also has textual echoes of Baudelaire, notably the image of 'l'Obscène confesseur' derived from 'Confesseur des pendus et des conspirateurs'.

For so isolated a figure as Corbière, who never associated with writers, there must have been a few books crucial for the potential they revealed which could then be exploited. It is difficult not to see *Les Fleurs du mal* as such a book. The presumed chronology of Corbière's poems shows the prime importance of autobiographical factors in his work, so it is significant that Corbière's time in Paris, Baudelaire's milieu, coincided with the darkest phases of his love for Marcelle, transmuted to passionate jealousy and hatred, which he must have seen mirrored in some of Baudelaire's poems about Jeanne Duval.

The argument that Corbière's Breton heritage enabled him to achieve a more balanced synthesis than Baudelaire's concern with exclusively urban life permitted[53] misinterprets the nature of *Les Amours jaunes*, which is neither thematically nor structurally 'architectural' like *Les Fleurs du mal*. Baudelaire also retained the terminology of Christianity with which Corbière, like most subsequent writers, dispensed, as *le néant* pre-empted any other vision.

In the direct line of succession of Baudelaire and Mallarmé, we must also range those poets who have considered it their principal mission to state, without recourse to aestheticism, the human condition in a nihilistic age. In this lineage we find the caustic poetry of Thomas Hardy, A. E. Housman, Corbière, Laforgue, and the Eliot of Prufrock, Sweeney, 'The Hollow Men,' and *The Waste Land*.[54]

*

Corbière reacted against the excessive formalism of the Parnassians, rejecting their aesthetic as well as that of the Romantics. His third 'Paris' sonnet mocks at Parnassian 'imitations of pretty nature'. The attitude of 'fatigué de pitié' in 'Décourageux' (p. 44) is a reaction against the 'belle ouvrage'. Corbière's 'I Sonnet' is aimed against Parnassian inflexibility, rather than traditional poetic forms in general. Using the sonnet form himself, albeit often with modifications, Corbière on the whole respected traditional prosody, while innovating in diction.

'Art doesn't know me. I don't know Art':* this was for too long taken literally, following Verlaine's belittling of Corbière's technique, which Laforgue, who was the first to examine *Les Amours jaunes* technically, corroborated. However, the modern researches of Christian Angelet and Marshall Lindsay have borne out Pol Kalig's testimony to Corbière's method of working:

> Corbière worked over his compositions a great deal, multiplying versions, then cutting, pruning, condensing, not to say quintessentializing and refining, torturing his theme which he often spoilt with childish concetti, but sometimes enhanced.†

In the only review of the first edition of *Les Amours jaunes*, the anonymous critic of *La Renaissance littéraire et artistique*, though by no means unsympathetic to the book generally, quoted the author's 'poet, despite his verse–and worse'‡ against him, because 'all the rules of poetry, rhyme and rhythm are too often ignored. If the author considers them useless encumbrances, why doesn't he write in prose?'§ Yet one of Corbière's two completed prose pieces,

---

* 'L'Art ne me connaît pas. Je ne connais pas l'Art', from 'Ça?', *Œuvres complètes de Tristan Corbière*, ed. P.-O. Walzer, 'Bibliothèque de la Pléiade', Paris, 1970, p. 705.

† 'Corbière travaillait beaucoup ses œuvres, multipliait les versions, puis coupait, émondait, condensait, quintessenssait et raffinait pour ne pas dire, bistournait son thème qu'il gâtait souvent par des concetti enfantins, mais quelquefois heureux.' From a letter from Pol Kalig to René Martineau, quoted by Micha Grin in *Tristan Corbière, Poète maudit*, Évian, 1972, p. 95.

‡ 'Poète, en dépit de ses vers', from 'Épitaphe', (p. 4).

§ '[. . .] toutes les règles de la poésie, la rime, le rhythme sont trop souvent mis de côté. Si l'auteur les considère comme des entraves inutiles, pourquoi n'a t-il pas écrit en prose.' *La Renaissance littéraire et artistique*, 26 October 1873, p. 304.

frequently termed prose poems, 'Casino des trépassés' (p. 130), has been claimed by Micha Grin as an early example of *vers libre*.[55] Édouard Corbière's achievements in prose, which like other contemporaries, Tristan seems to have overestimated, would surely have inhibited the son from attempting to work in the same medium.

Marshall Lindsay, admitting that Corbière's poetry 'abounds in lines that are merely prose in counted syllables, with a rhyme at the end', draws these conclusions from his prosodic analysis of *Les Amours jaunes*:

> Corbière's attitude towards the traditional rules of prosody seems to waver between passive acceptance, modified by negligence, and revolt. He did not deliberately plan to liberate poetry, but he was willing to transgress tradition when it threatened to restrain his poetic impulse. All of the poems of *Les Amours jaunes* are in lines of counted syllables, they have few forbidden hiatuses, and the rhymes are in general conservative. Corbière took many liberties in his counting of diphthongs and in the alternation of rhymes, and in his treatment of caesuras and enjambments, his independence made it possible for him to achieve a considerable variety of rhythmic effects.[56]

Corbière generally observed certain unreasonable rules, such as the prohibition of hiatus and of rhyming masculine and feminine, singular and plural words, since there appeared to be no particular effect to be gained by discarding them. Corbière was not interested in poetic theory. Just as he attacked the Romantics for the absurdity of their pretensions and the Parnassians for their rigidity, his attitude to prosody was pragmatic, an acceptance of the established form for lack of any other, unless he saw a way of gaining a more extreme effect by ignoring it. In 'Le poète contumace' (p. 28), the broken rhythms are deliberately intended to convey the changes of emotion in the course of the poem. The effort in this long, psychologically descriptive poem to make the verse follow the movement of consciousness presages the subsequent parallel development of *vers libre* and the interior monologue in the novel. In 'Femme' (p. 20), the rhymes are enhanced by the mixed metres. Repetition is a device handled effectively by Corbière;[57] in 'Cris d'aveugle' (p. 94) he repeats the sound 'or' forty-four

times in sixty-six lines, among other masculine rhymes, producing an almost hallucinatory effect.

Often, the repetition of sounds contributes to the rhythm of a line, as with the five sounds repeated in this line from 'Au vieux Roscoff', 'Il dort son lourd sommeille de rouille' (p. 112).

> The repeated *r*'s, *s*'s, *ou*'s, [ɔ]'s, and [j]'s are intermixed with and linked to each other, which, along with the weak tonic accents, gives the line a slow, even movement that coincides perfectly with its sense. The opposite occurs in a line from 'Rapsodie du Sourd': 'Hystérique tourment d'un Tantale acoustique!'[58]

Corbière's critics have deplored the absence of 'beaux vers', with the lack of modulation of consonants and vowels. This represents a complete divergence from the ideal of the 'serious-aesthetic' symbolists, the approximation of poetry to 'the condition of music'. But the obverse of this is the auditory conceit, which attempts to do for sounds what the verbal conceit does for reference. Such play on dissonance and alliteration is instanced in Corbière's lines,

> Tourne: nous sommes soûls! Et plats: Fais la cruelle!
> Cravache ton pacha, ton humble serviteur!...[59]

Further light was cast on Corbière's method of composition by Martineau's discovery in 1904 of an early draft of the satirical poem 'Veder Napoli poi mori', where the poet lets himself be guided above all by the sounds, although this auditory quality is played down in the final version. However, although earlier versions of other poems show the same tendency towards greater prosodic formalism, which the exclusion of 'La Balancelle', written in blank verse, from the final version of *Les Amours jaunes* perhaps also represents, revisions to 'Rapsodie d'un sourd' were directed towards irregularity, in key with the acuteness of the content. Corbière's poems are certainly not constructed by a technique of free association of sounds, since he applied the same technique with meanings in the terms of figures of speech, and with imagery, never allowing random suggestiveness to escape altogether from the underlying rationale of the particular poem.

The harsh sound of much of Corbière's work is probably sometimes due to carelessness. It was also the inevitable concomitant of

attempting to reproduce the rhythms of colloquial speech, elaborated by Laforgue into the 'conversational-ironic' tradition.[60] 'Depoetization and re-creation make use of the same methods. Corbière was responsible for the elaboration of this unique phenomenon in French literature: a burlesque and lyric conceptualism.'*

Aldous Huxley praised Laforgue for 'making real poetry out of science',[61] pinpointing another feature of symbolism, a widely flung diction, very prominent in Corbière's work also. An exotic flavour is imparted by the use of words from Latin, Italian, Spanish and English (often in incorrect forms), as well as Breton. His archaisms include 'palud', and his neologisms 'plangorer', doubtless from the Latin 'plangor', highlighted by Laforgue,[62] and the poem title 'Décourageux', a compound of 'découragé' and 'courageux'. Maritime terms are naturally prominent, frequently echoing terms used in his father's novels, such as 'pelletas' and 'amateloter',[63] but his use of specialized words also includes hunting terms.

Far more important though, was Corbière's use of slang, both sailors' and the Paris streets', coupled with his extensive use of colloquialisms, which gives *Les Amours jaunes* its tone. His use of slang in 'Le bossu Bitor' is comparable with Céline's. Familiar language and slang had not before been used on such a scale in poetry, since Villon. Perhaps related to the way Corbière had 'unclassed' himself by living at Roscoff there is an attitude of 'épater le bourgeois' in *Les Amours jaunes*.

The curious medley of terms ranging from romantic majesty to vulgarity and debasement are only the result of his almost sick taste for a poetry 'of shock'. Isn't this the best way to exorcize his contempt for contemporary literature, and for all literature?[. . .]

Paradoxically, however, the taste for rough drafts is coupled with a general fondness for word-play. Semantic manoeuvre lies at the heart of Corbière's poetic.†

* 'Dépoétisation et recréation recourent aux mêmes procédés. Il appartient à Corbière d'avoir élaboré ce phénomène unique dans la littérature française: un conceptisme burlesque et lyrique.' Christian Angelet, *La poétique de Tristan Corbière*, Brussels, 1961, p. 134.

† 'Le curieux bariolage de termes qui vont de la majesté romantique à la vulgarité et à l'encanaillement, ne résulte que de son goût presque maladif pour

Corbière's poetry combines elements from the literary tradition with extreme innovation. 'Far from being detached from literary language, he uses it in his own way, degrades the poetic vocabulary, makes use of the old rhetoric, of traditional syntax. . .'.* The jerkiness of rhythm, resulting from the colloquial style, fits the rapid shifts of sense of this 'writing in flashes and ellipses'.† 'A Corbière poem limps and breaks off and recovers when the poet wishes it to express the corresponding sentiment.'[64] The hiatuses in Corbière's work have to be crossed on the strength of an allusion, often contained in a single word. This omission of all extraneous material, even to the point of puzzlement, combined with Corbière's diction, produced the intensity so much admired by Pound.

Corbière's structuring of a poem is of a piece with his use of traditional prosody. Generally, he was content to use the traditional sonnet, rondel, and stanzaic forms, although he took liberties with these, for instance over the repetition of the refrain in his twelve-line 'Rondels pour après'. A few poems, including 'Sous un portrait de Corbière' (p. 124), are not written according to any pattern in line length, rhyme or stanzaic division. Laforgue was inconsistent in selecting one of these to redeem Corbière's technical deficiencies: 'He isn't an artist, but all is forgiven for the sake of perfect and immortal laments like: *Le poète contumace*.'‡

Corbière often used verbal associations structurally in a poem, to shift from one idea to another, to introduce additional connotations and to move from one stanza to another. The pun, a favourite device whether apposite or not, could be used pivotally; an elab-

---

une poésie "de choc". N'est-ce pas le meilleur moyen d'exorciser son mépris de la littérature contemporaine, et de toute littérature? [. . .]

Paradoxalement cependant, le goût du brouillon est allé de pair avec un enchérissement général des jeux de mots. C'est que la manœuvre sémantique est au centre de la poétique de Corbière.' Angelet, op. cit., pp. 38, 39.

* 'Bien loin d'être dégagé du langage littéraire, il l'utilise à sa guise, dégrade le vocabulaire poétique, se sert de la rhétorique ancienne, de la syntaxe traditionnelle [. . .].' Angelet, op. cit., p. 136.

† '[. . .] l'écriture en éclairs et en ellipses', André Breton, *Anthologie de l'humour noir*, Paris, 1950, p. 163.

‡ 'Il n'est pas artiste, mais on pardonne tout devant des plaintes parfaites et immortelles comme: *Le poète contumace*.' 'Une Étude sur Corbière', in *Mélanges posthumes, Œuvres complètes de Jules Laforgue*, Paris, 1903, p. 122.

orate example, involving a quotation from La Fontaine, occurs in
'Idylle coupée':

> – C'est le fonds qui manque le moins.
>
> C'est toujours un fond chaud qui fume [. . . .] [p. 62]

While Corbière made full use of traditional figures of speech,
especially the oxymoron, he turned them to his own incongruous
purposes by ignoring the classical preclusion of the metaphor with
terms excessively far removed from each other.

In stock phrases, Corbière was fond of replacing the expected
word by another, with humorous effects. In 'Matelots', 'le plancher
à vaches' becomes 'le plancher à bœufs' (p. 98). In 'Bonsoir', the
colloquialism 'taper dans l'œil' becomes 'taper dans un miroir'
(p. 28); this invented phrase is then used to structure ironically
the whole sonnet. In 'Le poète contumace', 'la harpe éolienne'
(the Aeolian harp, the wind harp) becomes (p. 36) 'la porte
éolienne' ('the Aeolian door') with burlesque effect. The section
title 'Sérénade des sérénades' is ironical at the expense of human
love, as well as of the Hebrew 'Song of Songs' from which it is
transposed.

Corbière found word play irresistible,[65] producing dazzling and
sometimes irritating effects. In an almost Joycean way he was
always alive to the various associations of each word, apart from
its temporary context. An aspect of artistic detachment, word-play
is here the poet's way of handling the ironic perception in the con-
fines of a single word.

Laforgue identified the psychological significance of Corbière's
paradoxes, used with particular éclat in 'Épitaphe' (p. 2), 'Litanie
du sommeil' (p. 50) and 'Décourageux' (p. 44).

> Besides, all these gongorisms of antithesis are not games in the
> air: they have roots. He is the man who declares his love and is
> disappointed if he's listened to, who flees society and complains that
> he's left alone. The spoilt child who doesn't know what he wants,
> refuses his soup because it's pressed on him and whimpers when it's
> taken away from him.*

* 'D'ailleurs tous ces gongorismes d'antithèse ne sont pas un jeu en l'air: il
y a des racines. C'est l'homme qui déclare son amour et qui est dépité si on
l'écoute, qui fuit la société et se lamente qu'on le laisse seul. L'enfant gâté qui

'Paria' (p. 70), though not among Corbière's most effective poems, expresses lucidly by means of antitheses the solitude of a mind perpetually *dédoublé*, anticipating the existentialist dilemma of the mind isolated from itself.

In his use of the plethora of imagery that characterizes his poetry, Corbière, disregards the classical insistence on analogous terms in a comparison, in favour of the most widely flung and surprising imagery. An apostrophe of insomnia, from 'Insomnie', illustrates the extent of this.

> Why, Pretty-by-night, blooming unclean,
> This black mask on your face? . . .
> – To complicate golden dreams? . . .
> Aren't you love in space,
> The breath of Messalina, exhausted,
> But not yet sated!   [p. 17]

The new element in Corbière's imagery was his hallucinatory perception, strikingly exemplified in 'Cris d'aveugle' (p. 94). 'Paris nocturne' (p. 124) illustrates Corbière's ability to integrate the subject with its setting, a mode of the 'objective correlative' in this poem given a hallucinatory character. In 'Heures' (p. 42), Corbière not only parodies Romantic medievalism in the first verse, but with 'charming brutality'* develops the Romantic conception of man's *rapport* with nature: 'Corbière takes up a position in a tradition at the same time turning it to new ends; from old material he makes a technique for exploring the "paranormal" regions of the individual.'†

Corbière's hallucinatory effect derives from a tendency in his work for the image to supplant the reality. This partly resulted from his favourite technique of attaching his imagery by means of apposition. 'The author's favourite formula of characterization consists of presenting the image by one or more appositions

---

ne sait ce qu'il veut, refuse sa soupe parce qu'on la lui prêche et pleurniche dès qu'on la lui enlève.' Laforgue, op. cit., p. 125.

  * '[. . .] brutalité charmante', Verlaine, op. cit., p. 9.

  † 'Corbière s'installe dans une tradition tout en la détournant à des fins nouvelles, il fait du matériel ancien un moyen d'exploration des régions "paranormales" de l'être.' Angelet, op. cit., p. 82.

following the term which explicates them.'* In the 'Litanie du sommeil' (p. 50), the images, unleashed by the association of ideas, are structured and heightened by the use of oxymoron and antithesis. Yet because these images remain comprehensive as symbols and never lose their hold on reality in attempting to delineate the sur-real, the 'Litanie du sommeil' is not comparable with 'automatic writing'. Corbière's technique exploits the multi-associations of words and phrases, but his syntax, though at times eccentric, and his grip on the poem's structuring rationale preclude total 'free association'.

Closely related to Corbière's activation of his images by means of apposition is his predilection for the noun, in turn imposing on his poetry characteristic constructions, as well as weakening the adjective and verb. 'Guitare' (p. 40) and 'Heures' (p. 42) are among Corbière's poems which have few adjectives, while 'Au vieux Roscoff' (p. 110) illustrates the typical poverty of those employed. Corbière's trick of using the noun as an adjective further weakens the verb, as in 'La mer . . . elle n'est plus *marin*!'

Eliot identified this trait in Corbière's work: 'With Corbière, the centre of gravity is more in the *word* and the phrase.'[66] Pol Kalig, too, perceived the same tendency, in less semantic terms, echoing 'Décourageux' (p. 46): 'It was the work of a true poet despite the lack of melody in his language, for poetry isn't in the harmony of words, [. . .] it's in *the thing*, the ocean, flowers, it's poetry itself, said Corbière–doesn't need painters or poets.'† This is a far cry from the mainstream of Symbolism, with its aspiration to the 'condition of music' and hermetic tendency, from which Corbière's use of colloquial speech and direct statement also diverged.

Laforgue, who developed these elements in Corbière's work, stressed its colloquial quality: 'half his verse is in the intonation, the gesture and the grimaces of the comedian'.‡ A characteristic

---

* 'La formule de caractérisation préférée de l'auteur consiste dans la présentation de l'image par une ou plusieurs appositions suivant le terme qui les glose.' Angelet, op. cit., p. 92.

† 'C'était l'œuvre d'un vrai poète malgré le peu de mélodie de sa langue, car la poésie n'est pas dans l'harmonie des mots, [. . .] elle est dans *la chose*, l'océan, les fleurs, c'est la poésie même, dit Corbière–pas n'est besoin de peintre ni de poète.' Pol Kalig quoted by René Martineau, in *Tristan Corbière*, Paris, 1904, p. 87.

‡ '[. . .] la moitié de son vers est dans l'intonation, le geste et les grimaces du

concern with the direct expression of feelings would have attracted
Corbière psychologically to this kind of language. 'For Corbière–
who knew how to be precious on occasion–spoken language is not
a source among others of equal or less importance, it is *the* source,
because only from there speech gushes out under the pulsations of
life like blood driven by the heart.'* Henri Thomas' qualification
here is important: Corbière could have used other idioms had he
wished. For 'it's by this surprising mixture of elements proper to
spoken language and artificial elements that Corbière achieves a
middle position between the oral and the literary'.†

Corbière's colloquial style made an effective break with the
poetic conventions respected by Baudelaire. In particular, it made
possible his use of the interior monologue, for instance in 'Femme'
(p. 20), 'Pauvre garçon' (p. 24) and 'Rapsodie d'un sourd' (p. 46).
This style lent itself generally to the treatment of more realistic,
so-called 'ordinary' themes, by contrast with Romantic-Symbolist
aestheticism.

Corbière's colloquialism also contributes to his pervasive irony,
whose literary roots were in his reaction against Romantic
attitudes. His syntactical fondness for apposition, making for swift
shifts of sense and the necessity for the reader to make quick
intuitive connections, facilitated a great deal of juxtaposition. A
detached perception of the simultaneity of unrelated experience
can scarcely fail to produce irony. Corbière's intensity is made
bearable only by his irony. Pound characterized Corbière by his
intensity, and what makes this intensity fully effective is the
detached ironic attitude which acts as a springboard: these two
aspects react together to give Corbière's work the explosive effect
of a proverbial immovable object meeting an irresistible force. The
ideal of the expression of emotion untrammelled by intellectual

---

diseur', 'Une Étude sur Corbière', in *Mélanges posthumes, Œuvres complètes de
Jules Laforgue*, Paris, 1903 p. 124.

* 'Pour Corbière–qui sait être précieux à l'occasion–la langue parlée n'est
pas une source parmi d'autres d'égale ou de moindre importance, elle est *la*
source, parce que là seulement le langage jaillit sous les pulsions de la vie
comme le sang lancé par le cœur.' Henri Thomas, *Tristan le Dépossédé*, Paris,
1972, p. 66.

† 'C'est par ce dosage surprenant d'éléments propres à la langue parlée et
d'éléments artificiels que Corbière atteint un moyen terme entre l'oral et le
littéraire.' Angelet, op. cit., p. 108.

schemata is not uncommon, at least outside France: what distinguishes Corbière is the thoroughgoing irony, safeguarding undoctored emotion that would otherwise evaporate off the page.

*

The achievements of Corbière and Laforgue have been strongly developed in English, but Verlaine's resurrection of *Les Amours jaunes*, a pivotal critical event in the development of Symbolism, also initiated a line of influence in France. Before that, *Les Amours jaunes* appears to have been appreciated by one small French literary group soon after its appearance:

> It's quite possible, in fact, and I willingly believe M. Luce and M. Paterne Berrichon, that a copy of the *Amours Jaunes*, discovered on the quays by the designer-poet, Parisel, was communicated early on to the 'Vivants', the poetic circle founded in 1875 by Jean Richepin, Raoul Ponchon, and Maurice Bouchor. But the members of the coterie must have kept this revelation jealously for themselves, for nothing about it came out in public until 1883.*

In particular, Richepin's use of slang seems to have been influenced by Corbière's. The realistic parts of *La Mer* reveal the influence of Corbière's 'Gens de mer', with which various textual parallels may be established.

In 1883 a copy of *Les Amours jaunes* was shown to Verlaine by Charles Morice and Léo Trézenik, the editor of *Lutèce*, whose attention had in turn been drawn to the book by Pol Kalig. Verlaine's study of Corbière was published in *Lutèce* later in the year, and in 1884 was reprinted as the opening chapter of his *Poètes maudits*, with his seminal studies of Rimbaud and Mallarmé.[67] Since *Les Amours jaunes* had passed quite unnoticed in 1873, and the edition had soon been remaindered, Verlaine's resurrection of the book was crucial.

In his essay, Verlaine praised Corbière so highly that it is not

---

* 'Il est fort possible, en effet, et j'en croirais volontiers M. Luce et M. Paterne Berrichon, qu'un exemplaire des *Amours Jaunes*, découvert sur les quais par le dessinateur-poète Parisel, ait été communiqué d'assez bonne heure aux "Vivants", le cénacle poétique fondé en 1875 par Jean Richepin, Raoul Ponchon, et Maurice Bouchor. Mais il faut donc que les membres du cénacle aient gardé jalousement pour eux cette révélation, car il n'en transpira rien dans le public jusqu'en 1883.' Charles Le Goffic, Introduction, *Les Amours jaunes*, Paris, 1912, p. iii.

surprising to trace the influence of the Breton in his later work, with the mutual 'realism in lyricism'.[68] In his study of Corbière he quoted the whole of 'Heures', whose influence may be found in 'L'Impudent' in *Parallèlement*, though the end of Verlaine's sonnet recalls the closing lines of 'Bonne fortune et fortune'. On the other hand, Verlaine doesn't mention the 'Rondels pour après', yet it is this section of Corbière's work that seems to have most influenced his own, especially syntactically.*

Soon after the publication of Verlaine's essay, J.-K. Huysmans published *À Rebours* (1884), 'the breviary of the Decadence'.[69] This book reached a wide circle of readers, and helped to publicize Corbière further. The term 'decadent', which had previously been applied to Baudelaire, now embraced, through Des Esseintes' predilection, Verlaine, Mallarmé and Corbière. Although Huysmans, like Verlaine, underestimated the technique of *Les Amours jaunes*, 'a fantastically eccentric book',† he stressed its energy and economy.

> It was scarcely French; the poet was talking 'pidgin', using a telegram idiom, suppressing far too many verbs, trying to be waggish, and indulging in cheap commercial-traveller jokes; but then, out of this jungle of comical conceits and smirking witticisms there would suddenly rise a sharp cry of pain, like the sound of a violoncello string breaking.‡

Yet the withdrawal trend in 'mainstream' Symbolism, of which the 'super-dreamer', Des Esseintes, is the personification, is not found in Corbière's work, or indeed in the 'conversational-ironic'

* Despite the similarity of Verlaine's famous 'Il pleure dans mon cœur / Comme il pleut sur la ville' ('Ariettes oubliées', III), with Corbière's 'Il pleut dans mon foyer, il pleut dans mon cœur feu' ('Le poète contumace'), it is clear from chronological evidence that all the *Romances sans paroles*, including this poem, were composed before even the publication of *Les Amours jaunes*. See Francis Burch, 'Corbière and Verlaine's "Romances sans Paroles" ', *Modern Language Review*, LIII, 2 (April 1958), pp. 217–18.

† '[. . .] un volume des plus excentriques', J.-K. Huysmans, *À Rebours*, Paris, 1919, p. 248.

‡ 'C'était à peine français; l'auteur parlait nègre, procédait par un langage de télégramme, abusait des suppressions de verbes, affectait une gouaillerie, se livrait à des quolibets de commis-voyageur insupportable, puis tout à coup, dans ce fouillis, se tortillaient des concetti falots, des minauderies interlopes, et soudain jaillissait un cri de douleur aiguë, comme une corde de violoncelle qui se brise.' Huysmans, op. cit., pp. 248–9. The English version is taken from Robert Baldick's translation, *Against Nature*, Penguin Classics, 1973, p. 188.

current generally. The analysis fits Corbière's life at Roscoff, but this has to be related to the peculiar circumstances of his illness. Contrary to G. M. Turnell's thesis,[70] Corbière did not use his Breton background to make a new synthesis, merely sharing to an extreme degree in the general contempt of artists for the bourgeois world. Equally false is the view of Corbière as anticipating the twentieth-century theme of the writer exiled in the city.[71] Corbière was an exile everywhere: 'My Country . . . is anywhere there's ground'.* Laforgue's metaphor of the man who 'flees society and complains that he's left alone'† is more applicable to himself than to Corbière, for whom circumstances at least initially beyond his control had created 'the brothel of life'.‡

Corbière's style diverged so sharply from the narrower Symbolist aesthetic as later defined as to subvert it; for the neo-classicist of the 1891 manifesto, Corbière was far too extreme and experimental. In the sense that the roots of their poetry are in daily life, albeit often in an off-beat milieu, Corbière, and Laforgue and Apollinaire and their followers, 'the modern realists', are 'the poets of the multitude',[72] though of course this very use of the quotidian was too sophisticated to appeal *to* the multitude. The withdrawal symptoms, of 'incessant speculations'[73] about the nature of poetry, diagnosed by Edmund Wilson in Corbière's admirer, T. S. Eliot, occurred when his own 'conversational-ironic' phase had been replaced by the rhetoric of the religious synthesis of the *Four Quartets*.

Léon Bloy compared Corbière favourably with Rimbaud and Mallarmé in his damning review of *Les Poètes maudits*, but he misunderstood his work. Concentrating on the Breton aspect, he denied that Corbière was a 'poète maudit'. He found 'La Rapsode foraine' 'an incontestable miracle of poetic beauty and simple sentiment',§ not only ignoring the religious irony, but reinforcing the exclusively Breton view of Corbière.

* '–Ma Patrie . . . elle est par le monde', from 'Paria' (p. 72).
† '[. . .] qui fuit la société et se lamente qu'on le laisse seul', 'Une Étude sur Corbière', in *Mélanges posthumes, Œuvres complètes de Jules Laforgue*, Paris,1903, p. 125.
‡ '[. . .] le bordel de la vie', Henri Thomas, Preface to *Les Amours jaunes*, ed Jean-Louis Lalanne, Paris, 1973, p. 12.
§ '[. . .] un incontestable miracle de beauté poétique et de sentiment naïf', Léon Bloy, 'On demande des malédictions', *Le Chat noir*, 3 May 1884; reprinted in *Le Pal, suivi des nouveaux propos d'un entrepreneur de démolitions*, Paris, 1925, p. 237.

In 1891 the second edition of *Les Amours jaunes* came out, from the 'Symbolist' publisher, Vanier, indicating the contemporary respect for those writers recognized by the Symbolists as their spiritual ancestors. The same year saw the posthumous publication of Laforgue's notes on Corbière,[74] the best nineteenth-century study of the poet. It is arguable that Corbière's most significant influence has not been direct, but via Laforgue. Yet controversy surrounds the exact measure of Laforgue's debt to Corbière, fifteen years his senior.

Léo Trézenik reviewing the *Complaintes* had seen Laforgue as a Decadent who 'steeped, soaked, completely saturated with Corbière, has taken to extravagant extremes the method of the author of "Les Amours jaunes" '.* This elicited an indignant letter from Laforgue, denying that he knew Corbière's work when writing the book, and faulting his technique: 'I've wanted to create symphonies and melody, and Corbière plays that everlasting fiddle of his.'† Yet Gustave Kahn stated that he introduced Laforgue to Corbière's work in 1880:

[. . .] I revealed to him Corbière, whom I had just come across in the conversations of one of his second cousins, who signed his light verses Pol Kalig, and tried to get the *Amours jaunes* known, without much success. We found him admirable for various reasons.‡

When in another chapter in *Symbolistes et décadents* he follows Laforgue in denying Corbière's influence on the *Complaintes*, he adds significantly that 'Laforgue scarcely knew Corbière'§ then.

* '[. . .] trempé, imbu, sursaturé de Corbière, a poussé jusqu'à l'extravagance le procédé de l'auteur de "Les Amours jaunes". . .', Léo Trézenik, *Lutèce*, 9 August 1885. Quoted by Micha Grin, *Tristan Corbière, Poète maudit*, Évian, 1972, p. 182.

† '[. . .] j'ai voulu faire de la symphonie et de la mélodie, et Corbière joue de l'éternel crincrin que vous savez.' Jules Laforgue, *Lutèce*, 4 October 1885; reprinted in *Œuvres complètes de Jules Laforgue*, V, ed. G. Jean-Aubry, Paris, 1925, p. 137.

‡ '[. . .] je lui révélais Corbière que je venais de découvrir dans les conversations d'un de ses petits cousins qui signait Pol Kalig des vers légers, essayait de faire connaître les *Amours Jaunes*, et y réussissait plutôt peu. Nous le trouvâmes admirable pour des raisons diverses.' Gustave Kahn, *Symbolistes et décadents*, Paris, 1902, p. 28. The previous paragraph on p. 27 dates it.

§ '[. . .] Laforgue ne connaissait presque pas Corbière', Kahn, op. cit., p. 136.

As Warren Ramsey concludes, 'a glance at his [Laforgue's] letters is enough to show that he had time, and his first book proves that he took occasion, to profit from the novel idiom that Corbière brought into French verse'.[75]

Highly significant, too, is Laforgue's 'Étude sur Corbière', which reveals almost despite itself the author's psychological attraction to *Les Amours jaunes*. Laforgue's insight suggests far more than the 'grain of cousinship'* which he reluctantly acknowledged. He implicitly admitted the importance of this 'ocean bohemian'† when he said, 'there is no other artist in verse, freer from poetic language than he is'.‡ Corbière and Laforgue together 'introduced a new variety of vocabulary and a new flexibility of feeling'.[76] By their use of the vernacular they prepared for the work of such twentieth-century poets as Blaise Cendrars, Max Jacob, Paul Éluard and Pierre Reverdy.

Laforgue's reputation has always overshadowed Corbière's; deservedly so, for the facility of his technical expertise and his fluency. His intellectualism enabled him both to smooth and to sharpen the chaotic feelings of *Les Amours jaunes*. He developed the techniques attendant on Corbière's colloquial style; his interior monologue, for instance, in the 'Complainte des consolations' resembles Corbière's 'Pauvre garçon'. He also took over themes, such as the tourism of some of Corbière's Italian poems, which Eliot was later to exploit. Laforgue's 'Avertissement', whose tone resembles Corbière's 'Bohème de chic' (p. 6), illustrates the psychological affinity between the two poets, though Laforgue's superior technique generally produced more sophisticated results.

> Mon père (un dur par timidité)
> Est mort avec un profil sévère;
> J'avais presque pas connu ma mère,
> Et donc vers vingt ans je suis resté.
>
> Alors, j'ai fait d'la littérature,
> Mais le Démon de la Vérité

* '[. . .] un grain de cousinage', Jules Laforgue, *Lutèce*, 4 October 1885.
† 'Bohême de l'océan', 'Une Étude sur Corbière', in *Mélanges posthumes, Œuvres complètes de Jules Laforgue*, Paris, 1903, p. 119.
‡ '[. . .]' il n'y a pas un autre artiste en vers, plus dégagé que lui du langage poétique.' Laforgue, op. cit., p. 121.

> Sifflotait tout l'temps à mes côtés:
> 'Pauvre! as-tu fini tes écritures . . .'[77]

Unfortunately, underestimation of Corbière's technique persisted even among his admirers. Rémy de Gourmont included him in his *Livre des masques* (1896) as a literary eccentric: 'Tristan Corbière is, like Laforgue, in some ways his disciple, one of those undeniable talents, defying classification, which occur in histories of literature'.* Though Gustave Kahn did not devote a separate study to Corbière in his *Symbolistes et décadents*, where he mentioned him briefly as a 'poète maudit', he discussed him sympathetically in his review of Martineau's first book on the poet, indicating his influence on the later Symbolists:

> [. . .] Tristan Corbière has taken his place among, in a way, the precursors of Symbolism, or rather among those in whom the writers of 1885 and the years immediately following, recognized enough independence towards the preceding literary forms and enough characteristic originality for them to appreciate them and to revise the judgements on them of their immediate predecessors.†

In the early twentieth century, Paul Fort's review, *Vers et Prose*, dedicated to the continuation of the lyric renaissance of 1885, recalled the Symbolist period in its poems and essays, including André Salmon's essay on Corbière. Praising the dizzy rhythms of the 'Litanie du sommeil', Salmon asked, 'isn't he one of those who prepared the fertile revolution from which, more dazzling, the new French poetry derives?'‡ Salmon himself later developed into

---

* '[. . .] Tristan Corbière est, comme Laforgue, un peu son disciple, l'un de ces talents inclassables et indéniables qui sont dans l'histoire des littératures', Rémy de Gourmont, *Le Livre des masques*, I, Paris, 1914, p. 155.

† '[. . .] Tristan Corbière a pris sa place parmi, en quelque sorte, les précurseurs du symbolisme, ou plutôt parmi ceux en qui les écrivains de 1885 et des années qui suivirent immédiatement, reconnurent assez d'indépendance envers les modes littéraires précédentes et une originalité assez particulière pour les aimer et reviser les arrêts de leurs immédiats devanciers à l'égard de ces artistes.' Gustave Kahn, 'Tristan Corbière', *La Nouvelle Revue*, Nouvelle série, XXIX (14 July 1904), p. 271.

‡ '[. . .] n'est-il pas de ceux qui préparèrent la révolution féconde dont vit plus éblouissante la jeune poésie française?' André Salmon, 'Nos Morts: Tristan Corbière', *Vers et Prose*, II (June–August 1905), p. 198.

a Cubist, and Corbière's influence is most marked in his early poems in *Les Clés ardentes* (1905) and *Les Féeries* (1907). 'Anvers', a slightly later poem reminiscent of Corbière, includes even the same typographical arrangement of the bar's name:

C'est à l'ESTAMINET DE L'ÉTOILE POLAIRE,
Tenu par une veuve hilaire et sans pudeur [. . . .][78]

This follows Corbière's

– C'est au boulevard excentrique,
Au–BON RETOUR DU CHAMP DU NORD–[. . . .]
[p. 62]

In 1908, in one of three lectures on poetry given at the Salon des artistes indépendants, P.-N. Roinard speaking on 'Nos Maîtres et nos Morts' claimed Corbière as one of the masters of those who had been important in the lyric renaissance of 1885.[79] Looking back, André Fontainas distinguished the line of Corbière's and Laforgue's influence: 'Following the originators Jules Laforgue and Tristan Corbière, a new mode of lyrical expression has developed at the height of the Symbolist period.'* With the 'Rondels pour après', the Paris poems chiefly attracted the Fantaisistes, preoccupied with modern civilization. Technically, they admired Corbière's demolition of the old lyric conception of poetry. Fontainas identified their typical manner 'mingling in-cessantly with irony of voice and attitude, badly controlled con-vulsions of disillusioned and painful bitterness',† continued by poets like Tristan Klingsor, Paul-Jean Toulet, Salmon and Apollinaire. The English critic, F. S. Flint, also recognized this influence: 'and above all [. . .] Laforgue, Rimbaud, Corbière, and M. Paul Fort himself: this seems to be the lineage of the younger Fantaisistes'.[80] Among the names listed by Flint in this connection were Salmon, Apollinaire, Max Jacob, Francis Carco, Tristan Derème and Toulet.

* 'A la suite de Jules Laforgue et de Tristan Corbière initiateurs, un mode nouveau d'expression lyrique s'est développé au fort de la période symboliste.' André Fontainas, *Mes Souvenirs du symbolisme*, Paris, 1928, p. 209.
† '[. . .] mêlant incessamment à l'ironie de la voix et de l'attitude les con-vulsions mal réfrénées d'une amertume désabusée et douloureuse', ibid.

Carco, too, mentioned Corbière with Rimbaud and Laforgue as precursors in his anthology of Fantaisiste poetry in *Vers et Prose*, 1913.[81] (Verlaine was at least equally important for the Fantaisistes, who were a very nebulous group.) Carco himself went so far as to include a line from Corbière's 'Un jeune qui s'en va' in his poem 'À l'amitié', which is a similar ironic invocation of the Muses, mentioning a string of poets, including Corbière, by name:

> Emporte-moi dans ton délire,
> Muse errante aux yeux clignotants,
> Qui vaticines et prétends:
> 'Mon bout de crayon, c'est ma lyre!
> Mais je n'ai plus de papier blanc.'[82]

Carco and Derème were the regular French contributors to John Middleton Murry's *Rhythm* for prose and poetry respectively. Writing there, Derème indicated as the sources of modern French verse, Baudelaire, Verlaine, Mallarmé and Corbière.[83] Corbière's influence is apparent in his own *La Verdure dorée*. Toulet's *Contrerimes*, too, appears indebted to Corbière and Laforgue in its use of the new style.

Apollinaire also referred to Corbière in his lecture at the Salon des artistes indépendants in 1908, comparing Henri Hertz to him and Laforgue.[84] Probably Apollinaire was very familiar with *Les Amours jaunes*. Corbière was sufficiently revered as a precursor of Symbolism for the book to be re-issued in 1891 and 1902.

> We must even suppose that Apollinaire read Corbière's verses very early. Indeed, how can we fail to recognize the latter's direct influence as much in the substance (the sarcasm) as in the form (cf. *Rondels pour après*) of the 'rondel' 'Au Ciel', signed Wilhelm de Kostrowitzki and dated, *Cannes, 1896?**

Corbière's bitter reversal of 'bien-aimé' to 'mal-aimé', in 'Femme' (p. 20) and 'À une camarade', became widespread after Apollin-

---

* 'On doit même supposer qu'Apollinaire lut très tôt les vers de Corbière. Comment, en effet, ne pas reconnaître l'influence directe de ce dernier aussi bien pour le fond (le sarcasme) que pour la forme (cf. *Rondels pour après*) dans le "rondel" "Au Ciel", signé Wilhelm de Kostrowitzki et daté de *Cannes, 1896?*' Antoine Fongaro, 'Le Poète et le Crapaud', *Revue des Lettres modernes*, 4 (104–7) (1964), p. 117

aire's 'Chanson du mal-aimé'. Though Apollinaire's dispensing with punctuation and his typographical innovations may be related to Mallarmé rather than to Corbière, his mixture of prose and verse and his use of popular songs, as well as his colloquialism and humour, link him with Corbière and Laforgue.

Corbière's early poem, the 'Légende incomprise de l'apothicaire Danet', shows his characteristic use of punctuation, developed in *Les Amours jaunes* almost as 'a kind of musical notation'.[85] His use of punctuation and his typographical arrangement have been further compared with Birot's and Marinetti's, as an aspiration towards 'total communication'.[86] Corbière's renunciation of punctuation in 'Cris d'aveugle' (p. 94), and also in the prose epigraph to 'Épitaphe' (p. 2), preceded Mallarmé's. Yet Corbière's punctuation was to an extent imposed by his appositional style.

More importantly, Corbière's use of the vernacular and his exploitation of irony influenced the early Expressionist poets, Hoddis and Lichtenstein, through the translations of his work by K. L. Ammer which came out in Germany in 1900 and 1907.[87] Stressing the Parisian poems and the 'Rondels pour après', in the Fantaisiste tradition, Léon Bocquet credited Corbière with the discovery of 'a new state of poetic sensibility':*

> Verlaine and the Symbolists will be honoured for this discovery, yet is it not Corbière who has been the originator of this poetry where the superimposed images and the colliding rhythms, 'seraphic choir and drunken versicles', together prolong and multiply the sensations and unforgettable resonances?†

In the defensive pride engendered by the circumstances of his life, Bocquet compared Corbière to Byron, as the anonymous reviewer in *La Renaissance littéraire et artistique* in 1873 had done.

Probably thinking of Poe, this reviewer also compared the book

* '[. . .] un état nouveau de sensibilité poétique', Léon Bocquet, *Les Destinées mauvaises*, Amiens, 1923, p. 77.

† 'On fera honneur de cette découverte à Verlaine et aux symbolistes, pourtant n'est-ce point Corbière qui a été initiateur de cette poésie où les images qui se superposent et les rhythmes qui se heurtent, "chant séraphique et chant d'ivrogne" tout ensemble prolongent et multiplient les sensations et d'inoubliables résonnances?' ibid.

to the work of 'certain American poets'.* In fact Poe, an aesthetic theorist whose ideal is 'anywhere out of this world' is the antithesis of Corbière, a pragmatic writer who did not enjoy being 'outside mankind's perimeter'.† This antithesis largely explains the appeal Poe and Corbière have had to the French and English respectively. Identifying linguistic and perceptual differences between French and English, Yves Bonnefoy instances the typical French critical attitude that considers Corbière and Laforgue minor, out of the mainstream of French poetry.[88] For the realism of Corbière and Laforgue, so attractive to English and American readers, is less acceptable in the more intellectual tradition of French poetry, though of course the current of their influence continued in twentieth-century French writers. The French point out that Villon himself has always been a great favourite of the Anglo-Saxons, in keeping with a poetic tradition derived from Chaucer.

There had already been some American fertilization of French literature in the Symbolist period, apart from Poe. The American, Francis Vielé-Griffin, laid so much stress on *vers libre* that he has been credited with breaking the alexandrine. Another American, Stuart Merrill, similarly celebrated as a French poet, at the end of the 1880s wrote articles for the *New York Times* and *Evening Post* on modern French literature.[89]

However, it was Pound who, in 1913 discovering in Corbière 'the greatest poet of the period',[90] was responsible for his introduction to English-speaking readers, beginning with his series of articles on modern French verse in *The New Age* the same year. Thenceforward, particularly as foreign correspondent for *Poetry*, he consistently publicized Corbière, for his 'modernity that we have not yet surpassed'.[91] Believing that 'the *technique* of French poets was *certainly* in a condition to serve to *educate* the poets of my language',‡ Pound later declared that the '*essential* poets'§ since Gautier were Corbière, Laforgue and Rimbaud. '[. . .] if our American bards would [. . .] get some idea of intensity from

* '[. . .] certains poètes américains', *La Renaissance littéraire et artistique*, 26 October 1873, p. 304.

† 'En dehors de l'humaine piste', from 'Le poète contumace' (p. 30).

‡ '[. . .] la *technique* des poètes français était *certainement* en état de servir d'*education* aux poétes [*sic*] de ma langue', letter to René Taupin, May 1928, *The Letters of Ezra Pound 1907–1941*, ed. D. D. Paige, New York, 1950, p. 217.

§ '[. . .] les poétes [*sic*] *essentials*', ibid.

Tristan Corbière (since they will not take their Villon in the original)', and if generally they would 'keep their eye on Paris instead of on London—the London of today or of yesterday—there might be some chance of their doing work that would not be *démodé* before it gets to the press'.[92] Pound has been accused of volatility in his sudden enthusiasm for the modern French poets, after some slight initial resistance to them,* but in fact he found in them the *same* qualities he admired in Catullus, Propertius and the troubadours, and they figured consistently in his lists of exemplars.

Corbière's influence on Pound's own work was particularly through his irony, his direct style, and his use of allusion and juxtaposition. Corbière's attack on Hugo and the Romantics was paralleled by Pound's and Eliot's reaction against Tennyson and the Victorians. Pound's 'Salutation the Third' reproduces Corbière's violence, controlled to an extent in both writers by the richness and curiosity of the imagery.

> Let us deride the smugness of 'The Times': GUFFAW!
> So much for the gagged reviewers,
> It will pay them when the worms are wriggling in their vitals;
> These are they who objected to newness,
> Here are their tomb-stones.
>   They supported the gag and the ring:
> A little BLACK BOX contains them.[93]

Pound came to overshadow Flint as the chief enthusiast for French poetry, in his influence on London, though Flint continued to publicize the younger Symbolists and their successors. Among these, he had compared Henri Hertz to Corbière, as Apollinaire had done: 'Just as with Laforgue, just as with Tristan Corbière, you will be aware that you have been attacked by a piercing criticism of life [. . .].'[94]

However, the Imagist most attracted to Corbière was the

---

* 'We were also very much influenced by modern French symbolist poetry.[. . .] Ezra Pound used to boast in those days that he was
      Nil praeter "Villon" et doctus cantare Catullum,
and he could not be made to believe that there was any French poetry after Ronsard.' F. S. Flint, 'The History of Imagism', *The Egoist*, 1 May 1915, p. 71. Flint's remarks refer to 1909–10.

American, John Gould Fletcher, who dedicated his *Fool's Gold*
(1913) to him and five other 'poètes maudits', placing Corbière at
the head of the list. At that time Fletcher read a French book a day.
He claimed to have introduced Pound to Corbière: '[. . .] on his
next visit to my flat, he borrowed an armful of my French books
and departed. When I next saw him, he was already enthusiastic
over de Gourmont, Corbière, and the early Francis Jammes.'[95]
Temperamentally, Fletcher would seem to have more affinity with
Corbière than would Flint. Pound's review of *Fool's Gold* and *The
Dominant City*, drawing attention to Fletcher's interest in French
poetry beyond that admired in England in the nineties and sanc-
tioned by the tradition, relates to his identification of 'the cult of
ugliness, Villon, Baudelaire, Corbière, Beardsley [. . .]':[96] 'His
[Fletcher's] art is an art that dares to go to the dust-bin for its
subjects.'[97]

Although Richard Aldington shared to an extreme degree in
the common confusion of Corbière and Laforgue–always to
Corbière's disadvantage–when he declared that, 'the new poet is
the "poète contumace" of Laforgue',[98] (while on another occasion
he appears to attribute Corbière's 'Heures' to Verlaine),[99] later
in the same article on 'The Poetry of T. S. Eliot', he differentiated
between the two French poets in connection with Eliot:

> The common perception of the affinity between 'Ara vos prec' and
> 'Les Complaintes' may be extended to 'Les Illuminations' and 'Les
> Amours Jaunes'. And when the reader has granted that, he has
> simply admitted that one side of Mr. Eliot's poetry is a development
> of the secular tradition of 'poètes contumaces' or 'poètes libertins',
> which runs from the poets of to-day to Laforgue and Verlaine, to
> Rimbaud and Corbière, to Aloysius Bertrand, to Saint-Amant, to
> Théophile, back to Villon, and beyond him to a shadowy host of
> mediaeval 'pinces-sans-rire' [. . .].[100]

Aldington concentrated on Eliot's French poems, where the
influence of Corbière is indeed most easily seen. 'Mélange Adultère
de Tout' 'depends for its full effect upon the reader's comprehend-
ing the reference to Corbière's "Épave mort-né" [in the sub-title
of the shorter "Épitaphe"]'.[101] Of Eliot's four French poems, this
one is closest to Corbière in inspiration, though, characteristically,
more impersonal; but 'Lune de Miel' suggests Corbière's 'Veder

Napoli poi mori',[102] and 'Dans le Restaurant', whose third stanza
is re-created in *The Waste Land*, suggests the French poet's 'Déjeuner
de soleil'. Eliot seems to have regarded these poems as more than
exercises, retaining them in the canon of his work, and Pound, too,
at one stage had thought of writing in French, in order to get his
vers libre published, but he found French less rich than English.[103]

Between 1915 and 1920, Eliot studied Corbière closely. In 1930
he stated how he came to Corbière through Symons's *The
Symbolist Movement in Literature* (published in 1899 without any
discussion of Corbière):

> I myself owe Mr. Symons a great debt: but for having read his book,
> I should not, in the year 1908, have heard of Laforgue or Rimbaud;
> I should probably not have begun to read Verlaine; and but for
> reading Verlaine, I should not have heard of Corbière. So the
> Symons book is one of those which have affected the course of my
> life.[104]

Later, Eliot defined the 'ability to receive and assimilate in-
fluences from abroad' as an essential condition for 'the possibility
of each literature renewing itself'.[105] He was attracted to the
French poets for similar stylistic reasons to Pound: 'And in poetry
[. . .] Rimbaud, Corbière and Laforgue were for us the masters
more than any English poet of their time.'[106] In 1924, when
Baudelaire's influence was stronger than Corbière's on his writing,
he expanded on this:

> It is not a permanent necessity that poets should be interested in
> philosophy, or in any other subject. We can only say that it appears
> likely that poets in our civilization, as it exists at present, must be
> *difficult*. Our civilization comprehends great variety and complexity,
> and this variety and complexity, playing upon a refined sensibility,
> must produce various and complex results. The poet must become
> more and more comprehensive, more allusive, more indirect, in
> order to force, to dislocate if necessary, language into his mean-
> ing.[. . .] Hence we get something which looks very much like the
> conceit—we get, in fact, a method curiously similar to that of the
> 'metaphysical poets', similar also in its use of obscure words and of
> simple phrasing.[. . .] Jules Laforgue, and Tristan Corbière in many
> of his poems, are nearer to the 'school of Donne' than any modern
> English poet.[107]

Such an image of conceit in Corbière's work is 'Tes cils, barreaux de fer!'[108] These images are concentrated in the 'Rondels pour après', on which Eliot laid great emphasis, particularly 'Petit mort pour rire' (p. 120), finding as with Laforgue 'the same product of thought-feeling and feeling-thought'.[109]

However, Eliot was indebted to Corbière in other ways, notably for the realism of his diction, which in 'Gerontion' echoes 'Le poète contumace' (p. 28):

My house is a decayed house,
And the Jew squats on the window sill, the owner,
Spawned in some estaminet of Antwerp,
Blistered in Brussels, patched and peeled in London.
The goat coughs at night in the field overhead;
Rocks, moss, stonecrop, iron, merds.
The woman keeps the kitchen, makes tea,
Sneezes at evening, poking the peevish gutter.[110]

A rarer echo of Corbière in Eliot's later work is in the opening sentence of 'East Coker', 'In my beginning is my end', recalling the epigraph to Corbière's 'Épitaphe' (p. 2): 'A recollection of this passage may have influenced Eliot's use of the motto from Mary Queen of Scots as well as the cyclical concept developed in *East Coker*.'[111]

Eliot borrowed devices and echoes from Corbière mostly at an intermediate stage in his own development, between the Prufrock poems when irony provided its own justification and viewpoint, and his later achievement of synthesis. Some critics, notably Francis Burch, have seen a close similarity in both structure and themes in *Les Amours jaunes* and *The Waste Land*, yet not only does this attribute a too clearly defined synthesis to Corbière, but also clashes with Eliot's remark that 'One difference between Baudelaire and the later poets–Laforgue, Verlaine, Corbière, Rimbaud, Mallarmé–is that Baudelaire not only reveals the troubles of his own age and predicts those of the age to come, but also foreshadows some issue from these difficulties.'[112] For Baudelaire is the chief French influence on *The Waste Land*.

Irony in Corbière is primarily a personal defence: the safeguarding of emotion through irony is 'the most strongly marked characteristic of *Les Amours jaunes*'.[113] Eliot was able to turn the

technique to his own uses, which initially through the mask of the
Prufrock poems were perhaps not so far removed from Corbière's,
though until 1915 Laforgue was his prime influence. Interior
monologue had already been used ironically by Browning, but
Eliot's psychological development of this was coloured by Corbière's work. Eliot may also have been influenced by the use of
the Spanish background in the section 'Sérénade des sérénades' in
realizing the possibilities of satirizing a type of society by the
parody of poetic convention.[114] Allusion is a key device of the
'conversational-ironic' tradition which Eliot developed from
Corbière and Laforgue. Eliot also uses snippets from songs, but in
a characteristically impersonal way, in contrast with the French
poet. In 'Le poète contumace', lines from 'Au clair de la lune' are
used to convey the poet's emotion by ostensibly undervaluing it:
in *The Waste Land*, Eliot applies the nursery rhyme 'London bridge
is falling down' to society.

The use of snippets of material transposed from other sources is
an aspect of the potent irony of juxtaposition, whose use relates to
the Symbolists' fidelity to the often illogical processes of thought.
From 'a recognition, implicit in the expression of every experience,
of other kinds of experience which are possible'[115] springs a fruitful
perception of the inherent irony of life, which Corbière of course
did not fail to carry to the extreme, in his assertion, in the epigraph
to the 'Épitaphe', of the contemporaneity of the beginning and end
of life. Juxtaposition can be a perception in itself, used effectively.
Without the intense degree of organization and synthesis achieved
by Eliot in *The Waste Land*, Pound used the device to great ironical
effect throughout the *Cantos*.

Subsequent interest in Corbière has been particularly strong in
America, while André Breton staged a minor 'revival' of Corbière
in France. Enid Starkie relates Wilfred Owen to Corbière, comparing 'Dulce et Decorum' to 'La pastorale de Conlie'.[116] Since
Owen worked in France as a teacher and tutor 1913–15, he had
very likely read *Les Amours jaunes*. Although Edith Sitwell's *A Poet's
Notebook* (1943) does not mention Corbière, among abundant
references to Baudelaire, Verlaine, Rimbaud and Cocteau, he
had made a major contribution to 'the tradition which it [her
poetry] presupposes',[117] and her use of dissonance and alliteration,
with the auditory conceit, in particular suggests familiarity with
Les Amours jaunes.

A far less fruitful line of interest in Corbière's work is the visionary one, though certainly the early date of the poems is remarkable, with the 'Litanie du sommeil' presaging 'le temps des *Assassins*'.

> When Tristan wrote this *Litany*, where the shock of the rhymes, the suction stimulated by the necessity of the echo, unleashed the image with unerring force, Rimbaud had not yet written the *Illuminations*, Lautréamont had not yet published *Maldoror*. Thus it would be difficult to exaggerate the prophetic innovation of this poem.*

Though both Tzara and Breton wrote perceptively about Corbière, there is little literary common ground between their work. Breton highlighted Corbière's 'Baudelairean dandyism [which] is here transposed into total spiritual solitude'.† In his *Anthologie de l'humour noir* (1940), he included a long extract from the 'Litanie du sommeil', which, for the Surrealists, is the first example of automatic writing.

> Without doubt, it's in the *Amours jaunes* that verbal automatism establishes itself in French poetry. Corbière must be chronologically the first to have allowed himself to be carried by the surge of words which, without any conscious direction, dies on our ears every second, and to which the majority of men opposes the barrier of immediate sense.‡

Yet when Breton went on to declare that, 'All the resources which the combination of words offers are here exploited without scruple, beginning with the pun',§ he was on the verge of demolishing his

---

* 'Quand Tristan écrit cette *Litanie*, où le choc des rimes, l'appel d'air provoqué par la nécessité de l'écho, déclenchent l'image à coup sûr, Rimbaud n'a pas encore écrit les *Illuminations*, Lautréamont n'a pas encore publié *Maldoror*. On ne saurait donc insister suffisamment sur la nouveauté prophétique de ce poème.' Rousselot, op. cit., p. 54.

† 'Le dandysme baudelairien est ici transposé en pleine solitude morale [. . .]', Breton, op. cit., p. 163.

‡ 'C'est sans doute avec les *Amours Jaunes* que l'automatisme verbal s'installe dans la poésie française. Corbière doit être le premier en date à s'être laissé porter par la vague des mots qui, en dehors de toute direction consciente, expire chaque seconde à notre oreille et à laquelle le commun des hommes oppose la digue du sens immédiat.' Breton, op. cit., pp. 163–4.

§ 'Toutes les ressources qu'offre l'assemblage des mots sont ici mises à contribution sans scrupule, à commencer par le calembour [. . .]', Breton, op. cit., p. 164.

own argument. Through *Les Amours jaunes*, the images remain comprehensible as symbols: 'translating without discontinuity the theme of communion with the sur-real, to the tenets of automatism they oppose a firm poetic outline.'*

Yet the 'Litanie du sommeil', 'second life' of dream bizarrely de Nerval's anticipated not only the Surrealists but Freud. Corbière's 'systematic pursuit of "bad taste" '† and exploitation of disorder also went beyond Symbolism, anticipating Surrealism. 'In Corbière, the will to express reached a kind of verbal exasperation which, far from being disorder, is, on the contrary, the coherent unfolding of his poetic thought.'‡ But more important than any explicit statement in the poems, Corbière's controlled disorder permitted his *mélange* of mystical and bawdy, cynical and sentimental elements, which fused into his predominantly, 'strident and satiric voice'.[118]

Latterly, several major American writers have been strongly attracted to Corbière. Yvor Winters considered 'La Rapsode foraine' and 'Cris d'aveugle' 'probably superior to any French verse of the nineteenth century save the best of Baudelaire'.[119] Randall Jarrell's translation of 'Le poète contumace' and adaptations from the 'Rondels pour après'[120] reveal his feeling for the French poet, of whose elliptical style he wrote:

> If nature, once, made no jumps, it was different from Corbière, who progresses by nothing else; one of his poems passes through its aggregation of exclamations, interjections, vocatives, imperatives as an electron passes through its orbits–now here, now there, and in between nowhere.[121]

More recently, John Berryman dedicated his penultimate book, *Love & Fame*,

* '[. . .] traduisant sans discontinuer le thème de la communion avec le surréel, elles opposent aux tenants de l'automatisme un tracé poétique solide.' Angelet, op. cit., p. 99.

† '[. . .] recherches systématiques "de mauvais goût" ', Breton, op. cit., p. 163.

‡ 'La volonté d'expression, chez Tristan Corbière, a atteint à une sorte d'exaspération verbale qui, loin d'être désordre, est, au contraire, le déroulement cohérent de sa pensée poétique.' Tzara, op. cit., p. 87.

To the memory of
the suffering lover & young Breton master
who called himself 'Tristan Corbière'

(I wish I versed with his bite)[. . . .][122]

In 'In & Out' in this book, he describes himself as a student 'watching Corbière doomed',[123] and in a radio talk he instanced
Corbière with Yeats, Auden, Rilke and Lorca as 'passions of those
remote days'.[124]

Through Laforgue, Corbière's influence may be traced to Hart
Crane, as well as to Jules Supervielle. It is in the 'conversational-
ironic' tradition with Laforgue that Corbière belongs primarily,
although, ironically, it was André Breton who identified the main-
spring of *Les Amours jaunes*: 'The contrast between physical
deformity and outstanding gifts of the first order could not avoid,
in Corbière's work, agitating humour as a defensive reflex.'*

Note on the Text

The text of the poems from *Les Amours jaunes* is taken from the
first edition, 1873. The text of the prose is taken from *La Vie
parisienne*, where 'Casino des trépassés' was first published 26
September 1874, and 'L'Américaine', 28 November 1874.

Acknowledgements

I would like to thank Pauline Francis and C. H. Sisson for reading
the manuscript, and Michael Schmidt, Anthony Rudolf and others
for their help; full responsibility for these versions must nevertheless be borne by me.

* 'Le contraste entre la disgrâce physique et les dons sensibles de premier
ordre ne peut manquer, dans l'œuvre de Corbière, de susciter l'humour comme
réflexe de défense [. . .]', Breton, op. cit., p. 163.

Notes

1. Ezra Pound, 'French Poets', *The Little Review*, February 1918; reprinted in *Make It New*, London, 1934, p. 181.
2. '[. . .] la structure morale', Albert Sonnenfeld, *L'Œuvre poétique de Tristan Corbière*, Paris, 1960, p. 120.
3. Warren Ramsey, *Jules Laforgue and the Ironic Inheritance*, New York, 1953, p. 192.
4. Ida Levi, 'New Light on Tristan Corbière', *French Studies* (July 1951), pp. 233–4.
5. Charles Le Goffic (ed.), *Les Amours jaunes*, Paris, 1912, pp. xxxiii–iv.
6. René Martineau, *Tristan Corbière*, Paris, 1904, p. 34.
7. Jean Vacher-Corbière, *Tristan Corbière, portrait de famille*, Monte Carlo, 1955, pp. 50–1.
8. Francis Burch, *Tristan Corbière: l'originalité des* Amours jaunes *et leur influence sur T. S. Eliot*, Paris, 1970, p. 73.
9. ibid., p. 85.
10. Alexandre Arnoux, *Tristan Corbière, une âme et pas de violon*, Paris, 1929, pp. 57–79.
11. Burch, op. cit., p. 232.
12. René Martineau, *Tristan Corbière*, Paris, 1925, p. 43.
13. See Jean Rousselot, *Tristan Corbière*, Paris, 1951.
    At the same time, 'Le Gad [the hotel proprietor at Roscoff and Corbière's friend] often insisted on the terrible ironist's admiration for his father, an admiration which remained constant.' ('[. . .] Le Gad [. . .] insista souvent sur cette admiration que le terrible ironiste avait pour son père, admiration qui ne se démentit jamais.') René Martineau, *Promenades biographiques*, Paris, 1920, p. 55.
14. René Martineau, *Tristan Corbière*, Paris, 1925, p. 66.
15. Edmund Wilson, *Axel's Castle*, London, 1971, p. 203.
16. '[. . .] un chef-d'œuvre de désespérance', quoted by René Martineau in *Promenades biographiques*, Paris, 1920, p. 44, from a letter from Pol Kalig, *Marches de Provence*, Aug.–Sept. 1912, pp. 26–7.
17. Jean Rousselot, *Tristan Corbière*, Paris, 1951, p. 67.
18. René Martineau, *Tristan Corbière*, Paris, 1904, p. 52.
19. ibid., p. 78.
20. Philip Stephan, 'Problems of Structure in the Poetry of Tristan Corbière', *Modern Language Quarterly*, XXII (1961), p. 343.
21. W. Branch Johnson, 'Death and the Beyond in Breton Folklore', *The French Quarterly*, VIII, 1 (March 1926), p. 32.
22. On the implications of the title, *Les Amours jaunes*, see Pauline Newman-Gordon, *Corbière, Laforgue, Apollinaire ou le rire en pleurs*, Paris, 1964, pp. 17–36.
23. René Martineau, *Tristan Corbière*, Paris, 1925, p. 77.
24. Levi, op. cit., p. 243.
25. Johnson, op. cit., p. 35.

26. René Martineau, *Tristan Corbière*, Paris, 1904, p. 54.
27. Cited by Yves-Gérard Le Dantec (ed.), *Les Amours jaunes*, Paris, 1953, p. 271.
28. Rousselot, op. cit., p. 80.
29. Johnson, op. cit., pp. 36–7.
30. Henri Thomas, *Tristan le Dépossédé*, Paris, 1972, p. 170.
31. '[. . .] la structure morale', Sonnenfeld, op. cit., p. 120.
32. G. M. Turnell, 'Introduction to the Study of Tristan Corbière', *The Criterion*, XV, 60 (April 1936), p. 397.
33. Charles Le Goffic (ed.), *Les Amours jaunes*, Paris, 1912, pp. xxvii–iii.
34. Paul Verlaine, *Les Poètes maudits*, Paris, 1888, p. 3.
35. Jules Laforgue, 'Une Étude sur Corbière', in *Mélanges posthumes (Œuvres complètes)*, Paris, 1903, p. 127.
36. René Martineau, *Promenades biographiques*, Paris, 1920, p. 43.
37. Édouard Corbière, *Le Négrier*, Paris, 1936, p. 47. The story-teller invariably begins his story with the formula, *'un tonnerre dans ton lit; une jeune fille dans mon hamac!'*
38. Burch, op. cit., pp. 145–7.
39. Sonnenfeld, op. cit., pp. 126–7.
40. Jean de Trigon, *Poètes d'océan*, Paris, 1958, pp. 165–91.
41. Burch, op. cit., pp. 37–58.
42. Christian Angelet, *La Poétique de Tristan Corbière*, Brussels, 1961, p. 102.
43. Verlaine, op. cit., p. 8.
44. Ezra Pound, *Literary Essays*, London, 1968, p. 282.
45. ibid., p. 33.
46. Louis Dimier (ed.), *Œuvres complètes de Villon*, Paris, 1927, p. 251. The other textual echo of Villon in *Les Amours jaunes* occurs in 'Le poète contumace', where Corbière's 'Lui, seul hibou payant, comme son *bail* le porte: / *Pour vingt-cinq écus l'an, dont: remettre une porte*' recalls Villon's lines in *Le Grand Testament*, 'Que maître Pierre Bobignon / M'arenta, en faisant refaire / L'huis et redresser le pignon' (Villon, op. cit., p. 141).
47. Wallace Fowlie, 'Corbière Translated', *Poetry*, LXXXIV, 6 (Sept. 1954), p. 355.
48. Jules Laforgue, 'Une Étude sur Corbière', in *Mélanges posthumes (Œuvres complètes)*, Paris, 1903, p. 123.
49. T. S. Eliot, 'Baudelaire', in *Selected Essays*, London, 1934, p. 388.
50. '[. . .] dandysme à la Baudelaire', Rémy de Gourmont, *Le Livre des masques*, I, Paris, 1914, p. 154.
51. Y.-G. Le Dantec (ed.), *Œuvres complètes de Baudelaire*, 'Bibliothèque de la Pléiade', Paris, 1954, p. 86.
52. ibid., p. 142.
53. Turnell, op. cit.
54. Claude Vigée, 'Metamorphoses of Modern Poetry', *Comparative Literature*, VII, 2 (Spring 1955), p. 105.
55. Micha Grin, *Tristan Corbière, Poète maudit*, Évian, 1972, pp. 137–8.
56. Marshall Lindsay, 'The Versification of Corbière's *Les Amours jaunes*', *Publications of the Modern Language Association of America*, LXXVIII, 4, part 1 (Sept. 1963), p. 363.

57. In the 'Litanie du sommeil', the word 'sommeil' (sleep) recurs thirty times, effectively suggesting insomnia.

58. Lindsay, op. cit., p. 366.

59. From 'Féminin singulier', *Œuvres complètes de Tristan Corbière*, ed. P.-O. Walzer, 'Bibliothèque de la Pléiade', Paris, 1970, p. 714.

60. Edmund Wilson, in *Axel's Castle*, London, 1971, p. 82, defines the two lines of symbolism, with reference to Eliot: 'But it is from the conversational-ironic, rather than from the serious-aesthetic, tradition of Symbolism that T. S. Eliot derives.'

61. Aldous Huxley, 'The Subject-Matter of Poetry', *The Chapbook*, II, 9 (March 1920), p. 11.

62. Jules Laforgue, 'Une Étude sur Corbière', in *Mélanges posthumes* (*Œuvres complètes*), Paris, 1903, p. 119.

63. This term is explained by Édouard Corbière, *Le Négrier*, Paris, 1936, p. 45, and is subsequently used by him in the course of the novel.

64. Fowlie, op. cit., p. 356.

65. An Italian edition of *Les Amours jaunes*, for instance, includes an extensive list, compiled by the translator, of Corbière's erotic *double entendre*, though of course the presence or not of a second meaning can only be inferred from the context each time such a word is used. I am grateful to Frances Fleetwood for translating this essay, from *Tristan Corbière, tutte le poesie*, introduced by Alfredo Giuliani, transl. by Claudio Rendina, Rome, 1973; translator's introductory note, pp. 15–30.

66. Quoted by Edward J. H. Greene, in *T. S. Eliot et la France*, Paris, 1951, p. 89, from the Clark Lectures, VIII (1926).

67. In the second edition of 1888, Verlaine added studies of Marceline Desbordes-Valmore, Villiers de l'Isle-Adam and Pauvre Lelian (Verlaine himself).

68. '[. . .] le réalisme dans le lyrisme', Charles Morice, *Tristan Corbière*, Paris, 1912, p. 24.

69. Arthur Symons, *The Symbolist Movement in Literature*, 2nd. ed. (revised), London, 1911, p. 139.

70. Turnell, op. cit.

71. Sonnenfeld, op. cit., pp. 89–90.

72. C. M. Bowra, *The Heritage of Symbolism*, London, 1943, p. 227.

73. Wilson, op. cit., p. 229.

74. Jules Laforgue, 'Une Étude sur Corbière', *Entretiens politiques et littéraires*, III (July 1891), pp. 2–13; reprinted in *Mélanges posthumes* (*Œuvres complètes*), Paris, 1903, pp. 119–28.

75. Ramsey, op. cit., p. 95.

76. Wilson, op. cit., p. 82.

77. Jules Laforgue, *Œuvres complètes*, II, Paris, 1922, p. 7.

78. André Salmon, *Créances 1905–10*, Paris, 1926, p. 224; (from *Le Calumet*, 1910).

79. P.-N. Roinard, *La Poésie Symboliste*, Paris, 1908, p. 22.

80. F. S. Flint, 'French Chronicle', *Poetry and Drama*, 5 (March 1914), p. 100.

81. Francis Carco (ed.), 'Les Poètes Fantaisistes', *Vers et Prose*, XXXV (Oct.–Dec. 1913), pp. 7–70.

82. Francis Carco, *Poésies complètes*, Paris, 1955, p. 197.

83. Tristan Derème, 'Lettre de France II', *Rhythm*, II, 3 (Aug. 1912), p. 114.

84. 'Henri Hertz [. . .] his soul, which is no doubt made up of the souls of Corbière and Laforgue [. . .]' ('[. . .] Son âme, que composent sans doute les âmes de Corbière et de Laforgue [. . .]'), 'La Phalange nouvelle', in *Œuvres complètes de Guillaume Apollinaire*, III, ed. Michel Décaudin, Paris, 1966, p. 764; and in *La Poésie Symboliste*, ed. Roinard, p. 178.

85. '[. . .] une espèce de notation musicale', Sonnenfeld, op. cit., p. 33.

86. Rousselot, op. cit., p. 79.

87. Michael Hamburger, *The Truth of Poetry*, London, 1969, pp. 48 and 317.

88. Yves Bonnefoy, 'La poésie française et le principe d'identité', in *Un Rêve fait à Mantoue*, Paris, 1967, p. 109.

89. A notable example: 'Gérard de Nerval', *New York Times*, 22 April 1888.

90. Ezra Pound, 'French Poets', *The Little Review*, February 1918; reprinted in *Make It New*, London, 1934, p. 173.

91. ibid., p. 184.

92. Ezra Pound, 'Paris', *Poetry*, III, 1 (Oct. 1913), pp. 26–7.

93. Ezra Pound, *Collected Shorter Poems*, London, 1973, p. 165; reprinted from *Blast*, 1914.

94. F. S. Flint, 'Contemporary French Poetry', *Poetry Review*, I, 8 (Aug. 1912), p. 408.

95. John Gould Fletcher, *Life is My Song*, New York, 1937, p. 73.

96. Ezra Pound, *Literary Essays*, London, 1968, p. 45.

97. Ezra Pound, 'In Metre', *The New Freewoman*, 15 Sept. 1913, p. 132.

98. Richard Aldington, *Literary Studies and Reviews*, London, 1924, p. 182.

99. Richard Aldington, *French Studies and Reviews*, London, 1926, p. 126.

100. Richard Aldington, *Literary Studies and Reviews*, London, 1924, pp. 186–7.

101. ibid., p. 184.

102. M.-J.-J. Laboulle, 'T. S. Eliot and Some French Poets', *Revue de Littérature comparée* (April–June 1936), p. 396.

103. René Taupin, *L'Influence du symbolisme français sur la poésie américaine 1910–20*, Paris, 1929, p. 139.

104. T. S. Eliot, in a review of *Baudelaire and the Symbolists* by Peter Quennell, *The Criterion*, IX, 35 (January 1930), p. 357.

105. T. S. Eliot, *Notes towards the Definition of Culture*, London, 1948, p. 113.

106. T. S. Eliot, 'Lettre d'Angleterre', *La Nouvelle Revue française* (November 1923), p. 620.

107. T. S. Eliot, 'The Metaphysical Poets', in *Selected Essays*, London, 1934, pp. 289–90.

108. From 'Libertà', *Œuvres complètes de Tristan Corbière*, ed. P.-O. Walzer, 'Bibliothèque de la Pléiade', Paris, 1970, p. 789.

109. Quoted by Edward J. H. Greene, in *T. S. Eliot et la France*, Paris, 1951, p. 89, from the Clark Lectures, VIII (1926).

110. T. S. Eliot, *Collected Poems 1909–1962*, London, 1965, p. 39.

111. Grover Smith, 'Tourneur and *Little Gidding*; Corbière and *East Coker*', *Modern Language Notes*, LXV, 6 (June 1950), pp. 420–1.

112. T. S. Eliot, in a review of *Baudelaire and the Symbolists* by Peter Quennell, *The Criterion*, IX, 35 (January 1930), pp. 358–9.

113. C. M. Shanahan, 'Irony in Laforgue, Corbière and Eliot', *Modern Philology*, LIII, 2 (November 1955), p. 121.

114. ibid., p. 127.

115. T. S. Eliot, 'Andrew Marvell', in *Selected Essays*, London, 1934, p. 303.

116. Enid Starkie, *From Gautier to Eliot*, London, 1960, p. 162.

117. Ihab H. Hassan, 'Edith Sitwell and the Symbolist Tradition', *Comparative Literature*, VII, 3 (Summer 1955), p. 241.

118. Ezra Pound, *Literary Essays*, London, 1968, p. 282.

119. Yvor Winters, *Primitivism and Decadence*, New York, 1937, p. 55.

120. Randall Jarrell, *The Complete Poems*, London, 1971, pp. 123–8 and 135–7.

121. Randall Jarrell, *Poetry and the Age*, London, 1973, p. 148.

122. John Berryman, *Love & Fame*, London, 1971, p. 7.

123. ibid., p. 31.

124. Howard Nemerov (ed.), *Contemporary American Poetry*, Voice of America Forum Lectures, *c.* 1965, p. 123.

Select Bibliography

For a full bibliography of Corbière, see Albert Sonnenfeld, *L'Œuvre poétique de Tristan Corbière*, Paris, 1960, pp. 199–209.

The standard edition of Corbière's work is the *Œuvres complètes de Tristan Corbière*, ed. P.-O. Walzer, 'Bibliothèque de la Pléiade', Paris, 1970 (in the same volume with Charles Cros). There is a Gallimard paperback edition of *Les Amours jaunes*, ed. Jean-Louis Lalanne, Paris, 1973.

Christian Angelet, *La Poétique de Tristan Corbière*, Brussels, 1961.

Léon Bocquet, *Les Destinées mauvaises*, Amiens, 1923.

Francis Burch, *Tristan Corbière: l'originalité des Amours jaunes et leur influence sur T. S. Eliot*, Paris, 1970.

Kenneth Cornell, *The Symbolist Movement*, New Haven, 1951.
The Post-Symbolist Period, New Haven, 1958.

Rémy de Gourmont, *Le Livre des masques*, I, Paris, 1914.

Edward J. H. Greene, *T. S. Eliot et la France*, Paris, 1951.

Micha Grin, *Tristan Corbière, Poète maudit*, Évian, 1972; (includes some hitherto unpublished material, but is sometimes inaccurate, and is inferior to Sonnenfeld's study).

Michael Hamburger, *The Truth of Poetry*, London, 1969.

Gustave Kahn, 'Tristan Corbière', *La Nouvelle Revue*, Nouvelle série, XXIX (14 July 1904), pp. 271–7.

Jules Laforgue, 'Une Étude sur Corbière', in *Mélanges posthumes* (*Œuvres complètes*), Paris, 1903, pp. 119–28.

Marshall Lindsay, *Le Temps jaune: Essais sur Corbière*, Berkeley, 1972.

René Martineau, *Tristan Corbière*, Paris, 1925; (an expanded version of his *Tristan Corbière* of 1904).

Warren Ramsey, *Jules Laforgue and the Ironic Inheritance*, New York, 1953.

Edgell Rickword, 'Tristan Corbière', in *Essays & Opinions 1921–31*, Cheadle, Cheshire, 1974, pp. 98–104.

Jean Rousselot, *Tristan Corbière* ('Poètes d'aujourd'hui' series), Paris, 1951.

Albert Sonnenfeld, *L'Œuvre poétique de Tristan Corbière*, Paris, 1960.

René Taupin, *L'Influence du symbolisme français sur la poésie américaine 1910–20*, Paris, 1929.

Henri Thomas, *Tristan le Dépossédé*, Paris, 1972.

G. M. Turnell, 'Introduction to the Study of Tristan Corbière', *The Criterion*, XV, 60 (April 1936), pp. 393–417.

Tristan Tzara, 'Tristan Corbière et les Limites du Cri', *Europe*, 60 (Dec. 1950), pp. 87–96.

Paul Verlaine, *Les Poètes maudits*, Paris, 1888.

Edmund Wilson, *Axel's Castle*, London, 1971.

THE CENTENARY CORBIÈRE

Les Amours jaunes – choix de poèmes

'Ça'

ÉPITAPHE

Sauf les amoureux commençans ou finis
qui veulent commencer par la fin il y a
tant de choses qui finissent par le commencement que le commencement commence à finir par être la fin la fin en sera
que les amoureux et autres finiront par
commencer à recommencer par ce commencement qui aura fini par n'être que la
fin retournée ce qui commencera par être
égal à l'éternité qui n'a ni fin ni commencement et finira par être aussi finale-
ment égal à la rotation de la terre où l'on
aura fini par ne distinguer plus où commence la fin d'où finit le commencement
ce qui est toute fin de tout commencement
égale à tout commencement de toute fin ce
qui est le commencement final de l'infini
défini par l'indéfini–Égale une épitaphe
égale une préface et réciproquement

(SAGESSE DES NATIONS)

Il se tua d'ardeur, ou mourut de paresse.
S'il vit, c'est par oubli; voici ce qu'il se laisse:

–Son seul regret fut de n'être pas sa maîtresse.–

Il ne naquit par aucun bout,
Fut toujours poussé vent-de-bout,
Et fut un arlequin-ragoût,
Mélange adultère de tout.

From *Yellow Loves*

From 'That'

EPITAPH

Except for lovers beginning or finished
who want to begin with the end there are
so many things that end with the beginning
that the beginning begins to end by being the
end the end of which will be that lovers and
others will end by beginning to begin again
with this beginning which will have ended by
being only the end reverted which will begin
by being equal to eternity which has neither
end nor beginning and will end by being
also finally equal to the rotation of the
earth when you'll have ended by no more
distinguishing when the end begins from
when the beginning ends which is every
end of every beginning equal to every final
beginning of the infinite defined by the
indefinite—This equals an epitaph which
equals a preface and conversely

(WISDOM OF THE NATIONS)

He killed himself with ardour, or died of laziness.
If he's alive, it's from forgetfulness; he leaves himself this, no less:

—His only regret was not being his mistress.—

He wasn't born tail-first nor head,
By a head wind was always driven ahead,
And was a motley stew of leavings,
Adulterous medley of everything.

Du *je-ne-sais-quoi.*–Mais ne sachant où;
De l'or,–mais avec pas le sou;
Des nerfs,–sans nerf. Vigueur sans force;
De l'élan,–avec une entorse;
De l'âme,–et pas de violon;
De l'amour,–mais pire étalon.
–Trop de noms pour avoir un nom.–

Coureur d'idéal,–sans idée;
Rime riche,–et jamais rimée;
Sans avoir été,–revenu;
Se retrouvant partout perdu.

Poète, en dépit de ses vers;
Artiste sans art,–à l'envers,
Philosophe,–à tort à travers.

Un drôle sérieux,–pas drôle.
Acteur, il ne sut pas son rôle;
Peintre: il jouait de la musette;
Et musicien: de la palette.

Une tête!–mais pas de tête;
Trop fou pour savoir être bête;
Prenant pour un trait le mot *très.*
–Ses vers faux furent ses seuls vrais.

Oiseau rare–et de pacotille;
Très mâle . . . et quelquefois très *fille;*
Capable de tout,–bon à rien;
Gâchant bien le mal, mal le bien.
Prodigue comme était l'enfant
Du Testament,–sans testament.
Brave, et souvent, par peur du plat,
Mettant ses deux pieds dans le plat.

Coloriste enragé,–mais blême;
Incompris . . .–surtout de lui-même;
Il pleura, chanta juste faux;
–Et fut un défaut sans défauts.

Of *je ne sais quoi*.–And nor did he;
Of gold,–but without a penny;
Of nerves,–without nerve. Vigour without efficacy;
Of dash,–bent like a hairpin;
Of soul,–and no violin;
Of love,–but as a stud, lame.
–Too many names to make a name.–

He ran after the ideal,–with no idea;
A *rime riche*, you couldn't hear;
Returning,–without having been there;
Finding himself again lost everywhere.

Poet, despite his verse–and worse;
Artless artist,–inverted,
Philosopher,–without rhyme or reason asserted.

A funny guy,–not droll.
An actor, he didn't know his role;
A painter: he played the cornet;
And a musician: with the palette.

A head!–but he had no head;
Too mad to know how to be dull-witted;
Using as a dash the word *very*.
–His false versification was his only verity.

A rare bird–and a load of rubbish;
Very male... and sometimes very *whorish*;
Capable of anything,–good for nothing;
Bungling bad well, and badly good things.
Prodigal like the son in the Testament
–Ultimately without a will. A gallant temperament,
And often, from fear of the unstimulating,
Putting his foot in it, unsimulating.

Dim,–but a rabid artist in colour;
Misunderstood...–by himself in particular;
His song was truly false, with tears fraught;
–And he was faultlessly in default.

Ne fut *quelqu'un*, ni quelque chose
Son naturel était la *pose*.
Pas poseur,—posant pour *l'unique*;
Trop naïf, étant trop cynique;
Ne croyant à rien, croyant tout.
—Son goût était dans le dégoût.

Trop cru,—parce qu'il fut trop cuit,
Ressemblant à rien moins qu'à lui,
Il s'amusa de son ennui,
Jusqu'à s'en réveiller la nuit.
Flâneur au large,—à la dérive,
Épave qui jamais n'arrive . . .

Trop *Soi* pour se pouvoir souffrir,
L'esprit à sec et la tête ivre,
Fini, mais ne sachant finir,
Il mourut en s'attendant vivre
Et vécut, s'attendant mourir.

Ci-gît,—cœur sans cœur, mal planté,
Trop réussi—comme *raté*.

'Les Amours jaunes'

BOHÈME DE CHIC

Ne m'offrez pas un trône!
À moi tout seul je fris,
Drôle, en ma sauce jaune
De *chic* et de mépris.

Que les bottes vernies
Pleuvent du paradis,
Avec des parapluies . . .
Moi, va-nu-pieds, j'en ris!

Was neither *someone*, nor something
A *pose* was his natural leaning.
Not to impose,–posing for *the one;*
Too cynical, therefore too homespun;
Taking nothing on trust, too trustful.
–His taste lay in the distasteful.

Too ripe,–because he was too raw,
Resembling nothing less
Than himself, boredom was a delight, and more
At night making him sleepless.
A lounger at large,–drifting,
Jetsam never arriving . . .

Too much *Himself* himself to be able to relish,
The head soaked and the spirit dry,
Finished, but not knowing how to make a finish,
With an expectation of life he died
And lived expecting to die.

Here lies,–a heartless heart, misplaced; a man
Too successful–as *an also-ran.*

From 'Yellow Loves'

CHIC BOHEMIA

Don't offer me a throne!
I prefer to fry alone,
In the scorn and *chic*
Of my yellow sauce, comic.*

Let the polished boots
Rain from paradise,
With umbrellas to boot...
A ragamuffin barefoot, these I despise!

*According to Florian Le Roy's interpretation, this poem is a satirical portrait
of Villiers de l'Isle Adam, with an allusion in the first verse to his candidature for
the Greek throne.

–Plate époque râpée,
Où chacun a du bien;
Où, cuistre sans épée,
Le vaurien ne vaut rien!

Papa,–pou, mais honnête,–
M'a laissé quelques sous,
Dont j'ai fait quelque dette,
Pour me payer des poux!

Son habit, mis en perce,
M'a fait de beaux haillons
Que le soleil traverse;
Mes trous sont des rayons.

Dans mon chapeau, la lune
Brille à travers les trous,
Bête et vierge comme une
Pièce de cent sous!

–Gentilhomme! . . . à trois queues:
Mon nom mal ramassé
Se perd à bien des lieues
Au diable du passé!

Mon blason,–pas bégueule,
Est, comme moi, faquin:
–*Nous bandons à la gueule,*
Fond troué d'arlequin.–

Je pose aux devantures
Où je lis:–DÉFENDU
DE POSER DES ORDURES–
Roide comme un pendu!

Et me plante sans gêne
Dans le plat du hasard,
Comme un couteau sans gaine
Dans un plat d'épinard.

-Insipid threadbare century,
When everyone has property;
When the swordless groundling,
The good-for-nothing's as good as nothing!

Papa,-a louse, but honest,-
Left me a few pence in bequest,
Which I turned to debt in a trice,
To treat myself to lice!

I've got glad rags from his apparel,
Broached like a wine-barrel
That the sun gashes;
My holes are flashes.

In my hat, the moon
Through the holes can glitter,
Stupid and virgin like a doubloon,
A coin with no hole in the centre!

-Gentleman!... with three tails:*
My name badly scraped all together fails
By many leagues to find its privy path
To the devil of the past!

My coat of arms,-not select,
Is, like me, cocky:
-*We bend gules at the gob, erect,*
On a ground bored with motley.-

I hang round the entrance
Of buildings where I scan:
-COMMIT NO NUISANCE-
Stiff like a hanged man!

And free and easy take my stance
In a basinful of chance,
Like a knife, keen
In a basin of bright greens.

*Following Le Roy's interpretation, this refers to the three names forming the patronymic, Villiers de l'Isle Adam.

Je lève haut la cuisse
Aux bornes que je voi:
Potence, pavé, suisse,
Fille, priape ou roi!

Quand, sans tambour ni flûte,
Un servile estafier
Au violon me culbute,
Je me sens libre et fier! . . .

Et je laisse la vie
Pleuvoir sans me mouiller,
En attendant l'envie
De me faire empailler.

–Je dors sous ma calotte,
La calotte des cieux;
Et l'étoile pâlotte
Clignotte entre mes yeux.

Ma Muse est grise ou blonde . . .
Je l'aime et ne sais pas;
Elle est à tout le monde . . .
Mais–moi seul–je la bats!

À moi ma Chair-de-poule!
À toi! Suis-je pas beau,
Quand mon baiser te roule
À cru dans mon manteau! . . .

Je ris comme une folle
Et sens mal aux cheveux,
Quand ta chair fraîche colle
Contre mon cuir lépreux!

Jérusalem.–Octobre.

I raise high my thigh
To the landmarks I spy:
Gallows, beadle, lane,
Whore, Priapus or sovereign!

When, without drum or flute,
A menial chucker-out
Tumbles me into clink, the brute,
I feel free, and in spirit stout!...

And life I let
Rain without making me wet,
While waiting till I fancy enough
Getting stuffed.

–Under my skull-cap I slumber,
The vaulting skull of the night skies;
And the stars, sombre,
Twinkle between my eyes.

My Muse is grey or fair ...
I don't know and I love her;
For any taker she's there ...
I–alone–beat her however!

For me my Goose-flesh! For you too!
Aren't I a handsome bloke,
When my kiss rolls you
Next to the skin inside my cloak!...

Like a mad woman I laugh in hoots
And my hair hurts at the roots,
When your cool flesh begins to slide
Against my leprous hide!

Jerusalem.–October.

SONNET À SIR BOB
Chien de femme légère, braque anglais pur sang.

Beau chien, quand je te vois caresser ta maîtresse,
Je grogne malgré moi–pourquoi?–Tu n'en sais rien . . .
–Ah! c'est que moi–vois-tu–jamais je ne caresse,
Je n'ai pas de maîtresse, et . . . ne suis pas beau chien.

–*Bob! Bob!*–Oh! le fier nom à hurler d'allégresse! . . .
Si je m'appelais *Bob* . . . Elle dit Bob si bien! . . .
Mais moi je ne suis pas *pur sang*.–Par maladresse,
On m'a fait *braque* aussi . . . mâtiné de chrétien.

–Ô Bob! nous changerons, à la métempsycose:
Prends mon sonnet, moi ta sonnette à faveur rose;
Toi ma peau, moi ton poil–avec puces ou non . . .

Et je serai *sir Bob*–Son seul amour fidèle!
Je mordrai les roquets, elle me mordrait, Elle! . . .
Et j'aurai le collier portant Son petit nom.

British channel.–15 may.

BONNE FORTUNE ET FORTUNE
Odor della feminita.

Moi, je fais mon trottoir, quand la nature est belle,
Pour la passante qui, d'un petit air vainqueur,
Voudra bien crocheter, du bout de son ombrelle,
Un clin de ma prunelle ou la peau de mon cœur . . .

Et je me crois content–pas trop!–mais il faut vivre:
Pour promener un peu sa faim, le gueux s'enivre . . .

SONNET TO SIR BOB
A fast woman's dog, a pure-bred English pointer.

Fine dog, when I see you caressing your mistress,
I growl in spite of myself–why?–You're befogged . . .
–Ah! it's because I–you see–never caress,
I have no mistress, and . . . am not a fine dog.

–*Bob! Bob!*–Oh! what a proud name to howl joyfully! . . .
If I were called *Bob* . . . She says Bob so nicely! . . .
But I'm not *pure-bred.*–Ineptly, I was also created
A pointer but hare-brained . . . from a Christian cross-bred.

–O Bob! we'll change places, by metempsychosis: take my sonnet
This belling round, I your round bell with its pink rosette;
You my skin, I your coat–with fleas or not . . .

And I'll be *Sir Bob*–Her faithful love! Her only!
I'll bite the mongrels, she'll bite me, She! . . .
And the collar with His Christian name will fall to my lot.

British Channel.–May 15th.

GOOD FORTUNE AND FORTUNE
Odor della feminita.

I go on the streets, when the weather's fair,
Lying in wait for that passer-by, with the slightly triumphant air,
Who, with her sunshade's tip, would very much like to wind in
A wink from me or my heart's skin . . .

And I think myself content–not too much!–but you must exist:
To get rid of his hunger a bit, the beggar gets pissed . . .

Un beau jour–quel métier!–je faisais, comme ça,
Ma croisière.–Métier! . . .–Enfin, Elle passa
–Elle qui?–La Passante! Elle, avec son ombrelle!
Vrai valet de bourreau, je la frôlai . . .–mais Elle

Me regarda tout bas, souriant en dessous,
Et . . . me tendit sa main, et . . .

                                    m'a donné deux sous.

                                              (*Rue des Martyrs.*)

INSOMNIE

Insomnie, impalpable Bête!
N'as-tu d'amour que dans la tête?
Pour venir te pâmer à voir,
Sous ton mauvais œil, l'homme mordre
Ses draps, et dans l'ennui se tordre! . . .
Sous ton œil de diamant noir.

Dis: pourquoi, durant la nuit blanche,
Pluvieuse comme un dimanche,
Venir nous lécher comme un chien:
Espérance ou Regret qui veille,
À notre palpitante oreille
Parler bas . . . et ne dire rien?

Pourquoi, sur notre gorge aride,
Toujours pencher ta coupe vide
Et nous laisser le cou tendu,
Tantales, soiffeurs de chimère:
–Philtre amoureux ou lie amère,
Fraîche rosée ou plomb fondu!–

Insomnie, es-tu donc pas belle? . . .
Eh pourquoi, lubrique pucelle,
Nous étreindre entre tes genoux?
Pourquoi râler sur notre bouche,

One fine day – what a life! – I was acting similarly,
Cruising. – My job! . . . – She passed, finally,
– What she? – The Passer-by! She, with her sunshade!
Veritable assistant-executioner, I swayed

Against her . . . – but She looked me up, and down, smiling furtively,
And . . . held out her hand, and . . .

has given me a halfpenny.

(*Rue des Martyrs.*)

INSOMNIA

Insomnia, impalpable Animal!
Is your love only cerebral?
That you come and are delighted to spy,
Under your evil eye, the man chewing
His sheets, writhing and stewing
With ennui! . . . Under your black diamond eye.

Tell me: why, in a night without repose,
Rainy like a Sunday, in you lope
To lick us like a dog: Hope
Or Regret keeping watch, close
At our ear throbbing
You speak low . . . and say nothing?

Why do you always pass
To our parched throats your empty glass
And leave us with our necks contorted,
Tantaluses, drunkards on chimera:
– Bitter dregs or loving philtre,
Cool dew or molten lead! –

Insomnia, aren't you a pretty miss? . . .
Well why, lewd maid,
Do you get us between your hips?
Why fade out on our lips,

Pourquoi défaire notre couche,
Et . . . ne pas coucher avec nous?

Pourquoi, Belle-de-nuit impure,
Ce masque noir sur ta figure? . . .
—Pour intriguer les songes d'or? . . .
N'es-tu pas l'amour dans l'espace,
Souffle de Messaline lasse,
Mais pas rassasiée encor!

Insomnie, es-tu l'Hystérie . . .
Es-tu l'orgue de barbarie
Qui moud l'*Hosannah* des Élus? . . .
—Ou n'es-tu pas l'éternel plectre,
Sur les nerfs des damnés-de-lettre,
Raclant leurs vers—qu'eux seuls ont lus.

Insomnie, es-tu l'âne en peine
De Buridan—ou le phalène
De l'enfer?—Ton baiser de feu
Laisse un goût froidi de fer rouge . . .
Oh! viens te poser dans mon bouge! . . .
Nous dormirons ensemble un peu.

LA PIPE AU POÈTE

Je suis la Pipe d'un poète,
Sa nourrice, et: j'endors *sa Bête*.

Quand ses chimères éborgnées
Viennent se heurter à son front,
Je fume. . .Et lui, dans son plafond,
Ne peut plus voir les araignées.

. . .Je lui fais un ciel, des nuages,
La mer, le désert, des mirages;
—Il laisse errer là son œil mort . . .

Why leave our bed unmade,
And . . . don't get laid?

Why, Pretty-by-night, blooming unclean,
This black mask on your face? . . .
—To complicate golden dreams? . . .
Aren't you love in space,
The breath of Messalina, exhausted,
But not yet sated!

Insomnia, are you Hysteria . . .
Are you the barrel organ grinding
The Elect's *Hosannah?* . . .
—Or aren't you the plectrum everlasting
On the nerves of the damned-of-letters, who tone
Up verses—read by them alone.

Insomnia, are you Buridan's
Ass in turmoil—or the moth
Of hell?—Your fiery kiss fans
A cold taste of iron red-hot . . .
Oh! come to my hovel and settle! . . .
We'll sleep together a little.

THE POET'S PIPE

A poet's Pipe, that's me,
His nurse, and: I make *his Animal* sleepy.

When his blinded dreams
Against his forehead clashing teem,
I smoke . . . And he can no longer see
The bats in his belfry.

. . . A horizon, clouds for him I fashion,
The desert, mirages, the ocean;
—Over that he lets his dead eye wander . . .

Et, quand lourde devient la nue,
Il croit voir une ombre connue,
–Et je sens mon tuyau qu'il mord . . .

–Un autre tourbillon délie
Son âme, son carcan, sa vie!
. . . Et je me sens m'éteindre.–Il dort–

. . . .

–Dors encor: la *Bête* est calmée,
File ton rêve jusqu'au bout . . .
Mon Pauvre! . . . la fumée est tout.
–S'il est vrai que tout est fumée . . .

(Paris.–Janvier.)

LE CRAPAUD

Un chant dans une nuit sans air . . .
–La lune plaque en métal clair
Les découpures du vert sombre.

. . . Un chant; comme un écho, tout vif
Enterré, là, sous le massif . . .
–Ça se tait: Viens, c'est là, dans l'ombre . . .

–Un crapaud!–Pourquoi cette peur,
Près de moi, ton soldat fidèle!
Vois-le, poète tondu, sans aile,
Rossignol de la boue . . .–Horreur!–

–Il chante.–Horreur!!–Horreur pourquoi?
Vois-tu pas son œil de lumière . . .
Non: il s'en va, froid, sous sa pierre.
. . . .

Bonsoir–ce crapaud-là c'est moi.

(Ce soir, 20 Juillet.)

And, when the cloud turns darker grey,
He thinks it's a familiar shadow he surveys,
–And I feel my stem bitten harder . . .

–Another eddy is untying
His life, his iron collar, his being!
. . . And I feel myself extinguished.–He slumbers–

. . . .

–Sleep on: the *Animal* is quietened,
Spin your dream to the end . . .
Poor Chap! . . . the smoke is all. No gleam
Of fire–if everything's a pipe dream . . .

(*Paris.–January.*)

THE TOAD

A song in a night without air . . .
–The moon plates like silverware
The cut-outs of dull jade.

. . . A song; like an echo, quite lively
Buried, there, under the greenery . . .
–It's silent: Come, it's there, in the shade . . .

–A toad!–Why this fearfulness,
Near me, your faithful warrior!
Look at him, a clipped poet, wingless,
Nightingale of the mud . . . –Horror!–

–He sings.–Horror!!–Why horror?
Don't you see his eye's lambency . . .
No: he goes off, cold, under his boulder.

. . . .

Good-evening–that toad there is me.

(*This evening, July 20th.*)

FEMME

La Bête féroce.

Lui—cet être faussé, mal aimé, mal souffert,
Mal haï—mauvais livre . . . et pire: il m'intéresse.—
S'il est vide après tout . . . Oh mon dieu, je le laisse,
    Comme un roman pauvre—entr'ouvert.

Cet homme est laid . . .—Et moi, ne suis-je donc pas belle,
    Et belle encore pour nous deux!—
En suis-je donc enfin aux rêves de pucelle? . . .
    —Je suis reine: Qu'il soit lépreux!

Où vais-je—femme!—Après . . . suis-je donc pas légère
    Pour me relever d'un faux pas!
Est-ce donc Lui que j'aime!—Eh non! c'est son mystère . . .
    Celui que peut-être Il n'a pas.

Plus Il m'évite, et plus et plus Il me poursuit . . .
    Nous verrons ce dédain suprême.
Il est rare à croquer, celui-là qui me fuit! . . .
    Il me fuit—Eh bien non! . . . Pas même.

. . . Aurais-je ri pourtant! si, comme un galant homme,
    Il avait allumé ses feux . . .
Comme Ève—femme aussi—qui n'aimait pas la Pomme,
    Je ne l'aime pas—et j'en veux!—

C'est innocent.—Et Lui? . . . Si l'arme était chargée . . .
    —Et moi, j'aime les vilains jeux!
Et . . . l'on sait amuser, avec une dragée
    Haute, un animal ombrageux.

De quel droit ce regard, ce mauvais œil qui touche:
    Monsieur poserait le fatal?
Je suis myope, il est vrai . . . Peut-être qu'il est louche;
    Je l'ai vu si peu—mais si mal.—

WOMAN

The Wild Beast.

Him–this twisted being, the unbeloved, not to be put up with
              hardly,
Hardly to be hated–a bad book . . . and worse: he's of interest
              to me.–
If he's empty, after all . . . Oh I'll leave him, good heavens,
          Like a poor novel–half-open.

This man is ugly . . . –And aren't I gorgeous,
          And gorgeous enough for the pair of us!–
Then am I indulging in a virgin's dream? . . .
          –He can be a leper: I'm a queen!

Where am I going–a woman!–Afterwards . . . aren't I a dab hand
          At recovering myself from a false stand?
Then is it Him I love?–Ah no! it's his mystery . . .
          Which He doesn't have maybe.

The more he avoids me, the more He haunts me again . . .
          We'll see about this supreme disdain.
He is singular to devour, this one who flees me! . . .
          He flees me–Well no! . . . No energy.

. . . Yet I'd have laughed! if, like a man of honour,
          He'd kindled his ardour . . .
Like she who didn't like the Apple–Eve, also feminine–
          I want some!–and I don't like him.–

It's innocent.–And Him? . . . If the weapon were loaded . . .
          –And I like a little foul play!
And . . . to amuse a touchy pet, you know the way
          With a grape shot up before his eyes, goaded.

By what right this look, this evil eye upon me:
          Does sir think his charm is fatal?
I'm myopic, yes . . . He's cross-eyed maybe;
          I've seen so little of him–and so ill.–

. . . Et si je le laissais se draper en quenouille,
      Seul dans sa honteuse fierté ! . . .
Non. Je sens me ronger, comme ronge la rouille,
      Mon orgueil malade, irrité.

Allons donc ! c'est écrit – n'est-ce pas – dans ma tête,
      En pattes-de-mouche d'enfer ;
Écrit, sur cette page où – là – ma main s'arrête.
      – Main de femme et plume de fer. –

Oui ! – Baiser de Judas – Lui cracher à la bouche
      Cet *amour !* – Il l'a mérité –
Lui dont la triste image est debout sur ma couche,
      Implacable de volupté.

Oh oui : coller ma langue à l'inerte sourire
      Qu'il porte là comme un faux pli !
Songe creux et malsain, repoussant . . . qui m'attire !

  . . . .

      – Une nuit blanche . . . un jour sali . . .

                                    ***

DUEL AUX CAMÉLIAS

J'ai vu le soleil dur contre les touffes
Ferrailler. – J'ai vu deux fers soleiller,
Deux fers qui faisaient des parades bouffes ;
Des merles en noir regardaient briller.

Un monsieur en linge arrangeait sa manche ;
Blanc, il me semblait un gros camélia ;
Une autre fleur rose était sur la branche,
Rose comme . . . Et puis un fleuret plia.

... If I were to leave him to stand erect – leaning to the distaff
        side,
    Alone in his shameful pride! ...
No. As rust corrodes, I feel corroding me
    My sick, offended vanity.

Well then! it's written in my head – isn't it –
    In a hellish script;
Written, on this page where – there – my hand jibs.
    – A woman's hand and an iron nib. –

Yes! – The kiss of Judas – To spit in his mouth
    This *love!* – He's deserved it –
He whose sorry image is upright on my couch,
    Implacably sybaritic.

Oh yes: to stick my tongue on to that dopey
    Smile like a crease that he displays!
A hollow and unhealthy dream, repellent ... that attracts me!

   . . . .

    – A wakeful night ... a darkened day ...

                                          * * *

DUEL WITH CAMELLIAS

I've seen the harsh sun against the clumps clash blades
Together. – I've seen two swords like the sun shining,
Two flashy blades comically on parade;
Watching their brilliance were blackbirds in mourning.

A gentleman, coatless, was arranging his shirt-sleeve;
White, a huge camellia, as I believed;
Another pink flower was adjacent,
Pink like ... And then a foil bent.

–Je vois rouge . . . Ah oui! c'est juste: on s'égorge–
. . . Un camélia blanc–là–comme Sa gorge . . .
Un camélia jaune,–ici–tout mâché . . .

Àmour mort, tombé de ma boutonnière.
–A moi, plaie ouverte et fleur printanière!
Camélia vivant, de sang panaché!

(Veneris Dies 13***)

FLEUR D'ART

Oui–Quel art jaloux dans Ta fine histoire!
Quels bibelots chers!–Un bout de sonnet,
Un cœur gravé dans ta manière noire,
Des traits de canif à coups de stylet.–

Tout fier mon cœur porte à la boutonnière
Que tu lui taillas, un petit bouquet
D'immortelle rouge–Encor ta manière–
C'est du sang en fleur. Souvenir coquet.

Allons, pas de pleurs à notre mémoire!
–C'est la male-mort de l'amour ici–
Foin du myosotis, vieux sachet d'armoire!

Double femme, va! . . . Qu'un âne te braie!
Si tu n'étais fausse, eh serais-tu vraie? . . .
L'amour est un duel:–Bien touché! Merci.

(***)

PAUVRE GARÇON
La Bête féroce.

Lui qui sifflait si haut, son petit air de tête,
Était plat près de moi; je voyais qu'il cherchait . . .

–I see red . . . They're cutting one another's throats.
    Ah yes!–
. . . A white camellia–there–like Her breast . . .
A yellow camellia,–here–perforated . . .

Dead love, fallen from my lapel.
–For me, the vernal flower and a wound as well!
Living camellia, with blood variegated!

                              (Veneris Dies 13***)

ARTIFICIAL FLOWER

Yes–Doesn't Your subtle story have a jealous skill!
What priceless knick-knacks!–A sonnet's frill,
A heart engraved in your black style,
Penknife digs with a stylet's spikes.–

My heart wears very proudly
In its buttonhole that you cut, a little posy
Of red everlasting flowers–In your style, ditto–
It's blood in bloom. A smart memento.

Come now, our memory doesn't need any tears!
–It's the violent death of love here–
Hay from forget-me-nots, an old lavender bag in a drawer!

Go, outsize woman! . . . Let a donkey bray to you!
If you weren't false, then would you be true? . . .
Love is a duel:–And I'm *touché*! No more.

                                      (***)

POOR BOY

                      The Wild Beast.

As he whistled a little tune in his head, so piercing,
He was insipid near me; I saw he was searching . . .

Et ne trouvait pas, et . . . j'aimais le sentir bête,
Ce héros qui n'a pas su trouver qu'il m'aimait.

J'ai fait des ricochets sur son cœur en tempête.
Il regardait cela . . . Vraiment, cela l'usait? . . .
Quel instrument rétif à jouer, qu'un poète! . . .
J'en ai joué. Vraiment–moi–cela m'amusait.

Est-il mort? . . .–Ah!–c'était, du reste, un garçon drôle.
Aurait-il donc trop pris au sérieux son rôle,
Sans me le dire . . . au moins.–Car il est mort, de quoi? . . .

Se serait-il laissé fluer de poésie . . .
Serait-il mort *de chic*, de boire, ou de phtisie.
Ou, peut-être, après tout: de rien . . .
                                        ou bien de Moi.

                                                    (***)

DÉCLIN

Comme il était bien, Lui, ce Jeune plein de sève!
Âpre à la vie *Ô Gué!* . . . et si doux en son rêve.
Comme il portait sa tête ou la couchait gaîment!
Hume-vent à l'amour! . . . qu'il passait tristement!

Oh comme il était Rien! . . .–Aujourd'hui, sans rancune
Il a vu lui sourire, au retour, la Fortune;
Lui ne sourira plus que d'autrefois; il sait
Combien tout cela coûte et comment ça se fait.

Son cœur a pris du ventre et dit bonjour en prose.
Il est coté fort cher . . . ce Dieu c'est quelque chose;
Il ne va plus les mains dans les poches tout nu . . .

And not finding, and . . . I loved his feeling silly,
This hero who couldn't discover he loved me.

I've played fast and loose with his heart a storm flayed.
He looked on . . . That tired him, really? . . .
What instrument more stubborn than a poet to play! . . .
I have played one. Really, that amused me.

Has he died? . . . –Ah!–besides, he was a strange
      youngster.
Then would he have taken too seriously his assumed
      character,
Without telling me . . . at least. –For what could the
      cause of his death be? . . .

Would he have let himself be drained into poetry . . .
Would he have died from *chic*, consumption, or whisky.
Or, perhaps, after all: of nothing . . .
                     or else of Me.

                               (***)

DECLINE

How fine He used to be, a Young Man full of vim!
Harsh on life *With a heigh-ho!* . . . and gentle dreams to the
      brim.
How he carried his head or rested it gaily!
A walking windmill for love! . . . how he passed on sadly!

Oh how he was Nothing! . . . –Today, without bile
He's seen, returning, Fortune on him smile;
He won't smile more than formerly; he doesn't doubt
How much all that costs him and how it comes about.

His heart's got a paunch and in prose says good-morning.
He's priced very dear . . . this God is something;
He no longer goes naked, hands in empty pockets . . .

Dans sa gloire qu'il porte en paletot funèbre,
Vous le reconnaîtrez fini, banal, célèbre...
Vous le reconnaîtrez, alors, cet inconnu.

BONSOIR

Et vous viendrez alors, imbécile caillette,
Taper dans ce miroir clignant qui se paillette
D'un éclis d'or, accroc de l'astre jaune, éteint.
Vous verrez un bijou dans cet éclat de tain.

Vous viendrez à cet homme, à son reflet mièvre
Sans chaleur . . . Mais, au jour qu'il dardait la fièvre,
Vous n'avez rien senti, vous qui – midi passé –
Tombez dans ce rayon tombant qu'il a laissé.

Lui ne vous connaît plus, Vous, l'Ombre déjà vue,
Vous qu'il avait couchée en son ciel toute nue,
Quand il était un Dieu! . . . Tout cela – n'en faut plus. –

Croyez – Mais lui n'a plus ce mirage qui leurre.
Pleurez – Mais il n'a plus cette corde qui pleure.
Ses chants . . . – C'était d'un autre; il ne les a pas lus.

LE POÈTE CONTUMACE

Sur la côte d'ARMOR, – Un ancien vieux couvent,
Les vents se croyaient là dans un moulin-à-vent,
    Et les ânes de la contrée,
Au lierre râpé, venaient râper leurs dents
Contre un mur si troué que, pour entrer dedans,
    On n'aurait pu trouver l'entrée.

– Seul – mais toujours debout avec un rare aplomb,
Crénelé comme la mâchoire d'une vieille,

In his glory that he puts on as funeral habiliment,
You'll recognize him done for, commonplace, eminent . . .
You'll recognize him then, this unknown ticket.

GOOD-EVENING

So you'll come down, silly tittle-tattler,
To preening in this blinking mirror that glitters
With a flicker of gold, a torn yellow star, extinguished.
In the mirror's silvering, you'll see a jewel flashed.

You'll come to this man, his miserable reflection
Without a glow . . . But, in the day when fire was on his
        breath,
You didn't feel anything,–as noon once gone–
You fall in this falling beam that he has left.

He doesn't know you any more, You, the outmoded Shadow,
Whom he'd put to bed in his sky quite naked,
When he was a God! . . . No more of that now.–

Believe–But he no longer has this mirage deceiving.
Cry–But he can no longer pull the tear-jerking string.
His songs . . . –They were by someone else; he hasn't read
        them.

THE CONTUMACIOUS POET

On the coast of ARMORICA,–A former, old monastery,
The winds thought they were in a windmill inside,
        And donkeys from far and wide,
Came to sharpen their teeth on the threadbare ivy
        Against a wall so holey,
That to go in, you couldn't have found the entry.

–Lonely–but still erect with singular aplomb,
Crenellated like an old woman's gum,

Son toit à coups-de-poing sur le coin de l'oreille,
Aux corneilles bayant, se tenait le donjon,

Fier toujours d'avoir eu, dans le temps, sa légende . . .
Ce n'était plus qu'un nid à gens de contrebande,
Vagabonds de nuit, amoureux buissonniers,
Chiens errants, vieux rats, fraudeurs et douaniers.

—Aujourd'hui l'hôte était de la borgne tourelle,
Un Poète sauvage, avec un plomb dans l'aile,
Et tombé là parmi les antiques hiboux
Qui l'estimaient d'en haut.—Il respectait leurs trous,—
Lui, seul hibou payant, comme son *bail* le porte:
Pour vingt-cinq écus l'an, dont: remettre une porte.—

Pour les gens du pays, il ne les voyait pas:
Seulement, en passant, eux regardaient d'en bas,
      Se montrant du nez sa fenêtre;
Le curé se doutait que c'était un lépreux;
Et le maire disait:—Moi, qu'est-ce que j'y peux,
      C'est plutôt un Anglais . . . un *Être*.

Les femmes avaient su—sans doute par les buses—
Qu'il *vivait en concubinage avec des Muses!* . . .
Un hérétique enfin . . . Quelque *Parisien*
De Paris ou d'ailleurs.—Hélas! on n'en sait rien.—
Il était invisible; et, comme *ses Donzelles*
Ne s'affichaient pas trop, on ne parla plus d'elles.

—Lui, c'était simplement un long flâneur, sec, pâle;
Un ermite-amateur, chassé par la rafale . . .
Il avait trop aimé les beaux pays malsains.
Condamné des huissiers, comme des médecins,
Il avait posé là, soûl et cherchant sa place
Pour mourir seul ou pour vivre par contumace . . .

      Faisant, d'un à-peu-près d'artiste,
      Un philosophe d'à peu près,
      Râleur de soleil ou de frais,
      En dehors de l'humaine piste.

The roof knocked over the corner of her ear,
Gaping to the sky, the keep reared,

Still proud of having had its legend, in other eras . . .
It was no more than a nest for the free-traders,
Nocturnal vagabonds, stray dogs, old rats, lovers
Lying low in the bushes, customs officers and smugglers.

–With wings clipped, in the one-eyed turret
Those days the inmate was a wild Poet,
Holed up there among the ancient owls
Who assessed him from above.–He respected their holes,–
He, the only owl that paid, *for four louis d'or*
–As his *lease* states, *of which: to replace one door.*–

He didn't notice the local folk: though
Going by, they watched him from below,
        With their noses pointing out his window;
The priest suspected he was a leper;
And the mayor said: 'What can I do in the matter,
        It's more likely an Englishman . . . some *Person* or
            other.'

The women had known–from the buzzards one surmises–
That he *was living in concubinage with the Muses!* . . .
In short a heretic . . . Some *Parisian,* from Paris
Or elsewhere.–Alas! they know nothing.–
He was invisible; and, as *not too much public notice*
Was attracted by his Damsels, there was no more gossiping.

–He was simply a rangy loafer, withered, pale;
An amateur hermit, blown in by the gale . . .
He'd loved too much the beautiful sick countries.
Condemned by bailiffs, also by doctors,
He'd perched there, fed-up and seeking quarters
To die alone or live through contumacy . . .

        Making a sort of philosopher,
        Of an artist of sorts, crass
        About rain or shine–except for brass,
        Outside mankind's perimeter.

Il lui restait encore un hamac, une vielle,
Un barbet qui dormait sous le nom de *Fidèle* ;
Non moins fidèle était, triste et doux comme lui,
Un autre compagnon qui s'appelait l'Ennui.

Se mourant en sommeil, il se vivait en rêve.
Son rêve était le flot qui montait sur la grève,
            Le flot qui descendait ;
Quelquefois, vaguement, il se prenait attendre ...
Attendre quoi ... le flot monter—le flot descendre—
            Ou l'Absente ... Qui sait ?

Le sait-il bien lui-même ? ... Au vent de sa guérite,
A-t-il donc oublié comme les morts vont vite,
Lui, ce viveur vécu, revenant égaré,
Cherche-t-il son follet, à lui, mal enterré ?

—Certe, Elle n'est pas loin, celle après qui tu brames,
Ô Cerf de Saint-Hubert ! Mais ton front est sans flammes ...
N'apparais pas, mon vieux, triste et faux déterré ...
Fais le mort si tu peux ... Car Elle t'a pleuré !

—Est-ce qu'il pouvait, Lui ! ... n'était-il pas poète ...
Immortel comme un autre ? ... Et dans sa pauvre tête
Déménagée, encor il sentait que les vers
Hexamètres faisaient les cent pas de travers.

—Manque de savoir-vivre extrême—il survivait—
Et—manque de savoir-mourir—il écrivait :

« C'est un être passé de cent lunes, ma Chère,
En ton cœur poétique, à l'état légendaire.
Je rime, donc je vis ... ne crains pas, c'est *à blanc*.
—Une coquille d'huître en rupture de banc !—
Oui, j'ai beau me palper : c'est moi !—Dernière faute—
En route pour les cieux—car ma niche est si haute !—
Je me suis demandé, prêt à prendre l'essor :
Tête ou pile ...—Et voilà—je me demande encor ... »

He still had a hammock, a hurdy-gurdy,
A spaniel who slept under the name of *Faithful*;
No less faithful, like him gentle and sorrowful,
Was another companion who was called Ennui.

At death's door in sleep, in dreams he lived more.
His dream was the tide that streamed up the shore,
     The tide that went out;
Sometimes, he began to wait in a hesitant way . . .
To wait for what . . . the tide to come in—the tide to go
       out—
     Or the Absent one . . . Who can say?

Does he know himself? . . . In his look-out
On the wind, has he forgotten how quickly the dead go out,
This dead gay dog, stray ghost, is he
Looking for his sprite, himself buried poorly?

—Indeed, She isn't far, she after whom you bell,
O Stag of Saint Hubert! But on your forehead no flames
     swell . . .
Old chap, sad and falsely dug up, don't appear . . .
Act a corpse if you can . . . Since for you She's shed tears!

—As if he could, He! . . . wasn't he a poet . . .
Immortal as another? . . . And in his poor head
With the door on the hinge, he still felt the queue
Of hexameters doing sentry duty askew.   ·

—Not knowing how to live—he survived—
And—not being able to die—he inscribed:

'He's a creature who has passed into legend, Sweetheart,
After a hundred moons, in your poetic heart.
I rhyme, therefore I live . . . drawing a *blank*, don't worry.
—An oyster-shell divorced from its bed in a flurry!—
Yes, I feel myself in vain: it's me!—Final defect—
On my way to heaven—for I have hope in that respect!—
I've asked myself, ready to take wing:
Heads or tails . . . —And see—I'm still asking . . .

«C'est à toi que je fis mes adieux à la vie,
À toi qui me pleuras, jusqu'à me faire envie
De rester me pleurer avec toi. Maintenant
C'est joué, je ne suis qu'un gâteux revenant,
En os et . . . (j'allais dire en chair).–La chose est sûre
C'est bien moi, je suis là–mais comme une rature.»

«Nous étions amateurs de curiosité:
Viens voir *le Bibelot.*–Moi j'en suis dégoûté.–
Dans mes dégoûts surtout, j'ai des goûts élégants;
Tu sais: j'avais lâché la Vie avec des gants;
L'*Autre* n'est pas même à prendre avec des pincettes . . .
Je cherche au mannequin de nouvelles toilettes.»

«Reviens m'aider: Tes yeux dans ces yeux-là! Ta lèvre
Sur cette lèvre! . . . Et, là, ne sens-tu pas ma fièvre
–Ma *fièvre de Toi?* . . .–Sous l'orbe est-il passé
L'arc-en-ciel au charbon par nos nuits laissé?
Et cette étoile? . . .–Oh! va, ne cherche plus l'étoile
        Que tu voulais voir à mon front;
        Une araignée a fait sa toile,
        Au même endroit–dans le plafond.»

«Je suis un étranger.–Cela vaut mieux peut-être . . .
–Eh bien! non, viens encor un peu me reconnaître;
Comme au bon saint Thomas, je veux te voir la foi,
Je veux te voir toucher la plaie et dire:–Toi!–

«Viens encor me finir–c'est très gai: De ta chambre,
Tu verras mes moissons–Nous sommes en décembre–
Mes grands bois de sapin, les fleurs d'or des genêts,
Mes bruyères d'Armor . . .–en tas sur les chenets.
Viens te gorger d'air pur–Ici j'ai de la brise
Si franche! . . . que le bout de ma toiture en frise.
Le soleil est si doux . . .–qu'il gèle tout le temps.
Le printemps . . .–Le printemps, n'est-ce pas tes vingt ans.
On n'attend plus que toi, vois: déjà l'hirondelle
Se pose . . . en fer rouillé, clouée à ma tourelle.–
Et bientôt nous pourrons cueillir le champignon . . .

'It's to you that I bade life good-bye,
To you who wept for me, and finally made me sigh
To stay and weep with you for myself. Now however
The die is cast, I'm only a drivelling spectre,
Of bone and . . . (I was going to say flesh).–Without a doubt
It's me all right, I'm there–but like a rubbing-out.

'We were collectors of curiosity:
Come and see *the Knick-knack*.–Personally I find it
            distasteful.–
Especially in my distastes, I'm most tasteful;
Wearing gloves I let go of Life: you know truly;
The *Other* isn't even to be touched with tongs, no fear . . .
I seek on tailor's dummies for new gear.

'Come back and help me: Your eyes in these eyes here!
Your lips on these lips! . . . And, here, don't you feel my
            fever
–My *fever for You?* . . . –Out of the sphere
Has the rainbow faded, by our nights left a cinder?
And that star? . . . —Oh! get along, don't go on looking
      For the star on my forehead you wanted to see;
      A spider's web is hanging,
      In the same place–the upper storey.

'I'm a stranger.–That's better maybe . . .
–Well! no, come and recognize me with a closer view;
Like good Saint Thomas, I want to see
The faith in you, see you touch the wound and say: "You!"

'Come and finish me off–it's delightful: From your room,
You'll see my harvest–We're in December–
My great woods of firs, the gold flowers of broom,
And heaped on the fire-dogs–my Armorican heather . . .
Come and stuff yourself with pure air–Here I've a wind
So free! . . . that my roof curls at the end.
The sun is so mild . . . –that it freezes continuously.
The spring . . . –The spring, isn't that your youth at twenty.
You're all that's missing, you see: the swallow already
Perches . . . in rusty iron, nailed to my tower.–
And soon there'll be mushrooms for gathering . . .

Dans mon escalier que dore . . . un lumignon.
Dans le mur qui verdoie existe une pervenche
Sèche.– . . . Et puis nous irons à l'eau *faire* la planche
–Planches d'épave au sec–comme moi–sur ces plages.
La Mer roucoule sa *Berceuse pour naufrages ;*
Barcarolle du soir . . . pour les canards sauvages.»

«En *Paul et Virginie*, et virginaux–veux-tu–
Nous nous mettrons au vert du paradis perdu . . .
Ou *Robinson avec Vendredi*–c'est facile–
La pluie a déjà fait, de mon royaume, une île.»

«Si pourtant, près de moi, tu crains la solitude,
Nous avons des amis, sans fard–Un braconnier ;
Sans compter un caban bleu qui, par habitude,
Fait toujours les cent-pas et contient un douanier . . .
Plus de clercs d'huissier ! J'ai le clair de la lune,
Et des amis pierrots amoureux sans fortune.»

–«Et nos nuits ! . . . *Belles nuits pour l'orgie à la tour !* . . .
Nuits à la Roméo !–Jamais il ne fait jour.–
La Nature au réveil–réveil de déchaînée–
Secouant son drap blanc . . . éteint ma cheminée.
Voici mes rossignols . . . rossignols d'ouragans–
Gais comme des pinsons–sanglots de chats-huants !
Ma girouette dérouille en haut sa tyrolienne
Et l'on entend gémir ma porte éolienne,
Comme chez saint Antoine en sa tentation . . .
Oh viens ! joli Suppôt de la séduction !»

–«Hop ! les rats du grenier dansent des farandoles !
Les ardoises du toit roulent en castagnoles !
Les Folles-du-logis . . .
                Non, je n'ai plus de Folles !»

. . . «Comme je revendrais ma dépouille à Satan
S'il me tentait avec un petit Revenant . . .

Up my staircase that's gilded by . . . the end of a taper.
A dried periwinkle subsists in the wall that's turning
Green.– . . . And then we'll go and *float* like boards
–Planks from wrecks dried–like me–on this seaboard.
The Sea coos its *Lullaby for shipwrecks' bad luck;*
Evening barcarolle . . . for the wild ducks.

'As *Paul and Virginia,* and virginal–if that's your price–
We'll graze on the green of a lost paradise . . .
Or *Robinson with Friday*–it's easy–
The rain has already made an island of my country.

'If moreover, you fear solitude, with me,
Frankly, we'll have friends–A poacher;
Besides a blue pea-jacket which, customarily,
Is on patrol and contains an excise officer . . .
No more bailiff's clerks! I have moonshine,
And loving feathered friends whose means are fine.*

–'And our nights! . . . *Fine nights for the orgies in the tower!* . . .
Nights for a Romeo!–Break of day never.–
Nature awaking–waking liberated on her path–
Shaking her white sheet . . . smothered my hearth.
Here are my nightingales . . . nightingales of the gale–
As merry as larks–tawny owls that wail!
My weathercock above takes the rust off its yodelling
And you can hear my Aeolian door groaning,
Like Saint Anthony unhinged during his temptation . . .
Oh come! pretty Tool of seduction!

–'Now then! the rats in the attic are farandoling!
Slates roll off the roof like the blocks of a galley's awning!
The Mad women of the dwelling . . .

No, I've no more Mad
women indwelling!

. . . 'I'd resell my sloughed-off skin with great expedition
To Satan if he'd tempt me with a little Apparition . . .

* A humorous adaptation of lines from the well-known French song by Lulli,
Au clair de la lune. Another reference below to this song is asterisked.

–Toi–Je te vois partout, mais comme un voyant blême,
Je t'adore . . . Et c'est pauvre: adorer ce qu'on aime!
Apparais, un poignard dans le cœur!–Ce sera,
Tu sais bien, comme dans *Inès de La Sierra* . . .
–On frappe . . . oh! c'est quelqu'un . . .

                     Hélas! oui, c'est un rat.

–«Je rêvasse . . . et toujours c'est *Toi*. Sur toute chose,
Comme un esprit follet, ton souvenir se pose:
Ma solitude–*Toi!*–Mes hiboux à l'œil d'or:
–*Toi!*–Ma girouette folle: Oh *Toi!* . . .–Que sais-je encor . . .
–*Toi:* mes volets ouvrant les bras dans la tempête . . .
Une lointaine voix: c'est Ta chanson!–c'est fête! . . .
Les rafales fouaillant Ton nom perdu–c'est bête–
C'est bête, mais c'est *Toi!* Mon cœur au grand ouvert
        Comme mes volets en pantenne,
        Bat, tout affolé sous l'haleine
        Des plus bizarres courants d'air.»

«Tiens . . . une ombre portée, un instant, est venue
Dessiner ton profil sur la muraille nue,
Et j'ai tourné la tête . . .–Espoir ou souvenir–
Ma sœur Anne, à la tour, voyez-vous pas venir? . . .

–Rien!–je vois . . . je vois, dans la froide chambrette.
Mon lit capitonné de *satin de brouette;*
Et mon chien qui dort dessus–Pauvre animal–
. . . Et je ris . . . parce que ça me fait un peu mal.»

«J'ai pris, pour t'appeler, ma vielle et ma lyre.
Mon cœur fait de l'esprit–le sot–pour se leurrer . . .
Viens pleurer, si mes vers ont pu te faire rire;
       Viens rire, s'ils t'ont fait pleurer . . .»

«Ce sera drôle . . . Viens jouer à la misère,
D'après nature:–*Un cœur avec une chaumière.*–
. . . Il pleut dans mon foyer, il pleut dans mon cœur feu.
Viens! Ma chandelle est morte et je n'ai plus de feu . . .»

               *

–You–I see you everywhere, but like a wan seer,
I adore you . . . And to adore where you love!–that's
              austere.
With a dagger in your heart, appear!
It would be like *Ines of Las Sierras*, you know that . . .
–A knock . . . oh! it's someone . . .
          Alas! yes, a rat.

–'I day-dream . . . and always it's *You*. Over everything,
Like a sprite, your memory is hovering:
My solitude–*You!*–My owls with the gold pupil:
–*You!*–My mad weathercock: Oh *You!* . . .–What do I know
              still . . .
–*You:* my shutters opening arms in the storm's fury . . .
A distant voice: it's Your song!–it's a festivity! . . .
The squalls lashing Your lost name–it's dotty–
It's dotty, but it's *You!* My heart wide open
        Like my shutters at sixes and sevens,
        Bangs about, in the wind that dements
        With stranger air currents.

'Look . . . a shadow projected, for an instant, falls
Tracing your profile on the bare wall,
And I've turned my head . . . –Hope or memory–
Sister Anne, in your tower, is no one coming you can see? . . .

–'Nothing!–I see . . . I see, in the small cold chamber,
My bed that with *bath-chair satin* spills;
And on it my dog–poor animal–slumbers
. . . And I laugh . . . because that makes me slightly ill.

'I've taken my lyre and my hurdy-gurdy to try
To call you. My heart cracks jokes–it's daft–
Self-cheat . . . Come and cry, if my verses made you laugh;
        Come and laugh, if they've made you cry . . .

'That will be amusing . . . Come and play at vagabondage,
Modelled from life:–*Love and a cottage.*–
. . . It rains in my hearth, it rains in my heart no more
          alight.
Come! My fire is dead and my candle gives no more light . . .'*

                    *

Sa lampe se mourait. Il ouvrit la fenêtre.
Le soleil se levait. Il regarda sa lettre,
Rit et la déchira . . . Les petits morceaux blancs,
Dans la brume, semblaient un vol de goëlands.

(*Penmarc'h—jour de Noël.*)

'Sérénade des sérénades'

GUITARE

Je sais rouler une amourette
    En cigarette,
Je sais rouler l'or et les plats!
Et les filles dans de beaux draps!

Ne crains pas de longueurs fidèles:
Pour mules mes pieds ont des ailes;
Voleur de nuit, hibou d'amour,
    M'envole au jour.

Connais-tu Psyché?—Non?—Mercure? . . .
Cendrillon et son aventure?
—Non?—. . . Eh bien! tout cela, c'est moi:
    Nul ne me voit.

Et je te laisserais bien fraîche
Comme un petit Jésus en crèche,
Avant le rayon indiscret . . .
    —Je suis si laid!—

Je sais flamber en cigarette,
    Une amourette,
Chiffonner et flamber les draps,
Mettre les filles dans les plats!

His lamp was dying. He opened the shutter.
The sun was rising. He looked at his letter,
Laughed and tore it up . . . The white pieces were a sight
In the mist, like gulls in flight.

(Penmarc'h—Christmas Day.)

From 'Serenade of Serenades'

GUITAR

I know how to roll a light affair
       Like a cigarette,
I know how to roll greenhorns to stuff my wallet!
And girls into a predicament not rare!

Don't fear long faithful loving:
For slippers my feet have wings;
Owl of love, thief in the night,
       I flit at first light.

You know Psyche?—No?—Mercury? . . .
Cindarella and her story?
—No?—. . . Well! all those are me:
       Seen by nobody.

And I would leave you fresher
Than a little Jesus in the manger,
Before dawn comes revealingly . . .
       —I'm so ugly!—

I know how to light like a cigarette,
       A light affair,
How to tangle and light the blankets,
And how to get girls into trouble, there!

TOIT

Tiens non! J'attendrai tranquille,
    Planté sous le toit,
Qu'il me tombe quelque tuile,
    Souvenir de Toi!

J'ai tondu l'herbe, je lèche
    La pierre,—altéré
Comme *la Colique-sèche*
    De Miserere!

Je crèverai—Dieu me damne!—
Ton tympan ou la peau d'âne
    De mon bon tambour!

Dans ton boîtier, ô Fenêtre!
Calme et pure, gît peut-être . . .

   . . . .

Un vieux monsieur sourd!

HEURES

Aumône au malandrin en chasse
Mauvais œil à l'œil assassin!
Fer contre fer au spadassin!
—Mon âme n'est pas en état de grâce!—

Je suis le fou de Pampelune,
J'ai peur du rire de la Lune,
Cafarde, avec son crêpe noir . . .
Horreur! tout est donc sous un éteignoir.

J'entends comme un bruit de crécelle . . .
C'est la male heure qui m'appelle.
Dans le creux des nuits tombe: un glas . . . deux glas

ROOF

I'll wait quietly, 'struth!
    Stationed under the roof,
Until a tile falls on me askew,
    Memento of You!

I've cut the grass, I lick the tarmac,
    – In a parched condition
Like *the dry Iliac*
    Passion!

– God damn me! – I'll knock in
Your tympanum, or the ass's skin
    Of my good drum!

In your frame, O Window!
Perhaps, calm and pure, lies below . . .

. . . .

    An old gentleman, deaf and dumb!

HOURS

Alms to the highwayman giving chase
The evil eye to the eye that's a killer!
For the bravo sabre against sabre!
– My soul is not in a state of grace! –

I'm Pamplona's loon,
I'm frightened of the laughter of the Moon,
    Hypocritically mooning about, with a black pall . . .
Horror! so a candle-snuffer covers all.

I hear a noise like a hand-rattle briskly . . .
It's the evil hour calls me.
In the hollow of nights falls: a knell . . . two knells

J'ai compté plus de quatorze heures . . .
L'heure est une larme–Tu pleures,
Mon cœur! . . . Chante encor, va–Ne compte pas.

'Raccrocs'

DÉCOURAGEUX

Ce fut un vrai poète: Il n'avait pas de chant.
Mort, il aimait le jour et dédaigna de geindre.
Peintre: il aimait son art–Il oublia de peindre . . .
Il voyait trop–Et voir est un aveuglement.

–Songe-creux: bien profond il resta dans son rêve;
Sans lui donner la forme en baudruche qui crève,
Sans *ouvrir le bonhomme*, et se chercher dedans.

–Pur héros de roman: il adorait la brune,
Sans voir s'elle était blonde . . . Il adorait la lune;
Mais il n'aima jamais–Il n'avait pas le temps.

–Chercheur infatigable: Ici-bas où l'on rame,
Il regardait ramer, du haut de sa grande âme,
Fatigué de pitié pour ceux qui ramaient bien . . .

Mineur de la pensée: il touchait son front blême,
Pour gratter un bouton ou gratter le problème
        Qui travaillait là–Faire rien.–

–Il parlait: «Oui, la Muse est stérile! elle est fille
«D'amour, d'oisiveté, de prostitution;
«Ne la déformez pas en ventre de famille
«Que couvre un étalon pour la production!»

«Ô vous tous qui gâchez, maçons de la pensée!
«Vous tous que son caprice a touchés en amants,
«–Vanité, vanité–La folle nuit passée,
«Vous l'affichez *en charge* aux yeux ronds des manants!

I've been a teller for the hours, for a start
Fourteen . . . Each hour is a tear—My heart,
You weep! . . . Go on singing—Don't tell.

From 'Flukes'

DISENTHUSIAST

This was a true poet: He had no refrain.
Dead, he loved daylight and disdained to complain.
A painter: he loved his art—He forgot about painting . . .
He saw too much—And sight is blinding.

—A dreamer: he stayed in his dream very far under;
Without forming it in a gold-beater's skin that tears asunder,
Without *opening up the good chap*, and looking inside for his prime.

—The complete hero of romance: he adored the red-head,
Without seeing if she was blonde . . . To the moon he was devoted;
But he never loved—He didn't have time.

—Indefatigable seeker: Where they slog here below,
He watched the slog, from his great soul's plateau,
Weary with pity for the best of the slogging . . .

Miner of maxims: he touched his wan brow,
To scratch a pimple or to scratch the vow
    That laboured there—To do nothing.—

—He spoke: 'Yes, the Muse is sterile! she
Is the daughter of love, idleness, prostitution;
Don't deform her with a family belly
That a stud covers for production!

'O all you bunglers, thought's bricklayers!
All you whom her caprice has turned into lovers,
—Vanity, vanity—The mad night elapsed,
You parade her *with a load of it* to round-eyed peasants!

«Elle vous effleurait, vous, comme chats qu'on noie,
«Vous avez accroché son aile ou son réseau,
«Fiers d'avoir dans vos mains un bout de plume d'oie,
«Ou des poils à gratter, en façon de pinceau!»

–Il disait: «Ô naïf Océan! Ô fleurettes,
«Ne sommes-nous pas là, sans peintres, ni poètes! . . .
«Quel vitrier a peint! quel aveugle a chanté! . . .
«Et quel vitrier chante en raclant sa palette,

«Ou quel aveugle a peint avec sa clarinette!
«Est-ce l'art? . . .»
                        –Lui resta dans le Sublime Bête
Noyer son orgueil vide et sa virginité.

(*Méditerranée.*)

RAPSODIE DU SOURD
*À Madame D****

L'homme de l'art lui dit:–Fort bien, restons-en là.
Le traitement est fait: vous êtes sourd. Voilà
Comme quoi vous avez l'organe bien perdu.–
Et lui comprit trop bien, n'ayant pas entendu.

–«Eh bien, merci Monsieur, vous qui daignez me rendre
            La tête comme un bon cercueil.
Désormais, à crédit, je pourrai tout entendre
            Avec un légitime orgueil . . .

À l'œil–Mais gare à l'œil jaloux, gardant la place
De l'oreille au clou! . . .–Non–À quoi sert de braver?
. . . Si j'ai sifflé trop haut le ridicule en face,
En face, et bassement, il pourra me baver! . . .

Moi, mannequin muet, à fil banal!–Demain,
Dans la rue, un ami peut me prendre la main,
En me disant: vieux pot . . ., ou rien, en radouci;
Et je lui répondrai–Pas mal et vous, merci!–

'She stroked you, like cats for drowning
–You! You've hooked her net or her wing,
Proud to have in your hands a goose feather's quill,
Or some hairs as a paint-brush to fulfil!'

–He said: 'O artless Ocean! O sweet nothings,
Aren't we there, without a painter, or poet! . . .
What glazier has painted! what blind man was singing! . . .
And what glazier sings scraping his palette,

Or what blind man has painted with his clarinet!
Is that art? . . .'
                    –It's left to him to drown his pride's vacuity
In the Foolish Sublime, with his virginity.

                                        (*Mediterranean.*)

DEAF MAN'S RHAPSODY
*To Mrs D****

The specialist said: 'Let's leave it at that, couldn't be better.
The treatment's completed: you're deaf. The fact of the matter
Is you've completely lost the faculty.'
And not having heard, he understood perfectly.

–'Well, thank you sir, for having condescended
        To make a fine coffin of my head.
From now on, I'll be able to understand everything
        On trust, with legitimate vaunting . . .

Like window-shopping–But beware the jealous eye, in the place
Of the nailed-up ear! . . . –No–Why bother to defy?
. . . If in the face of ridicule I've whistled too high,
Below the belt it will sling mud in my face! . . .

I'm a dumb puppet, on a trite string!–
Tomorrow, a friend could take my hand, along the avenue,
Calling me: a bloody post . . ., or more kindly, nothing;
And I would answer 'Not bad, thanks, and you!'

Si l'un me corne un mot, j'enrage de l'entendre;
Si quelqu'autre se tait: serait-ce par pitié? . . .
Toujours, comme un *rebus*, je travaille à surprendre
Un mot de travers . . . –Non.–On m'a donc oublié!

–Ou bien–autre guitare–un officieux être
Dont la lippe me fait le mouvement de paître,
Croit me parler . . . Et moi je tire, en me rongeant,
Un sourire idiot–d'un air intelligent!

–Bonnet de laine grise enfoncé sur mon âme!
Et–coup de pied de l'âne . . . Hue!–Une bonne-femme,
Vieille Limonadière, aussi, de la Passion!
Peut venir saliver sa sainte compassion
Dans ma *trompe-d'Eustache*, à pleins cris, à plein cor,
Sans que je puisse au moins lui marcher sur un cor!

–Bête comme une vierge et fier comme un lépreux,
Je suis là, mais absent . . . On dit: Est-ce un gâteux,
Poète muselé, hérisson à rebours? . . . –
Un haussement d'épaule, et ça veut dire: un sourd.

–Hystérique tourment d'un Tantale acoustique!
Je vois voler des mots que je ne puis happer;
Gobe-mouche impuissant, mangé par un moustique,
Tête-de-turc gratis où chacun peut taper.

Ô musique céleste: entendre, sur du plâtre,
Gratter un coquillage! un rasoir, un couteau
Grinçant dans un bouchon! . . . un couplet de théâtre!
Un os vivant qu'on scie! un monsieur! un rondeau! . . .

–Rien–Je parle sous moi . . . Des mots qu'à l'air je jette
De chic, et sans savoir si je parle en indou . . .
Ou peut-être en canard, comme la clarinette
D'un aveugle bouché qui se trompe de trou.

–Va donc, balancier soûl affolé dans ma tête!
Bats en branle ce bon tam-tam, chaudron fêlé
Qui rend la voix de femme ainsi qu'une sonnette,
Qu'un coucou! . . . quelquefois: un moucheron ailé . . .

If someone trumpets me a word, I go mad to understand;
If another is silent: would that be through pity? . . .
Always, like a *rebus*, I work to land
One word askew . . . –No.–So they've forgotten me!

–Or–the reverse of the coin–some officious being
Whose blubber lip makes the motion of grazing,
Believes he's conversing . . . While in torment
I put on an imbecile smile–with an air of discernment!

–Over my soul a dunce's cap in wool a shade of donkey!
And–for an ass–the hardest knock . . . Gee-up!–That good lady,
The vinegary Lemonade-seller, Passion-trader in addition!
Can come and drool her blessed compassion
Into my *Eustachian tube*, in full hue and cry,
While I'm unable even to tread on her corn, as an outcry!

–Foolish as a virgin and stand-offish as a leper,
I am there, but absent . . . They say: Is that a doddering
Old idiot, a muzzled poet, some crab in a temper? . . . –
A shrug of the shoulders: 'deaf' is the meaning.

–An acoustic Tantalus' hysterical suffering!
I can't apprehend the words I see flying;
Impotent fly-catcher, eaten by a mosquito,
A free butt where everyone can have a go.

O celestial music: to hear, on plaster,
A shell scrape! a razor,
A knife grinding in a cork! . . . a stage couplet!
A living bone being sawn! a gentleman! a sonnet! . . .

–Nothing–I babble to myself . . . Words that I toss into the air
Off the cuff, and not knowing if it's in Hindi I declare . . .
Or perhaps in goose language, like a clarinet sounded
By a blind man muddling the stops, with perceptions muted.

–Go then, pendulum, distracted in my head, boozed!
Beat with a swing this fine tom-tom, a tinny piano so flat
It makes the female voice like a cuckoo's!
Like a door bell . . . sometimes: a circling gnat . . .

–Va te coucher, mon cœur! et ne bats plus de l'aile.
Dans la lanterne sourde étouffons la chandelle,
Et tout ce qui vibrait là–je ne sais plus où–
Oubliette où l'on vient de tirer le verrou.

–Soyez muette pour moi, contemplative Idole,
Tous les deux, l'un par l'autre, oubliant la parole,
Vous ne me direz mot: je ne répondrai rien ...
Et rien ne pourra dédorer l'entretien.

Le silence est d'or (Saint Jean Chrysostome).

LITANIE DU SOMMEIL

«J'ai scié le sommeil!»
(MACBETH.)

Vous qui ronflez au coin d'une épouse endormie,
RUMINANT! Savez-vous ce soupir: L' INSOMNIE?
–Avez-vous vu la Nuit, et le Sommeil ailé,
Papillon de minuit dans la nuit envolé,
Sans un coup d'aile ami, vous laissant sur le seuil,
Seul, dans le pot-au-noir au couvercle sans œil?
–Avez-vous navigué? ... La pensée est la houle
Ressassant le galet: ma tête ... votre boule.
–Vous êtes-vous laissé voyager en ballon?
–Non?–bien, c'est l'insomnie.–Un grand coup de talon
Là!–Vous voyez cligner des chandelles étranges:
Une femme, une Gloire en soleil, des archanges ...
Et, la nuit s'éteignant dans le jour à demi,
Vous vous réveillez coi, sans vous être endormi.

*

SOMMEIL! écoute-moi: je parlerai bien bas:
Sommeil–Ciel-de-lit de ceux qui n'en ont pas!

TOI qui planes avec l'Albatros des tempêtes,
Et qui t'assieds sur les casques-à-mèche honnêtes!

-Go to bed, heart! and stop flapping your wings.
In the dark lantern let's snuff out the candle,
And, I no longer know where-all that used to be vibrating
There-dungeon where someone has just turned the handle.

-Meditative Idol, for me be dumb,
Both, the one through the other, forgetting phraseology,
You won't say a word: I'll keep mum . . .
And then nothing will be able to tarnish our colloquy.

Silence is golden (St John Chrysostom).

THE LITANY OF SLEEP

'I've murdered sleep!'
(MACBETH.)*

You snorers in the angle of a sleeping partner,
RUMINATING! Do you know this sigh: INSOMNIA?
-Have you seen winged Sleep, with Night,
Midnight butterfly in the night in flight,
Without a friendly flutter, leaving you on the threshold,
Alone, in the pitch-pot whose lid has no hole?
Have you been sailing? . . . Thought is the sea's rise and fall
Sifting the shingle again: my head . . . your ball.
-Have you let yourself in a balloon travel around?
-No?-very well, it's insomnia.-Run aground
There!-You see blinking candles that ensorcell:
A woman, a haloed Glory in the sun, archangels . . .
And, night dying away in the early morning,
You awake quiet, without sleeping.

*

SLEEP! listen to me: I'll speak very softly:
Sleep-For those who haven't got one, a bed-canopy!

YOU hover with the Albatross of the tempest,
And sit on the night-caps of the honest!

* Misquotation or adaptation of *Macbeth*, II. ii. 35-6.

SOMMEIL!–Oreiller blanc des vierges assez bêtes!
Et Soupape à secret des vierges assez faites!
–Moelleux Matelas de l'échine en arête!
Sac noir où les chassés s'en vont cacher leur tête!
Rôdeur de boulevard extérieur! Proxénète!
Pays où le muet se réveille prophète!
Césure du vers long, et Rime du poète!

SOMMEIL!–Loup-Garou gris! Sommeil Noir de fumée!
SOMMEIL!–Loup de velours, de dentelle embaumée!
Baiser de l'Inconnue, et Baiser de l'Aimée!
–SOMMEIL! Voleur de nuit! Folle-brise pâmée!
Parfum qui monte au ciel des tombes parfumées!
Carrosse à Cendrillon ramassant *les Traînées!*
Obscène Confesseur des dévotes mort-nées!

TOI qui viens, comme un chien, lécher la vieille plaie
Du martyr que la mort tiraille sur sa claie!
Ô sourire forcé de la crise tuée!
SOMMEIL! Brise alizée! Aurorale buée!

TROP-PLEIN de l'existence, et Torchon neuf qu'on passe
Au CAFÉ DE LA VIE, à chaque assiette grasse!
Grain d'ennui qui nous pleut de l'ennui des espaces!
Chose qui court encor, sans sillage et sans traces!
Pont-levis des fossés! Passage des impasses!

SOMMEIL!–Caméléon tout pailleté d'étoiles!
Vaisseau-fantôme errant tout seul à pleines voiles!
Femme du rendez-vous, s'enveloppant d'un voile!
SOMMEIL!–Triste Araignée, étends sur moi ta toile!

SOMMEIL auréolé! féerique Apothéose,
Exaltant le grabat du déclassé qui pose!
Patient Auditeur de l'incompris qui cause!
Refuge du pécheur, de l'innocent qui n'ose!
Domino! Diables-bleus! Ange-gardien rose!

VOIX mortelle qui vibre aux immortelles ondes!
Réveil des échos morts et des choses profondes,
–Journal du soir: TEMPS, SIÈCLE et REVUE DES DEUX
    MONDES!

SLEEP!–White pillow of virgins sufficiently silly!
And secret Safety-valve of virgins developed sufficiently!
–For the backbone like herring-bone, a soft Mattress!
Black sack where the hunted man runs to hide his head in distress!
Prowler along the outward avenue! Procuress!
Land where the mute awakens prophet!
Caesura of the long line, and Rhyme of the poet!

SLEEP!–Grey werewolf! Black Sleep fuming!
SLEEP!–Wolfish mask of scented lace for illicit meetings!
Kiss of the Unknown Woman, and Kiss of the Darling!
–SLEEP! Thief of night! Mad breeze swooning!
Fragrance from fumigated tombs to the sky rising!
Cindarella's coach picking up *the Street-walking!*
Obscene Confessor of the still-borns' revering!

YOU come, like a dog, to lick the old pain
Of the martyr on death's execution-hurdle strained!
O forced smile of the crisis slain!
SLEEP! Trade-wind! Dawn steam on the window-pane!

EXCESS of existence, and clean Duster to chase
Trash in the CAFÉ OF LIFE, on each table's greasy surface!
Squall of tedium raining on us from the tedium of space!
Thing that runs on, without wake or trace!
Drawbridge of moats! Way through a no-through place!

SLEEP!–Chameleon that many stars scale!
Phantom ship roving alone in full sail!
Covered by a net, the woman for sale!
SLEEP!–Sad Spider, stretch over me your web's veil!

SLEEP crowned with a halo! fairy Apotheosis,
Exalting the pallet of the posing misfit!
Patient Listener to the misunderstood who gossips!
Refuge of the sinner, of the innocent who doesn't risk it!
Domino! Pink guardian-angel! Blue-devils!

MORTAL voice that vibrates in immortal waters!
Awakening of dead echoes and deep matters,
–Evening paper: THE TIMES, EVERGREEN REVIEW and
        ENCOUNTER!

FONTAINE de Jouvence et Borne de l'envie!
—Toi qui viens assouvir la faim inassouvie!
Toi qui viens délirer la pauvre âme ravie,
Pour la noyer d'air pur au large de la vie!

TOI qui, le rideau bas, viens lâcher la ficelle
Du Chat, du Commissaire, et de Polichinelle,
Du violoncelliste et de son violoncelle,
Et la lyre de ceux dont la Muse est pucelle!

GRAND Dieu, Maître de tout! Maître de ma Maîtresse
Qui me trompe avec toi—l'amoureuse Paresse—
Ô Bain de voluptés! Éventail de caresse!

SOMMEIL! Honnêteté des voleurs! Clair de lune
Des yeux crevés!—SOMMEIL! Roulette de fortune
De tout infortuné! Balayeur de rancune!

Ô corde-de-pendu de la Planète lourde!
Accord éolien hantant l'oreille sourde!
—Beau Conteur à dormir debout: conte ta bourde?...
SOMMEIL!—Foyer de ceux dont morte est la falourde!

SOMMEIL—Foyer de ceux dont la falourde est morte!
Passe-partout de ceux qui sont mis à la porte!
Face-de-bois pour les créanciers et leur sorte!
Paravent du mari contre la femme forte!

SURFACE des profonds! Profondeur des jocrisses!
Nourrice du soldat et Soldat des nourrices!
Paix des juges-de-paix! Police des polices!
SOMMEIL!—Belle-de-nuit entr'ouvrant son calice!
Larve, Ver-luisant et nocturne Cilice!
Puits de vérité de monsieur La Palisse!

SOUPIRAIL d'en haut! Rais de poussière impalpable,
Qui viens rayer du jour la lanterne implacable!

*

SOMMEIL—Écoute-moi, je parlerai bien bas:
Crépuscule flottant de l'*Être ou n'Être pas!*...

FOUNTAIN of Youth and longing's Frontier!
– You come to satiate the insatiable hunger!
You come to madden the poor transported sensitivity,
To drown it with pure air in life's open sea!

YOU come, when the curtain's dropped, to the aid
Of Punch and the Policeman, untying their braid,
Of the Cat, and the cellist and his serenade,
And the lyre of those whose Muse is maid!

GREAT God, Master of all! Master of my Mistress
Who deceives me with you – loving Laziness –
O Bath of voluptuousness! Fan of caresses!

SLEEP! Thieves' integrity! Moonlight
Of the blind! – SLEEP! For all in an unfortunate plight
Roulette of fortune! Scavenger of spite!

O hangman's rope by which the heavy Planet is suspended!
Aeolian harmony by which the deaf ear is haunted!
– Fine Story-teller of tall stories: telling your tommy rot? . . .
SLEEP! – Hearth of those who've burnt their faggots!

SLEEP – Hearth of those whose faggot has burnt out!
Skeleton key for those who are turned out!
Moonlight flit from the creditors and their band!
Screen against the strong woman for the husband!

SURFACE of the depths! Depth of imbeciles!
Nanny of the soldier and Soldier to nannies!
Force of the police force! Peace of J.P.s!
SLEEP! – Pretty-by-night half-opening her calyx!
Larva, Glow-worm and nocturnal Cilice!
For Peter crying wolf, the howl of peace!

VENTILATOR from above! Impalpable dust's ray,
Coming to rub out the implacable lantern from the day!

*

SLEEP – Listen to me, I'll speak very softly:
Floating twilight of *to Be or not to Be!* . . .

SOMBRE lucidité! Clair-obscur! Souvenir
De l'Inouï! Marée! Horizon! Avenir!
Conte des *Mille-et-une-nuits* doux à ouïr!
Lampiste d'*Aladin* qui sais nous éblouir!
Eunuque noir! muet blanc! Derviche! Djinn! Fakir!
Conte de Fée où *le Roi* se laisse assoupir!
Forêt vierge où *Peau-d'Âne* en pleurs va s'accroupir!
Garde-manger où l'*Ogre* encor va s'assouvir!
Tourelle où *ma sœur Anne* allait voir rien venir!
Tour où *dame Malbrouck* voyait page courir . . .
Où *Femme Barbe-Bleue* oyait l'heure mourir! . . .
Où *Belle-au-Bois-Dormant* dormait dans un soupir!

CUIRASSE du petit! Camisole du fort!
Lampion des éteints! Éteignoir du remord!
Conscience du juste, et du pochard qui dort!
Contre-poids des poids faux de l'épicier du Sort!
Portrait enluminé de la livide Mort!

GRAND fleuve où Cupidon va retremper ses dards
SOMMEIL!–Corne de Diane, et corne du cornard!
Couveur de magistrats et Couveur de lézards!
Marmite d'*Arlequin*!–bout de cuir, lard, homard–
SOMMEIL!–Noce de ceux qui sont dans les beaux-arts.

BOULET des forcenés, Liberté des captifs!
Sabbat du somnambule et Relais des poussifs!–

SOMME! Actif du passif et Passif de l'actif!
Pavillon de *la Folle* et *Folle* du poncif! . . .
–Ô viens changer de patte au cormoran pensif!

Ô brun Amant de l'Ombre! Amant honteux du jour!
Bal de nuit où Psyché veut démasquer l'Amour!
Grosse Nudité du chanoine en jupon court!
Panier-à-salade idéal! Banal four!
Omnibus où, dans l'Orbe, on fait pour rien un tour!

DARK lucidity! Chiaroscuro! Horizon near!
Memory of the Unheard of! Tide! The coming years!
Story of the *Arabian Nights* sweet to hear!
Lamp-maker of *Aladdin* who can dazzle us clear!
Black eunuch! white mute! Dervish! Jinnee! Fakir!
Fairy-tale where *the King* lets himself grow blear!
Virgin forest where *Donkey-Skin* goes to crouch in tears!
Larder where the *Ogre* goes to stuff himself queer!
Turret where *my sister Anne* went to see nothing appear!
Tower where *Lady Marlborough* saw the page running near . . .
Where *Blue-Beard's Wife* to the hour dying gave ear! . . .
Where *Sleeping Beauty* was sleeping in a tear!

BREAST-PLATE of the weak! Strait-jacket of the men of force!
Fairy lights for the extinct branch! Candle-snuffer of remorse!
Conscience of the just man, and of the sleeping drunkard!
Counterweight to the false weights of the grocer of Hazard!
A highly coloured portrait of Death, who's discoloured and haggard!

WIDE river where Cupid goes to re-soak his darts
SLEEP!—Horn of Diana, and horn of the greenhorn cuckold's
                    heart!
Cover for the magistrate and to Cover the hart!
Casserole of *Left-overs*!—fag-end of hide, lobster, tart—
SLEEP!—Wedding of those who are in the fine arts.

BALL and chain of the mad, Liberty of the captive!
Sabbath of the sleep-walker and Breathing-space of the
                    convulsive!—

TOTAL of liabilities! Active of the passive and Passive of the
                    active!
Colours of *the Mad Woman* and *Mad Imagination* of the sketch
                    that's derivative . . .
—O come and change the claw of the cormorant so pensive!

O dusky Lover of the Shade! Lover ashamed of daylight!
Masked ball where Psyche wants to unmask Love at midnight!
In short petticoats the canon's bulk, Nude and white!
Black Hole of Calcutta! Black Maria entered without fright!
Omnibus in which, along the Orbit, you go on a trip gratis
                    overnight!

SOMMEIL! Drame hagard! Sommeil, molle Langueur!
Bouche d'or du silence et Bâillon du blagueur!
Berceuse des vaincus! Perchoir des coqs vainqueurs!
Alinéa du livre où dorment les longueurs!

Du jeune homme rêveur Singulier Féminin!
De la femme rêvant pluriel masculin!

SOMMEIL!–Râtelier du Pégase fringant!
SOMMEIL!–Petite pluie abattant l'ouragan!
SOMMEIL!–Dédale vague où vient le revenant!
SOMMEIL!–Long corridor où plangore le vent!

NÉANT du fainéant! Lazzarone infini!
Aurore boréale au sein du jour terni!

SOMMEIL!–Autant de pris sur notre éternité!
Tour du cadran *à blanc!* Clou du Mont-de-Piété!
Héritage en Espagne à tout déshérité!
Coup de rapière dans l'eau du fleuve Léthé!
Génie au nimbe d'or des grands hallucinés!
Nid des petits hiboux! Aile des déplumés!

IMMENSE Vache à lait dont nous sommes les veaux!
Arche où le hère et le boa changent de peaux!
Arc-en-ciel miroitant! Faux du vrai! Vrai du faux!
Ivresse que la brute appelle le repos!
Sorcière de Bohême à sayon d'oripeaux!
Tityre sous l'ombrage essayant des pipeaux!
Temps qui porte un chibouck à la place de faux!
Parque qui met un peu d'huile à ses ciseaux!
Parque qui met un peu de chanvre à ses fuseaux!
Chat qui joue avec le peloton d'Atropos!

SOMMEIL!–Manne de grâce au cœur disgracié!
. . . .

LE SOMMEIL S'ÉVEILLANT ME DIT: TU M'AS SCIÉ.
. . . .

*

SLEEP! Haggard drama! Sleep, flabby Lethargy!
Golden mouth of silence and Gag of the joker in motley!
Lullaby of the defeated! Roost of the cocks after victory!
Indentation in the book where sleeps prolixity!

FOR the dreamy young man the Singular Feminine!
For the woman dreaming the plural masculine!

SLEEP!—Rack of frisky Pegasus' stall!
SLEEP!—Small rain laying great dust in a pall!
SLEEP!—Hazy maze, haunts where the haunting ghost comes to
            call!
SLEEP!—Long corridor where the wind bawls!

NOTHINGNESS of the good-for-nothing! Lazzaroni in relay!
Northern lights at the heart of the tarnished day!

SLEEP!—So much snatched from our eternity!
Round the clock *sleeplessly!* Nail from the Mount-of-Piety!
Patrimony of Spanish castles for all cut off paternally!
Rapier-thrust in the water of the River Lethe!
Spirit in the golden halo of the great dreamy!
Nest of little owls! Wing of those plucked rapaciously!

HUGE milch cow whose calves we are, lo!
Ark where the stag changes skin with a boa!
Falsehood of truth! Truth of falsehood! Shimmering rainbow!
So-called peace of the brute in drunk vertigo!
Bohemian sorceress dressed like a hobo!
Tityrus testing reed-pipes in the shadow!
Father Time with a Turkish pipe instead of a scythe in tow!
The Fate who puts on her scissors a bit of tallow!
The Fate who puts on her spindles a bit of hemp also!
Cat playing with Atropos' ball in tempo!

SLEEP!—Manna of grace to the heart in disgrace!
. . . .

YOU'VE MURDERED ME : SLEEP WAKING SAID IN MY FACE.
. . . .

*

TOI qui souffles dessus une épouse enrayée,
RUMINANT! dilatant ta pupille éraillée;
Sais-tu?... Ne sais-tu pas ce soupir–LE RÉVEIL!–
Qui bâille au ciel, parmi les crins d'or du soleil
Et les crins fous de ta Déesse ardente et blonde?...
–Non?...–Sais-tu le réveil du philosophe immonde
–Le Porc–rognonnant sa prière du matin;
Ou le réveil, extrait-d'âge de la catin?...
As-tu jamais sonné le réveil de la meute;
As-tu jamais senti l'éveil sourd de l'émeute,
Ou le réveil de plomb du malade fini?...
As-tu vu s'étirer l'œil des Lazzaroni?...
Sais-tu?... ne sais-tu pas le chant de l'alouette?
–Non–Gluants sont tes cils, pâteuse est ta luette,
Ruminant! Tu n'as pas L'INSOMNIE, éveillé;
Tu n'as pas LE SOMMEIL, ô Sac ensommeillé!

(Lits divers – Une nuit de jour)

IDYLLE COUPÉE

Avril.

C'est très parisien dans les rues
Quand l'Aurore fait le trottoir,
De voir sortir toutes les Grues
Du violon, ou de leur boudoir...

Chanson pitoyable et gaillarde:
Chiffons fanés papillotants,
Fausse note rauque et criarde
Et petits traits crus, turlutants:

Velours ratissant la chaussée;
Grande-duchesse mal chaussée,
Cocotte qui court becqueter
Et qui dit bonjour pour chanter...

YOU on top of a jammed wife panting,
RUMINATING! your bloodshot pupil dilating;
Do you know? . . . Don't you know this sigh—AWAKING!—
Yawning to the sky, among the sun's golden tresses
And the mad tresses of your ardent and blond Goddess? . . .
—No? . . .—Do you know the unclean philosopher's awaking
—The Pig—grumbling his prayers in the morning;
Or the awaking, superannuation certificate of the harlot? . . .
Have you ever sounded the pack's awaking;
Have you ever felt the mute awaking of the riot,
Or the terminal patient's leaden awaking? . . .
Have you seen the eyes extended by the Lazzaroni? . . .
Do you know? . . . don't you know the lark's melody?
—No—Your eye-lashes are sticky, your tongue is furry,
Ruminating! Awake, you don't have INSOMNIA;
Old bag heavy with sleep, you don't have SLUMBER!

(Various beds—A sleepless night)

TRUNCATED IDYLL

April.

It's very Parisian on the streets
When Aurora's doing her beat,
To watch all the Whores
Emerge from clink, or their boudoir doors . . .

A gay and pitiful melody:
Gaudy faded finery,
A shrill wrong note, raucous
And sharp raw features, monotonous:

Sweeping the pavement in a velvet gown;
A grand duchess, but down at heel,
A tart running for a kiss and a feel
Who is friendly so as to let you down . . .

J'aime les voir, tout plein légères,
Et, comme en façon de prières,
Entrer dire—Bonjour, gros chien—
Au *merlan*, puis au pharmacien.

J'aime les voir, chauves, déteintes,
Vierges de seize à soixante ans,
Rossignoler pas mal d'absinthes,
Perruches de tout leur printemps;

Et puis *payer le mannezingue*,
Au *Polyte* qui sert d'Arthur,
Bon jeune homme né *brandezingue*,
Dos-bleu sous la blouse d'azur.

—C'est au boulevard excentrique,
Au—*BON RETOUR DU CHAMP DU NORD*—
Là: toujours vert le jus de trique,
Rose le nez des Croque-mort . . .

Moitié panaches, moitié cire,
Nez croqués vifs au demeurant,
Et gais comme un enterrement . . .
—Toujours le petit *mort* pour rire!—

Le voyou siffle—vilain merle—
Et le poète de charnier
Dans ce fumier cherche la perle,
Avec le peintre chiffonnier.

Tous les deux fouillent la pâture
De leur art . . . à coups de groins;
Sûrs toujours de trouver l'ordure.
—C'est le fonds qui manque le moins.

C'est toujours un fond chaud qui fume,
Et, par le soleil, lardé d'or . . .
Le rapin nomme ça: bitume;
Et le marchand de lyre: accord.

I like to see them flit here and there,
And, as if going to say their prayers,
Look in and say 'Hullo, you old sinner'
To the chemist, then the hairdresser.

I like to see them bald, dingy,
Virgins from sixteen to sixty,
Swigging absinthes without counting,
And parroting their own spring;

And then *to the barman who has to be paid*
A pimp, the closest they get to a Prince Charming,
A nice young man born *to the trade*,
Under his working jacket *a good-for-nothing*.

–It's on the far-out boulevard,
At–*HAPPY RETURN FROM THE NORTHERN*
                 FRONT–the bar,
There: prison liquor is always green,
The Undertakers' noses have a pink sheen . . .

Half feathers and half wax,
Noses hooked on a survival,
And jolly as a funeral . . .
–The little *corpse* is good for cracks!–

The loafer whistles–the louse–
And the poet of the charnel-house
Seeks for the pearl in this dunghill,
With the rag-picker painter as well.

Both are trying to find a bit
For their art . . . using their snout;
Sure at least of finding shit.
–Stocks of that–like work–lie about.

The background's well stocked, hot and smoky,
And, by the sun, larded golden . . .
The dauber calls that: bitumen;
And the lyre-pedlar: harmony.

–Ajoutez une pipe en terre
Dont la spirale fait les cieux . . .
Allez: je plains votre misère,
Vous qui trouvez qu'on trouve mieux!

C'est le *Persil* des gueux sans poses,
Et des riches sans un radis . . .
–Mais ce n'est pas pour vous, ces choses,
Ô provinciaux de Paris! . . .

Ni pour vous, essayeurs de sauces,
Pour qui l'azur est un ragoût!
Grands empâteurs d'emplâtres fausses,
Ne fesant rien, fesant partout!

–Rembranesque! Raphaélique!
–Manet et Courbet au milieu–
. . . Ils donnent des noms de fabrique
À la pochade du bon Dieu!

Ces *Galimard cherchant la ligne*,
Et ces *Ducornet-né-sans-bras*,
Dont la blague, de chic, vous signe
N'importe quoi . . . qu'on ne peint pas.

Dieu garde encor l'homme qui glane
Sur le soleil du promenoir,
De flairer jamais la soutane
De la vieille dame au bas noir!

. . . On dégèle, animal nocturne,
Et l'on se détache en vigueur;
On veut, aveugle taciturne,
À soi tout seul être blagueur.

Savates et chapeau grotesque
Deviennent de l'antique pur;
On se colle comme une fresque
Enrayonnée au pied d'un mur.

–Add a clay-pipe, earthen
Whose spiral makes the skies . . .
Go on: I pity your dearth,
You who realize there's better to be realized!

It's the *Soliciting* of beggars without posing,
And the poorly endowed rich . . .
–But they aren't for you, such things,
O provincials of Paris! . . .

Nor for you, tasters of sauces, you
For whom the colour of sky is a stew!
Anointing with false ointments unctiously,
Not making anything, on the make universally!

–Rembrandtesque! Raphaelesque!
–Manet and Courbet in the centre–
. . . They give the names of a manufacturer
To the Almighty's rough sketch!

These *looking-for-the-line-Galimard*,
And these *Ducornet-born-without-arms*,*
Who'll have you subscribe, with their unique feint
No matter what . . . for them not to paint.

God still keeps the man gleaning
In the sun along the alleys,
From ever sniffing the old lady's
Cassock, over black stockings!

. . . Detaching themselves from the masses, and the hoar,
Nocturnal animals, they thaw;
These taciturn blind hanker
To be their own only joker.

Outlandish hats and old slippers
Take on ancient purity;
At the foot of the wall they lie together
Like a fresco, shiny.

* Two painters currently in fashion: Nicolas Galimard, pupil of Ingres, and
Louis Ducornet who, born without arms, painted with his feet.

Il coule une divine flamme,
Sous la peau; l'on se sent avoir
Je ne sais quoi qui fleure l'âme . . .
Je ne sais—mais ne veux savoir.

La Muse malade s'étire . . .
Il semble que l'huissier sursoit . . .
Soi-même on cherche à se sourire,
Soi-même on a pitié de soi.

Volez, mouches et demoiselles! . . .
Le gouapeur aussi vole un peu
D'idéal . . . Tout n'a pas des ailes . . .
Et chacun vole comme il peut.

—Un grand pendard, cocasse, triste,
Jouissait de tout ça, comme moi,
Point ne lui demandais pourquoi . . .
Du reste—une gueule d'artiste—

Il reluquait surtout la tête
Et moi je reluquais le pié.
—Jaloux . . . pourquoi? c'eût été bête,
Ayant chacun notre moitié.—

Ma béatitude nagée
Jamais, jamais n'avait bravé
Sa silhouette ravagée
Plantée au milieu du pavé . . .

—Mais il fut un Dieu pour ce drille:
Au soleil loupant comme ça,
Dessinant des yeux une fille . . .
—Un omnibus vert l'écrasa.

There flows a divine glow,
Under the skin; they feel they hold
I don't know what that smells of the soul . . .
I don't know—but don't want to know.

The sick Muse stretches herself . . .
The bailiff delays apparently . . .
Oneself, one tries to smile at oneself,
Oneself, one's full of self-pity.

Fly, flies and butterfly missies! . . .
The loafer also steals in his way
Something from the ideal . . . Everyone's wingless . . .
And each must fly—by night—as he may.

—Droll, sad, a great thug,
Was revelling in all that, like me,
Why, I didn't query . . .
Besides—an artist's mug—

He ogled the head especially
And myself I ogled the calf.
—Jealous . . . why? that would have been silly,
Each having our better half.—

My buoyant bliss hadn't yet
Ever, ever dared to meet
Her ruined silhouette
Fixed in the middle of the street . . .

—But he was a God for this guy:
In the sun failing to focus,
Drawing a girl with his eyes . . .
—He was crushed by a green omnibus.

LE CONVOI DU PAUVRE

(Paris, le 30 avril 1873,
Rue Notre-Dame-de-Lorette.)

Ça monte et c'est lourd – Allons, Hue!
– Frères de renfort, votre main? . . .
C'est trop! . . . et je fais le gamin;
C'est mon Calvaire cette rue!

Depuis Notre-Dame-Lorette . . .
– Allons! *la Cayenne* est au bout,
Frère! du cœur! encore un coup! . . .
– Mais mon âme est dans la charrette:

Corbillard dur à fendre l'âme.
Vers en bas l'attire un aimant;
Et du piteux enterrement
Rit la Lorette notre dame . . .

C'est bien ça – Splendeur et misère! –
Sous le voile en trous a brillé
Un bout du tréteau funéraire;
Cadre d'or riche . . . et pas payé.

La pente est âpre, tout de même,
Et les stations sont des *fours*,
Au tableau remontant le cours
De l'Élysée à la Bohème . . .

– Oui, camarade, il faut qu'on sue
Après son harnais et son art! . . .
Après les ailes: le brancard!
Vivre notre métier – ça tue . . .

Tués l'idéal et le râble!
Hue! . . . Et le cœur dans le talon!
. . . .

– Salut au convoi misérable
De peintre écrémé du Salon!

A POOR MAN'S FUNERAL PROCESSION

*(Paris, April 30th, 1873,
Rue Notre-Dame-de-Lorette.)*

The way is steep and it's heavy—Come on, Gee-
Up!—More help, your hand, brothers? . . .
It's too much! . . . and I act like the teenagers;
This street is my Calvary!

From Our-Lady-the-Courtesan . . .
—Come on! *the Boneyard* ends the caravan,
Brother! one more shove! take heart! . . .
—But my soul is in the cart:

It's heart-breaking, the leaden hearse.
A magnet attracts the worms below, as a lover verse;
And this pathetic burial
The Courtesan our lady finds comical . . .

That's it—Splendour and squalor!—
Beneath the holey pall has glistened
The tip of a funeral trestle;
A richly gilded frame . . . and not paid for.

All the same, the slope is bitter,
And *oven-hot* are the blessed stations,
For the picture-sque in procession
From the Élysée to Bohemia . . .

—Yes, comrade, you have to be sweating
After your harness and your art! . . .
After the wings: the shafts of an ambulance cart!
To live after our calling—is killing . . .

Twisted the ideal and the back en route!
Gee-up! . . . And your heart is in your boots!
. . . .

—Cheers to the wretched funeral party
Of the painter skimmed by the Salon's hanging
committee!

—Parmi les martyrs ça te range;
C'est prononcé comme l'arrêt
De Raphaël, peintre au nom d'ange,
Par le Peintre au nom de ... courbet!

À L'ETNA

Sicelides Musae, paulo majora canamus.
(VIRGILE.)

Etna—j'ai monté le Vésuve ...
Le Vésuve a beaucoup baissé:
J'étais plus chaud que son effluve,
Plus que sa crête hérissé ...

—Toi que l'on compare à la femme ...
—Pourquoi?—Pour ton âge? ou ton âme
De caillou cuit? ...—Ça fait rêver ...
—Et tu t'en fais rire à crever!—

—Tu ris jaune et tousses: sans doute,
Crachant un vieil amour malsain;
La lave coule sous la croûte
De ton vieux cancer au sein.

—Couchons ensemble, Camarade!
Là—mon flanc sur ton flanc malade:
Nous sommes frères, par Vénus,
Volcan! ...
              Un peu moins ... un peu plus ...

                          (*Palerme.—Août.*)

PARIA

Qu'ils se payent des républiques,
Hommes libres!—carcan au cou—
Qu'ils peuplent leurs nids domestiques! ...
—Moi je suis le maigre coucou.

–That turns you too into a martyr;
It's declared like the judgement of Raphael,
The angel-named painter,
By the Painter named . . . Bill Hook (Courbet!)

TO MOUNT ETNA

Sicilides Musae, paulo majora canamus.
(VIRGIL.)

Etna–I've climbed Vesuvius . . .
Vesuvius has somewhat flopped:
I was hotter than its effluvium,
Hotter than its bristling top . . .

–They compare you to the female . . .
–Why?–For your age? or the cooked shale
That's your heart? . . . –Think of it . . .
–And you make me laugh fit to split!–

–You laugh on the wrong side of your face and splutter:
Spitting out an old unwholesome love, no doubt;
From your old breast cancer
Beneath the crust, lava trickles out.

–Comrade, let's sleep together!
There–my side on your side's sickness:
By Venus, we're brothers,
Vulcan-ic! . . .
                        More . . . or less . . .

                                    (*Palermo.–August.*)

PARIAH

They can keep their republics,
Free men!–on whose necks iron collars click–
Let them feather their nests of domesticity! . . .
–The lean cuckoo, that's me.

—Moi,—cœur eunuque, dératé
De ce qui mouille et ce qui vibre . . .
Que me chante leur Liberté,
À moi? toujours seul. Toujours libre.

—Ma Patrie . . . elle est par le monde;
Et, puisque la planète est ronde,
Je ne crains pas d'en voir le bout . . .
Ma patrie est où je la plante:
Terre ou mer, elle est sous la plante
De mes pieds—quand je suis debout.

—Quand je suis couché: ma patrie
C'est la couche seule et meurtrie
Où je vais forcer dans mes bras
Ma moitié, comme moi sans âme;
Et ma moitié: c'est une femme . . .
Une femme que je n'ai pas.

—L'idéal à moi: c'est un songe
Creux; mon horizon—l'imprévu—
Et le mal du pays me ronge . . .
Du pays que je n'ai pas vu.

Que les moutons suivent leur route,
De Carcassonne à Tombouctou . . .
—Moi, ma route me suit. Sans doute
Elle me suivra n'importe où.

Mon pavillon sur moi frissonne,
Il a le ciel pour couronne:
C'est la brise dans mes cheveux . . .
Et, dans n'importe quelle langue;
Je puis subir une harangue;
Je puis me taire si je veux.

Ma pensée est un souffle aride:
C'est l'air. L'air est à moi partout.
Et ma parole est l'écho vide
Qui ne dit rien—et c'est tout.

—A eunuch heart, robbed
Of what casts your moorings and throbs . . .
What does their Liberty mean to me?
Always alone. Always free.

—My Country . . . is anywhere there's ground;
And, since the planet is round,
I'm not afraid of seeing its finish . . .
My country is solely what I establish:
Under the sole of my foot is she
—When I'm on my feet—by land or sea.

—My country, when I lie down to rest
Is the bruised mattress for my sole
Repose, where I shall force to my breast
My other half, like me without a soul;
And my other half: is a lady . . .
A lady not possessed by me.

—My ideal: is a hollow dream;
My horizon—the unforeseen—
And my homesickness is extreme . . .
For a land I've never seen.

Let the sheep follow their thoroughfare,
From Timbuktu to the Carcassonne . . .
—Behind me, my road follows on.
No doubt it will follow me anywhere.

Over me my ensign flies,
For a crown it has the skies:
It's the breeze in my hair . . .
And, in any tongue;
I can sustain a harangue;
I can shut up if I care.

My thought is an arid breath: it's the air.
The air belongs to me everywhere.
And my speech is an empty echo
Which says—and this is all—zero.

Mon passé: c'est ce que j'oublie.
La seule chose qui me lie
C'est ma main dans mon autre main.
Mon souvenir–Rien–C'est ma trace.
Mon présent, c'est tout ce qui passe
Mon avenir–Demain . . . demain

Je ne connais pas mon semblable;
Moi, je suis ce que je me fais.
–*Le Moi humain est haïssable* . . .
–Je ne m'aime ni ne me hais.

–Allons! la vie est une fille
Qui m'a pris à son bon plaisir . . .
Le mien, c'est: la mettre en guenille,
La prostituer sans désir.

–Des dieux? . . .–Par hasard j'ai pu naître;
Peut-être en est-il–par hasard . . .
Ceux-là, s'ils veulent me connaître,
Me trouveront bien quelque part.

–Où que je meure: ma patrie
S'ouvrira bien, sans qu'on l'en prie,
Assez grande pour mon linceul . . .
Un linceul encor: pour que faire? . . .
Puisque ma patrie est en terre
Mon os ira bien là tout seul . . .

'Armor'

PAYSAGE MAUVAIS

Sables de vieux os–Le flot râle
Des glas: crevant bruit sur bruit . . .
–Palud pâle, où la lune avale
De gros vers, pour passer la nuit.

What I forget: is my past.
The only thing to bind me fast
Is my hand in its fellow.
My memory—This is my wake—Nothing.
My present, this is all that is passing
My future—Tomorrow . . . tomorrow

I don't know anyone comparable
With me; I'm what I make myself.
—*The human Ego is detestable* . . .
—I neither love nor hate myself.

—So what! life is a girl who's taken me
For her fine sensuality . . .
Mine is: to dress her in a tatter,
Without desire to prostitute her.

—Gods? . . .—By chance I was able to be given
        birth;
Perhaps there are some—by chance . . .
If they want to know me, in that circumstance,
Somewhere they'll certainly run me to earth.

—Wherever I die: my country
Without any entreaty,
For my winding-sheet will open sufficiently wide . . .
One more winding-sheet: why bother besides? . . .
Since my country is the earth, my bones
Will easily go there on their own . . .

From 'Armorica'

EVIL LANDSCAPE

Sands of old bones—The tide rattles in its gullet
Passing-bells: cracking racket on racket . . .
—Pale salt-marsh, where the moon swallows fat worms
To go through the night's term.

–Calme de peste, où la fièvre
Cuit . . . Le follet damné languit.
–Herbe puante où le lièvre
Est un sorcier poltron qui fuit . . .

–La Lavandière blanche étale
Des trépassés le linge sale,
Au *soleil des loups* . . .–Les crapauds,

Petits chantres mélancoliques
Empoisonnent de leurs coliques,
Les champignons, leurs escabeaux.

(Marais de Guérande.–Avril.)

NATURE MORTE

Des coucous l'*Angelus* funèbre
A fait sursauter, à ténèbre,
Le coucou, pendule du vieux,

Et le chat-huant, sentinelle,
Dans sa carcasse à la chandelle
Qui flamboie à travers ses yeux.

–Écoute se taire la chouette . . .
–Un cri de bois: C'est *la brouette*
De la Mort, le long du chemin . . .

Et, d'un vol joyeux, la corneille
Fait le tour du toit où l'on veille
Le défunt qui s'en va demain.

(Bretagne.–Avril.)

–The calm of pestilence, where
Fever cooks . . . The accursed marsh-light
Sinks. –Fetid grass where the hare
Is a craven sorcerer in flight . . .

–The white Laundress makes a spread
Of the dirty linen of the dead,
In *the wolves' midnight sun* . . . –Little ghouls

Who chant, the toads,
Poison with their bellies' loads
The mushrooms, their stools.

(*Guérande Marsh.–April.*)

STILL LIFE

The cuckoos' mournful *Angelus* was a shock
To the cuckoo-pint, the old man's clock,
Cuckooing in the twilight,

And to the tawny owl, sentry
In his carcass, with a candle incandescently
Through his eyes alight.

–Hear the wood owl fall silent in a breath . . .
–A creak of the wood: It's *Death's*
Wheelbarrow, along the hedgerow . . .

And the crow is merrily on the wing
Above the cottage, where they're watching
By the deceased who will leave tomorrow.

(*Brittany.–April.*)

LA RAPSODE FORAINE ET LE PARDON
DE SAINTE-ANNE

La Palud, 27 août, jour du Pardon.

Bénite est l'infertile plage
Où, comme la mer, tout est nud.
Sainte est la chapelle sauvage
De Sainte-Anne-de-la-Palud . . .

De la Bonne Femme Sainte Anne,
Grand'tante du petit Jésus,
En bois pourri dans sa soutane
Riche . . . plus riche que Crésus!

Contre elle la petite Vierge,
Fuseau frêle, attend l'*Angelus;*
Au coin, Joseph tenant son cierge,
Niche, en saint qu'on ne fête plus . . .

. . . .

C'est le *Pardon.* — Liesse et mystères —
Déjà l'herbe rase a des poux . . .
— *Sainte Anne, Onguent des belles-mères!*
Consolation des époux! . . .

Des paroisses environnantes:
De Plougastel et Loc-Tudy,
Ils viennent tous planter leurs tentes,
Trois nuits, trois jours, — jusqu'au lundi.

Trois jours, trois nuits, la palud grogne,
Selon l'antique rituel,
— Chœur séraphique et chant d'ivrogne —
Le *CANTIQUE SPIRITUEL.*

* *

Mère taillée à coups de hache,
Tout cœur de chêne dur et bon;
Sous l'or de ta robe se cache
L'âme en pièce d'un franc-Breton!

*

THE TRAVELLING MINSTREL AND THE
PARDON OF SAINT ANNE
La Palud, August 27th, the day of the Pardon.

Hallowed are the beach's infertile levels
Where everything, like the sea, is harsh.
Holy is the primitive chapel
Of Saint-Anne-of-the-Marsh . . .

Of the Good-hearted Woman Saint Anne,
Great-aunt of the little Jesus,
With rotten wood in her cloth, fustian,
Rich . . . richer than Croesus!

The little Virgin is contiguous,
A fragile spindle, waiting for the *Angelus*;
In the corner, Joseph, holding his taper,
Nestles, as a saint no more held in honour . . .
. . . .

It's the Pardon.—Revels and mystery—
Lice in the trodden grass already . . .
—Saint Anne, for mothers-in-law a Lotion!
For husbands consolation! . . .

From the parishes round about:
From Plougastel and Loc-Tudy,
They all come with tents to camp out,
Three nights, three days,—till Monday early.

The salt-marsh grunts three days, three nights,
According to the ancient rites,
—Seraphic choir and drunken versicles—
The *SPIRITUAL CANTICLE*.

**
Mother with hatchet blows made,
All heart of oak, hard and good;
Under the gold of your dress is laid
A free Breton's soul like wine in the wood!

*

—Vieille verte à face usée
Comme la pierre du torrent,
Par des larmes d'amour creusée,
Séchée avec des pleurs de sang . . .

*

— Toi dont la mamelle tarie
S'est refait, pour avoir porté
La Virginité de Marie,
Une mâle virginité!

*

—Servante-maîtresse altière,
Très-haute devant le Très-Haut;
Au pauvre monde, pas fière,
Dame pleine de comme-il-faut!

*

—Bâton des aveugles! Béquille
Des vieilles! Bras des nouveau-nés!
Mère de madame ta fille!
Parente des abandonnés!

*

— Ô Fleur de la pucelle neuve!
Fruit de l'épouse au sein grossi!
Reposoir de la femme veuve . . .
Et du veuf Dame-de-merci!

*

—Arche de Joachim! Aïeule!
Médaille de cuivre effacé!
Gui sacré! Trèfle-quatre-feuille!
Mont d'Horeb! Souche de Jessé!

*

— Ô toi qui recouvrais la cendre,
Qui filais comme on fait chez nous,
Quand le soir venait à descendre,
Tenant l'ENFANT sur tes genoux;

*

—Green old woman with a face worn
Like a stone the torrent has borne,
By tears of love rived,
By tears of blood dried . . .

*

—You whose breasts were arid
And recovered strength, by having carried
The Virginity of Mary,
A male virginity!

*

—Lofty servant and mistress,
All mighty before the Almighty;
To the poor in society, without haughtiness,
Lady replete with a proper courtesy!

*

—Crutches for old women! For the blind
A stick! Arms for the new-born!
Mother of madam your child!
Kin to the forlorn!

*

—O Flower of the new maiden!
Fruit of the wife with the swollen womb!
For the widow an altar and haven . . .
And Lady-of-Mercy for the widowed groom!

*

—Arc of Joachim! Ancestor!
Copper medal that can't be read!
Holy mistletoe! A four-leafed clover!
Stem of Jesse! Mount Horeb!

*

—O you who covered the cinders,
And spun as hereabouts they do,
In the light growing dimmer,
Holding the CHILD *against you;*

*

— Toi qui fus là, seule, pour faire
Son maillot neuf à Bethléem,
Et là, pour coudre son suaire
Douloureux, à Jérusalem! . . .

*

Des croix profondes sont tes rides,
Tes cheveux sont blancs comme fils . . .
— Préserve des regards arides
Le berceau de nos petits-fils!

*

Fais venir et conserve en joie
Ceux à naître et ceux qui sont nés.
Et verse, sans que Dieu te voie,
L'eau de tes yeux sur les damnés!

*

Reprends dans leur chemise blanche
Les petits qui sont en langueur . . .
Rappelle à l'éternel Dimanche
Les vieux qui traînent en longueur.

*

— Dragon-gardien de la Vierge,
Garde la crèche sous ton œil.
Que, près de toi, Joseph-concierge
Garde la propreté du seuil!

*

Prends pitié de la fille-mère,
Du petit au bord du chemin . . .
Si quelqu'un leur jette la pierre,
Que la pierre se change en pain!

*

— Dame bonne en mer et sur terre,
Montre-nous le ciel et le port,
Dans la tempête ou dans la guerre . . .
Ô Fanal de la bonne mort!

*

— You, alone, were there sewing
His new swaddling-bands at Bethlehem,
And there, to make his afflicting
Shroud at Jerusalem! . . .

*

Deep crosses are your wrinkles,
White as thread your hair . . .
— Keep our grandsons' cradles
From the sterile stare!

*

Aid their coming and keep in felicity
Those to be born and those arrived.
And pour, without letting God see,
Water from your eyes on the damned!

*

In their white shirts take up again
The children who are weakly . . .
Let the old an eternal Sunday regain
Instead of lingering interminably.

*

— As the Virgin's dragon-guardian,
Keep the crib under your eye.
Near you may Joseph the doorman
Keep the threshold spry!

*

Have pity on the unmarried mother,
On the child in the gutter . . .
If someone casts a stone at her head,
Let the stone be changed to bread!

*

— Lady kind by land and ocean,
Show us heaven and a mooring,
In war or in the weather's commotion . . .
O Beacon of a good dying!

*

Humble : à tes pieds n'a point d'étoile,
Humble . . . et brave pour protéger !
Dans la nue apparaît ton voile,
Pâle auréole du danger.

*

—Aux perdus dont la vie est grise,
(—Sauf respect—perdus de boisson)
Montre le clocher de l'église
Et le chemin de la maison.

*

Prête ta douce et chaste flamme
Aux chrétiens qui sont ici . . .
Ton remède de bonne femme
Pour les bêtes-à-corne aussi !

*

Montre à nos femmes et servantes
L'ouvrage et la fécondité . . .
—Le bonjour aux âmes parentes
Qui sont bien dans l'éternité !

*

Nous mettrons un cordon de cire,
De cire-vierge jaune, autour
De ta chapelle ; et ferons dire
Ta messe basse au point du jour.

*

—Préserve notre cheminée
Des sorts et du monde-malin . . .
À Pâques te sera donnée
Une quenouille avec du lin.

*

Si nos corps sont puants sur terre,
Ta grâce est un bain de santé ;
Répands sur nous, au cimetière,
Ta bonne odeur-de-sainteté.

*

Humble: at your feet there's no star,
Humble . . . and valiantly tutelar!
In the clouds you veil appears
Danger's halo, sear.

*

– To the lost whose life is boozy,
(–Saving your presence – through drink thrown away)
Show the church's belfry
And the homeward way.

*

Lend your flame, gentle and pure,
To the Christians here below . . .
Your wise woman's cure
For the horned beasts also!

*

To our women and maidservants disclose
Work and fertility . . .
– Good-day to the souls of kinsfolk
Who are snug in eternity!

*

We shall put a border of wax,
Virgin and the colour of flax,
Around your chapel; and have the rite
Of your low mass said at first light.

*

– Keep our threshold
From the evil world and every spell . . .
At Easter we shall not withhold
A distaff and some wool as well.

*

If our bodies on earth are cess,
Your grace is a bath of healthiness;
Sprinkle on us, in the cemetery,
Your good essence-of-sanctity.

*

– À l'an prochain! – Voici ton cierge:
(C'est deux livres qu'il a coûté)
. . . Respects à Madame la Vierge,
Sans oublier la Trinité.

. . . Et les fidèles, en chemise,
– Sainte Anne, ayez pitié de nous! –
Font trois fois le tour de l'église
En se traînant sur leurs genoux;

Et boivent l'eau miraculeuse
Où les Job teigneux ont lavé
Leur nudité contagieuse . . .
– Allez: la Foi vous a sauvé! –

C'est là que tiennent leurs cénacles
Les pauvres, frères de Jésus.
– Ce n'est pas la cour des miracles,
Les trous sont vrais: *Vide latus!*

Sont-ils pas divins sur leurs claies,
Qu'auréole un nimbe vermeil,
Ces propriétaires de plaies,
Rubis vivants sous le soleil! . . .

En aboyant, un rachitique
Secoue un moignon désossé,
Coudoyant un épileptique
Qui travaille dans un fossé.

Là, ce tronc d'homme où croît l'ulcère,
Contre un tronc d'arbre où croît le gui;
Ici, c'est la fille et la mère
Dansant la danse de Saint-Guy.

Cet autre pare le cautère
De son petit enfant malsain:
– L'enfant se doit à son vieux père . . .
– Et le chancre est un gagne-pain!

—Here's your taper.—To next year!
(Two pounds, that dear)
... Respects to Madam the Virgin Mary,
Not forgetting the Trinity.

... And the faithful, in only their shirts,
—Saint Anne, have pity!—
Three times go round the church
Dragging themselves on their knees;

And drink miraculous water where the scurvy
Jobs have washed the varioles
Of their infectious nudity ...
—Go: thy Faith hath made thee whole!—

It's there that conventicles
Are held by the poor, brothers of Jesus.
—This isn't the court of miracles,
The holes are real: *Vide latus!*

On their stretchers for execution aren't they divine
Crowned with a ruddy halo, colour of wine,
These owners of injuries,
Under the sun living rubies! ...

Barking, a man with rickets
Shakes a flabby stump,
Elbowing an epileptic
Who labours on a dump.

There, a man's trunk where an ulcer begins to grow,
Against a tree-trunk where grows the mistletoe;
Here, it's a mother and daughter who prance
Dancing St Vitus's dance.

This other tends the abscess
Of her little child's sickness:
—The child owes that to his old father ...
—And the tumour is a bread-winner!

Là, c'est l'idiot de naissance,
Un *visité par Gabriel*,
Dans l'extase de l'innocence . . .
—L'innocent est près du ciel!—

—Tiens, passant, regarde: tout passe . . .
L'œil de l'idiot est resté.
Car il est en état-de-grâce . . .
—Et la Grâce est l'Éternité!—

Parmi les autres, après vêpre,
Qui sont d'eau bénite arrosés,
Un cadavre, vivant de lèpre,
Fleurit—souvenir des croisés . . .

Puis tous ceux que les Rois de France
Guérissaient d'un toucher de doigts . . .
—Mais la France n'a plus de rois,
Et leur dieu suspend sa clémence.

—Charité dans leurs écuelles! . . .
Nos aïeux ensemble ont porté
Ces fleurs de lis en écrouelles
Dont ces *choisis* ont hérité.

—*Miserere* pour les ripailles
Des *Ankokrignets* et *Kakous!* . . .
Ces moignons-là sont des tenailles,
Ces béquilles donnent des coups.

Risquez-vous donc là, gens ingambes,
Mais gare pour votre toison:
Gare aux doigts crochus! gare aux jambes
En *kyriè-éleison!*

There, it's the naturally retarded,
One *by Gabriel visited,*
In the ecstasy of innocence . . .
– The innocent is near God's presence! –

– Here, passer-by, look: everything must fade . . .
The idiot's eye is stayed.
For a state of grace is his case . . .
– And Eternity is Grace! –

Among the others, after vespers,
Who are sprinkled with holy water,
A corpse, alive with leprosy, flowers
– A memento of the crusaders' era . . .

Next all those that the French Kings
Used to cure by their fingers touching . . .
– But there are no more kings in France,
And their god defers his forbearance.

– Alms in their platters! . . .
Together, our ancestors have carried
These fleur-de-lis of scrofula
Which these *chosen ones* have inherited.

– *Miserere* for the revels and songs
Of the *Kakous* and *Ankokrignets!* . . . *
Those stumps there are tongs,
Those crutches deal buffets.

Therefore, active folk, venture there,
As for your woolly heads, beware:
Beware the hooked fingers! beware the legs in unison
In *kyrie-eleison!*

* *Ankokrignets:* possibly a word made up by Corbière; in any case, constructed
on *Ankou,* the personification of death, it probably comes to mean 'gnawed
skeletons'. *Kakous:* lepers. (*Les Amours jaunes,* ed. Y.-G. Le Dantec, Paris, 1953,
p. 263.)

... Et détourne-toi, jeune fille,
Qui viens là voir, et prendre l'air ...
Peut-être, sous l'autre guenille,
Percerait la guenille en chair ...

C'est qu'ils chassent là sur leurs terres!
Leurs peaux sont leurs blasons béants:
—Le droit-du-seigneur à leurs serres! ...
Le droit du Seigneur de céans!—

Tas d'*ex-voto* de carne impure,
Charnier d'élus pour les cieux,
Chez le Seigneur ils sont chez eux!
—Ne sont-ils pas sa créature ...

Ils grouillent dans le cimetière
On dirait des morts déroutés
N'ayant tiré de sous la pierre
Que des membres mal reboutés.

—Nous, taisons-nous! ... Ils sont sacrés.
C'est la faute d'Adam punie
Le doigt d'En-haut les a marqués:
—La droite d'En-haut soit bénie!

Du grand troupeau, boucs émissaires
Chargés des forfaits d'ici-bas,
Sur eux Dieu purge ses colères! ...
—Le pasteur de Sainte-Anne est gras.—

. . . .

Mais une note pantelante,
Écho grelottant dans le vent
Vient battre la rumeur bêlante
De ce purgatoire ambulant.

Une forme humaine qui beugle
Contre le *calvaire* se tient;
C'est comme une moitié d'aveugle:
Elle est borgne, et n'a pas de chien ...

... And you, young lady, out for the air
And to look on, retire ...
Perhaps, beneath these rags and tears,
Rags of a body might transpire ...

So they go hunting there on their domain!
Their coats of arms gaping are their skin:
–*Droit de seigneur* for their claws that strain! ...
The Lord's right of way within!–

Heaps of *ex-voto* of meat gone rotten,
Charnel-houses of the elect for heaven,
In the Lord's house they're at home!
–Aren't these creatures his own ...

They swarm in the cemetery
You'd say the dead all at sea
Who've dragged from beneath the stones
Only limbs with badly set bones.

–Let's be quiet! ... They're sanctified.
It's Adam's lapse that was penalized
The finger from On-high on them has set a sign:
–Blessed be the right hand of the On-high!

From the great flock, scapegoats whose cargo
Is crimes from here below,
On them God purges his furies! ...
–The shepherd of Saint Anne is obese.–

. . . .

But a note of thick breathing,
An echo in the wind, nugatory,
Comes beating on the confused bleating
Of this peripatetic purgatory.

Bellowing, the form is human,
Against the *calvary* leaning;
Like half–the better one–of a blind man:
She's one-eyed, and has no dog guiding ...

C'est une rapsode foraine
Qui donne aux gens pour un liard
L'*Istoyre de la Magdalayne*,
Du *Juif-Errant* ou d'*Abaylar*.

Elle hâle comme une plainte,
Comme une plainte de la faim,
Et, longue comme un jour sans pain,
Lamentablement, sa complainte . . .

–Ça chante comme ça respire,
Triste oiseau sans plume et sans nid
Vaguant où son instinct l'attire:
Autour des Bon Dieu de granit . . .

Ça peut parler aussi, sans doute.
Ça peut penser comme ça voit:
Toujours devant soi la grand'route . . .
–Et, quand ç'a deux sous . . . ça les boit.

–Femme: on dirait hélas–sa nippe
Lui pend, ficelée en jupon;
Sa dent noire serre une pipe
Éteinte . . .–Oh, la vie a du bon!–

Son nom . . . ça se nomme Misère.
Ça s'est trouvé né par hasard.
Ça sera trouvé mort par terre . . .
La même chose–quelque part.

–Si tu la rencontres, Poète,
Avec son vieux sac de soldat:
C'est notre sœur . . . donne–c'est fête–
Pour sa pipe, un peu de tabac! . . .

Tu verras dans sa face creuse
Se creuser, comme dans du bois,
Un sourire; et sa main galeuse
Te faire un vrai signe de croix.

It's a travelling minstrel
Who for a farthing will tell
Mary Magdalen's Historie,
Or of *The Wandering Jew,* or *Abelard's* story.

She heaves like a moan,
Like a hunger groan,
And, woefully like a day without bread,
Her tragic ballad, just as extended . . .

– It sings as it takes breath,
A sad bird without feather or nest
Wandering where its instinct draws it:
Around these holy statues of granite . . .

It can also speak, unquestionably.
It can think as it can see:
Always in front of it the highway . . .
– And, when it's got two halfpence . . . it drinks them away.

– A woman: you'd wonder, alas – her old clouts
Hang her, got up in a petticoat with string;
Her black tooth grips a pipe, gone out . . .
– Oh, life has its good things! –

Her name . . . it's called Dearth.
It found it was born on the off chance.
It will be found dead on the earth . . .
Somewhere – the same circumstance.

– Poet, if you cross her track,
With her old soldier's knapsack:
It's our sister . . . give her – it's a festivity –
For her pipe, a little baccy! . . .

You will see in her hollow face,
As in wood, hollowing itself anew
A smile; and her scabby hand trace
A true sign of the cross for you.

CRIS D'AVEUGLE
Sur l'air bas-breton: *Ann hini goz*.

L'œil tué n'est pas mort
Un coin le fend encor
Encloué je suis sans cercueil
On m'a planté le clou dans l'œil
L'œil cloué n'est pas mort
Et le coin entre encor

Deus misericors
Deus misericors
Le marteau bat ma tête en bois
Le marteau qui fera la croix
Deus misericors
Deus misericors

Les oiseaux croque-morts
Ont donc peur à mon corps
Mon Golgotha n'est pas fini
Lamma lamma sabacthani
Colombes de la Mort
Soiffez après mon corps

Rouge comme un sabord
La plaie est sur le bord
Comme la gencive bavant
D'une vieille qui rit sans dent
La plaie est sur le bord
Rouge comme un sabord

Je vois des cercles d'or
Le soleil blanc me mord
J'ai deux trous percés par un fer
Rougi dans la forge d'enfer
Je vois un cercle d'or
Le feu d'en haut me mord

BLIND MAN'S CRIES*
To the Low Breton tune: *The Old Woman*.

The slaughtered eye is not dead
Still by a wedge it's penetrated
Nailed I'm without a coffin
In my eye the nail's been stuck in
The nailed eye is not dead
And the wedge is still insinuated

Deus misericors
Deus misericors
The hammer on my wooden head flails
The hammer that the cross will nail
Deus misericors
Deus misericors

The mute undertaker birds are jumpy
Still over my body
Golgatha has not ended for me
Lamma lamma sabacthani
Then be boozy
Doves of Death at my body

Like a port-hole painted red
Round the edge the sore is spread
Like the gum dribbling
Of a toothless old woman giggling
Round the edge the sore is spread
Like a port-hole painted red

I see circles of gold
The white sun scalds
I have two holes pierced by branding-irons
Reddened at the forge in hell's environs
I see a circle of gold
Fire from on high scalds

* Corbière rhymes lines 1, 2, 5 and 6 of each stanza with the same sound, used throughout the poem.

Dans la moelle se tord
Une larme qui sort
Je vois dedans le paradis
Miserere, De profundis
Dans mon crâne se tord
Du soufre en pleur qui sort

Bienheureux le bon mort
Le mort sauvé qui dort
Heureux les martyrs, les élus
Avec la Vierge et son Jésus
Ô bienheureux le mort
Le mort jugé qui dort

Un Chevalier dehors
Repose sans remords
Dans le cimetière bénit
Dans sa sieste de granit
L'homme en pierre dehors
A deux yeux sans remords

Ho je vous sens encor
Landes jaunes d'Armor
Je sens mon rosaire à mes doigts
Et le Christ en os sur le bois
À toi je baye encor
Ô ciel défunt d'Armor

Pardon de prier fort
Seigneur si c'est le sort
Mes yeux, deux bénitiers ardents
Le diable a mis ses doigts dedans
Pardon de crier fort
Seigneur contre le sort

J'entends le vent du nord
Qui bugle comme un cor
C'est l'hallali des trépassés
J'aboie après mon tour assez
J'entends le vent du nord
J'entends le glas du cor

(*Menez-Arrez.*)

Out of the marrow twists
A tear that mists
Wherein is paradise I notice
Miserere, De profundis
Out of my skull twists
Weeping sulphur that mists

The good dead man is blest
The saved dead man at rest
Happy the martyrs, the chosen few
With the Virgin and her Jesu
O the dead man is blest
The judged dead man at rest

A Knight by the gorse
Sleeps without remorse
In the consecrated cemetery
In his granite reverie
The man of stone by the gorse
Has two eyes without remorse

Ah for you I still hanker
Yellow moors of Armorica
Between my fingers I feel my rosary
And the Christ in bone on the tree
I gape at you still blanker
O dead sky of Armorica

Forgive my praying late
Lord if it is fate
My eyes, two burning stoups
Where the devil's fingers scooped
Forgive my crying late
Lord against fate

I hear the north wind of storm
Sounding like a horn
It's the kill of the dead in the hunt
I bay after my turn in the brunt
I hear the north wind of storm
I hear the knell of the horn

(*Menez-Arrez.*)

'Gens de mer'

MATELOTS

Vos marins de quinquets à l'Opéra . . . comique,
Sous un frac en bleu-ciel jurent «Mille sabords!»
Et, sur les boulevards, le survivant chronique
Du *Vengeur* vend l'onguent à tuer les rats morts.
Le Jûn'homme infligé d'un bras–même en voyage–
Infortuné, chantant par suite de naufrage;
La femme en bain de mer qui tord ses bras au flot;
Et l'amiral ***–Ce n'est pas matelot!
–Matelots–quelle brusque et nerveuse saillie
Fait cette *Race à part* sur la race faillie!
Comme ils vous mettent tous, *terriens*, au même sac!
–*Un curé dans ton lit, un' fill' dans mon hamac!*–

. . . .

–On ne les connaît pas, ces gens à rudes nœuds.
Ils ont le mal de mer sur vos *planchers à bœufs;*
À terre–oiseaux palmés–ils sont gauches et veules.
Ils sont mal culottés comme leurs brûle-gueules.
Quand le roulis leur manque . . . ils se sentent rouler:
–*À terre, on a beau boire, on ne peut désoûler!*

–On ne les connaît pas.–Eux: que leur fait la terre? . . .
Une relâche, avec l'hôpital militaire,
Des filles, la prison, des horions, du vin . . .
Le reste: Eh bien, après?–Est-ce que c'est marin? . . .

–Eux ils sont matelots.–À travers les tortures,
Les luttes, les dangers, les larges aventures,
Leur *face-à-coups-de-hache* a pris un tic nerveux
D'insouciant dédain pour ce qui n'est pas Eux . . .
C'est qu'ils se sentent bien, ces chiens! Ce sont des mâles!
–Eux: l'Océan!—et vous: les plates-bandes sales;
Vous êtes des *terriens*, en un mot, des *troupiers:*
–*De la terre de pipe et de la sueur de pieds!*–

From 'Sailors'

SEAMEN

Your sailors of the Opera footlights . . . the comic opera,
In sky-blue frock-coats swear 'A thousand portholes!'
And the chronic survivor of *The Avenger*
Along the boulevards sells ointment to kill dead moles.
The Young man–even on a voyage–*in one arm afflicted,*
Ill-fated, singing–that's what a shipwreck inflicted;
The woman sea-bathing who wrings her hands at the breakers;
And Admiral ***–These aren't sailors!
–Sailors–what sudden vigorous gush
Creates this *Race apart* out of the race that's done for!
How they tar you all, *landlubbers*, with the same brush!
–*A reverend in your bed, in my hammock a whore!*–

. . . .

–You don't know them, these roughly hitched types.
They're sea-sick on your *dry land for pussy-footing;*
On land–web-footed birds–they're awkward and gangling.
They're as ill-breeched as their badly seasoned pipes.
When the rollers are missing . . . they feel themselves rolling:
–*You can't get sober on land, it's all very well to be boozing!*

–You don't know them.–What does the land mean to them? . . .
A port of call, with punches, wine, scars,
Prison, the military hospital, women . . .
The rest: Well, so what?–Is this what makes Jack tar? . . .

–They *are* sailors.–Through the tortures,
The struggles, the dangers, the wide adventures,
Their *hatchet-faces* have taken on a nervous twitching
Of careless contempt for all not of Their calling . . .
It's because these dogs feel themselves at ease! They're men!
–For them: the Ocean!–and for you: flower-beds of phlegm;
You're *landlubbers, troopers*, worse yet,
–*Pipe-clay and foot-sweat!*–

Eux sont les *vieux-de-cale* et *les frères-la-côte*,
Gens au cœur sur la main, et toujours la main haute;
Des natures en barre!—Et capables de tout . . .
—Faites-en donc autant! . . .—Ils sont *de mauvais goût* . . .
—Peut-être . . . Ils ont chez vous des amours tolérées
Par un *grippe-Jésus** accueillant leurs entrées . . .
—Eh! faut-il pas du cœur au ventre quelque part,
Pour entrer en plein jour là—bagne-lupanar,
Qu'ils nomment le *Cap-Horn*, dans leur langue hâlée:
—Le cap Horn, noir séjour de tempête grêlée—
Et se coller en vrac, sans crampe d'estomac,
De la chair à chiquer—comme un nœud de tabac!
Jetant leur solde avec leur trop-plein de tendresse,
À tout vent; ils vont là comme ils vont à la messe . . .
Ces anges mal léchés, ces durs enfants perdus!
—Leur tête a du requin et du petit-Jésus.

Ils aiment à tout crin: Ils aiment plaie et bosse,
La Bonne-Vierge, avec le gendarme qu'on rosse;
Ils font des vœux à tout . . . mais leur vœu caressé
A toujours l'habit bleu d'un *Jésus-christ*† rossé.

—Allez: ce franc cynique a sa grâce native . . .
Comme il vous toise un chef, à sa façon naïve!
Comme il connaît son maître:—*Un d'un seul bloc de bois!*
—*Un mauvais chien toujours qu'un bon enfant parfois!*

. . . .

—Allez: à bord, chez eux, ils ont leur poésie!
Ces brutes ont des chants ivres d'âme saisie
Improvisée aux quarts sur le gaillard-d'avant . . .
—Ils ne s'en doutent pas, eux, poème vivant.

—Ils ont toujours, pour leur *bonne femme de mère*,
Une larme d'enfant, ces héros de misère;
Pour leur *Douce-Jolie*, une larme d'amour! . . .

*Grippe-Jésus: petit nom marin du gendarme.
†*Jésus-Christ*: du même au même.

They're *old salts* and *shore brothers*,
Folk with their hearts on their sleeves, and *de rigueur*
Their sleeves on raised hands; iron characters!–
And capable of anything . . . –Do as much yourselves then! . . .
    –They're *vulgar* . . .
–Perhaps . . . In your town they have loves that the *raw lobster**
Winks at, greeting them as they enter . . .
–Well! you must have a heart somewhere in your stomach, just
   think,
To enter there in daylight–brothel-clink,
Called in their sunburnt tongue, the *Cape Horn*:
–Cape Horn, dark home of the poxy hailstorm–
And higgledy-piggledy, without an ache in the belly,
To adhere to flesh to chew–like a knot of baccy!
With their excess tenderness throwing what pay they've amassed
To the winds; they go there as they go to mass . . .
These roughly finished angels, these hard children without a clue!
–Their heads have something of the shark and of the infant Jesu.

They love frantically: They love sores and protuberances,
The Holy-Virgin, along with the policeman they batter;
They make vows to everybody . . . but their fondest of assurances
Always has the blue uniform of a beaten *copper*.†

–So what: this open cynic has his natural good . . .
How he sizes up a boss, in his simple fashion!
How he knows his master: *One from a single block of wood!*
–*Always a surly dog but a good child on occasion!*

. . . .

–So what: at home on board, they have their poetry!
These brutes have intoxicated songs of the ravished spirit
Extemporized in the fo'c's'le on watch duty . . .
–A living poem, themselves, they don't suspect it.

–Always, for their *good woman of a mother*,
These heroes of wretchedness have a child's tear;
A tear of love, for the *girl who's dear*! . . .

   * *Raw lobster*: sailors' name for a policeman. [T.C.]
   † *Copper*: the same for the same. [T.C.]

Au pays—loin—ils ont, espérant leur retour,
Ces gens de cuivre rouge, une pâle fiancée
Que, pour la mer jolie, un jour ils ont laissée.
Elle attend vaguement . . . comme on attend là-bas.
Eux ils portent son nom tatoué sur leur bras.
Peut-être elle sera veuve avant d'être épouse . . .
—Car la mer est bien grande et la mer est jalouse.—
Mais elle sera fière, à travers un sanglot,
De pouvoir dire encore:—Il était matelot! . . .

—C'est plus qu'un homme aussi devant la mer géante,
Ce matelot entier! . . .
                  Piétinant sous la plante
De son pied marin le pont près de crouler:
Tiens bon! Ça le connaît, ça va le désoûler.
Il finit comme ça, simple en sa grande allure,
D'un bloc:—*Un trou dans l'eau, quoi! . . . pas de fioriture.*—

. . . .

On en voit revenir pourtant: bris de naufrage,
Ramassis de scorbut et hachis d'abordage . . .
Cassés, défigurés, dépaysés, perclus:
—Un œil en moins.—Et vous, en avez-vous en plus?
—La fièvre-jaune.—Eh bien, et vous, l'avez-vous rose?
—Une balafre.—Ah, c'est signé! . . . C'est quelque chose!
—Et le bras en pantenne.—Oui, c'est un biscaïen,
Le reste c'est le bel ouvrage au chirurgien.
—Et ce trou dans la joue?—Un ancien coup de pique.
—Cette bosse?—À *tribord?* . . . excusez: c'est ma chique.
—Ça?—Rien: une *foutaise*, un pruneau dans la main,
Ça sert de baromètre, et vous verrez demain:
Je ne vous dis que ça, sûr! quand je sens ma crampe . . .
Allez, on n'en fait plus de coques de ma trempe!
On m'a pendu deux fois . . .—
                  Et l'honnête forban
Creuse un bateau de bois pour un petit enfant.

—Ils durent comme ça, reniflant la tempête
Riches de gloire et de trois cents francs de retraite,

In their own–distant–country, these men of red copper
Have a pale betrothed, hoping for their return,
Whom one day for the pretty sea they spurned.
She waits . . . as they wait there, vaguely.
Meanwhile, tattooed on their arms they carry
Her name. Perhaps she'll be a widow before a bride . . .
–For the sea is wide and the sea is jealous.–
But through a sob, with pride,
–He was a sailor! . . . She'll be able to repeat, tremulous.

–This complete sailor before the giant ocean
Is more than a man too! . . .
                                                Treading
Under his sailor's sole the deck near to destruction:
Hold fast! This will sober him up, what's coming he knows.
He ends like that, simple in his noble bearing,
In one piece:–*A hole in the water! . . . no furbelows.–*

. . . .

Still you see some come back: shipwrecks' debris,
Minced meat from boardings and a rabble of scurvy . . .
Disfigured, uprooted, crippled, and breaking:
–One eye the less.–And do you have one extra, you?
–Yellow fever.–What about you, do you have the blue?
–A scar.–Ah, it's signed! . . . That's something!
–And the arm askew.–Yes, that's musket-fire,
The rest is the surgeon's handiwork, quite inspired.
–And this hole in your cheek?–An old pike blow.
–This lump?–To *starboard?* . . . pardon: that's my tobacco.
–That?–Nothing: a *bagatelle*, a bullet in my hand,
It serves as a barometer, and tomorrow you'll understand:
I'm not just saying that either!
When I feel a twinge . . . Ah, they don't any longer
Make hulls of my stamp! They hanged me twice . . .–
                                                And the honest adventurer
Hollows for a small child a wooden schooner.

–They last like that, sniffing the storm, wealthy
With fame and three hundred francs of pension money,

Vieux culots de gargousse, épaves de héros! . . .
—Héros?—ils riraient bien! . . .—Non merci: matelots!

—Matelots!—Ce n'est pas vous, jeunes *mateluches*,
Pour qui les femmes ont toujours des coqueluches . . .
Ah, les vieux avaient de plus fiers appétits!
En haussant leur épaule ils vous trouvent petits.
À treize ans ils mangeaient de l'Anglais, les corsaires!
Vous, vous n'êtes que des *pelletas* militaires . . .
Allez, on n'en fait plus de ces *purs, premier brin!*
Tout s'en va . . . tout! La mer . . . elle n'est plus *marin!*
De leur temps, elle était plus salée et sauvage.
Mais, à présent, rien n'a plus de pucelage . . .
La mer . . . La mer n'est plus qu'une fille à soldats! . . .

—Vous, matelots, rêvez, en faisant vos cent pas
Comme dans les grands quarts . . . Paisible rêverie
De carcasse qui geint, de mât craqué qui crie . . .
—Aux pompes! . . .
                          —Non . . . fini!—Les beaux jours sont passés:
—*Adieu mon beau navire aux trois mâts pavoisés!*

. . . .

Tel qu'une vieille coque, au sec et dégréée,
Où vient encor parfois clapoter la marée:
Âme-de-mer en peine est le vieux matelot
Attendant, échoué . . .—quoi: la mort?
                                        —Non, le flot.
                              (*Île d'Ouessant.—Avril.*)

BAMBINE

Tu dors sous les panais, capitaine Bambine
Du remorqueur havrais *l'Aimable-Proserpine*,
Qui, vingt-huit ans, fis voir au Parisien béant,
Pour vingt sous: *L'OCÉAN! L'OCÉAN!! L'OCÉAN!!!*

Old cartridge ends, flotsam of heroes! . . .
—At that they'd laugh heartily! . . . Sailors!—Heroes, thank you,
    no!

—Sailors!—This isn't you, young *sailor lads*,
For whom the women always cater to every fad . . .
Ah, the old ones' appetites were prouder!
They find you small, shrugging their shoulders.
At thirteen they were eating Englishmen, these freebooters!
You, you're only army *sappers* . . .
Get along, they don't make any more these *genuine first-raters!*
Everything passes . . . everything! The sea . . . is no longer
    maritime!
It was saltier and wilder, in their time.
But, now, nothing is virginal any more . . .
The sea . . . The sea is nothing but a soldiers' whore! . . .

—Dream, sailors, while you pace five score
As during the long watches . . . A peaceful dream
Of moaning hulls and cracking masts that scream . . .
—To the pumps! . . .
                    —No . . . over!—The good old days are past:
—*Farewell my fine ship with three dressed masts!*

. . . .

Like an old hull high and dry, without rigging,
Where sometimes the waves still slide:
The old sailor is a sea-soul suffering
Waiting, stranded . . . for what: death?
                        —No, the tide.

                        (*Isle of Ouessant.—April.*)

BAMBINE

You're pushing up the daisies, Captain Bambine
Of the tug from Le Havre *The Fair-Proserpine*,
Who, for twenty-eight years, gave gaping Parisians an impression
For a shilling of: *THE OCEAN! THE OCEAN!! THE
    OCEAN!!!*

Train de plaisir au large.–On double la jetée–
En rade: *y-a-z-un peu d'gomme* . . .–Une mer démontée–
Et *la cargaison* râle:–Ah! commandant! assez!
Assez, pour notre argent, de tempête! cessez!–

Bambine ne dit mot. Un bon coup de mer passe
Sur les infortunés:–Ah, capitaine! grâce! . . .
–C'est bon . . . si ces messieurs et dam's ont leur content? . . .
C'est pas pour mon plaisir, moi, v's'êt's mon chargement:
Pare à virer . . .–

        Malheur! le coquin de navire
Donne en grand sur un banc . . .–Stoppe!–Fini de rire . . .
Et talonne à tout rompre, et roule bord sur bord
Balayé par la lame:–À la fin, c'est trop fort! . . .–

Et la *cargaison* rend des cris . . . rend tout! rend l'âme.
Bambine fait les cent pas.
            Un ange, une femme
Le prend:–C'est ennuyeux ça, conducteur! cessez!
Faites-moi mettre à terre, à la fin! c'est assez!–

Bambine l'élongeant d'un long regard austère:
–À terre! q'vous avez dit? . . . vous avez dit: à terre . . .
À terre! pas dégoûtaî . . . Moi-z'aussi, foi d'mat'lot,
J'voudrais ben! . . . attendu q'si t'-ta-l'heure l'prim'flot
Ne soulag' pas la coque: vous et moi, mes princesses
J'bêrons ben, sauf respect, la lavure éd'nos fesses!–

Il reprit ses cent pas, tout à fait mal bordé:
–À terre! . . . j'crâis f . . . tre ben! Les femm's! . . . pas dégoûté!

                     (*Havre-de-Grâce. La Hève.–Août.*)

An excursion train at sea.–They round the pier–
In the roadstead: *a bit of all right* . . . –Waves start to rear–
And *the cargo* are at the last gasp: 'Ah! sir! that's plenty!
Give over! that's enough storm, for our money!'

Bambine says nothing. Over the unfortunates rushes the sea,
A sizeable wave: 'Ah, captain! mercy! . . .'
'If these ladies and gentlemen are 'aving their fill? . . . that's all
   right . . .
You're my consignment, this ain't for my delight:
Get ready to tack . . .'

               Bad luck! the rogue of a boat
Lunges on to a shoal . . .–Stop!–The end of the joke . . .
And she grounds so's to break everything, and rolls gunwale under
Swept by the billow: 'It's too much, just consider! . . .'

And the *cargo* throw up screams . . . throw up everything! throw
   up their spirits.
Bambine paces the bridge.
               An angel, a woman hits
Out at him: 'It's annoying, that! give over!
Now then, have me put ashore! that's enough, driver!'

Bambine lay alongside her with a long severe scan: 'Cor!
Ashore you said? . . . you said: ashore . . .
Ashore! you don't want much . . . Me too, on my word as a sailor,
I'd like that a lot! . . . seeing if the first roller
Don't budge the boat: you and me, my princesses
Will most likely get, with respect, a swill for our arses!'

He went on pacing the bridge, crossly resting on his oars:
–Women! . . . not much! . . . I'm scared we've fucking had it!
   Ashore!
               (*Havre-de-Grâce. La Hève.–August.*)

LETTRE DU MEXIQUE

La Vera-Cruz, 10 février.

«Vous m'avez confié le petit.–Il est mort.
«Et plus d'un camarade avec, pauvre cher être.
«L'équipage . . . y en a plus. Il reviendra peut-être
      «Quelques-uns de nous.–C'est le sort–

«Rien n'est beau comme ça–Matelot–pour un homme;
«Tout le monde en voudrait à terre–C'est bien sûr.
«Sans le désagrément. Rien que ça: Voyez comme
      «Déjà l'apprentissage est dur.

«Je pleure en marquant ça, moi, vieux *Frère-la-côte.*
«J'aurais donné ma peau joliment sans façon
«Pour vous le renvoyer . . . Moi, ce n'est pas ma faute:
      «Ce mal-là n'a pas de raison.

«La fièvre est ici comme Mars en carême.
«Au cimetière on va toucher sa ration.
«Le zouave a nommé ça—Parisien quand-même–
      «*Le jardin d'acclimatation.*»

«Consolez-vous. Le monde y crève comme mouches.
«. . . J'ai trouvé dans son sac des souvenirs de cœur:
«Un portrait de fille, et deux petites babouches,
      «Et: marqué–*Cadeau pour ma sœur.*–

«Il fait dire à *maman:* qu'il a fait sa prière.
«Au père: qu'il serait mieux mort dans un combat.
«Deux anges étaient là sur son heure dernière:
      «Un matelot. Un vieux soldat.»

Toulon, 24 mai.

LETTER FROM MEXICO

Vera Cruz, February 10th.

'You've entrusted the kid to me.–He's dead.
And more than one of his pals too, poor little chap.
The crew . . . all gone. Some of us perhaps
    Will return.–Fate: take it as read–

'Nothing so fine as that for a man–Sailor–
Everybody wants to be on shore–That's the stuff.
Without any kind of trouble. No more:
    You see apprenticeship is really tough.

'I weep recording it, old *Shore-brother*.
I'd have given my life without a second thought
To send him back to you . . . Weren't my fault:
    There's no sense in this distemper.

'Like clock-work the fever's here inevitably.
You get your ration in the cemetery.
The Zouave—after all, a Parisian–
    Calls it *the zoo's acclimatizing garden*.

'Don't be too upset. They die off here like flies.
. . . I've found some mementoes in his bag:
A girl's picture, Turkish slippers in a small size,
    And:–*Present for my sister*–on the tag.

'His message to *Ma* was that he'd kept his religion.
To his father: that he'd rather have died in action.
Two angels watched him growing paler:
    An old soldier. A sailor.'

Toulon, May 24th.

LE MOUSSE

Mousse: il est donc marin, ton père?...
–Pêcheur. Perdu depuis longtemps.
En découchant d'avec ma mère,
Il a couché dans les brisants...

Maman lui garde au cimetière
Une tombe–et rien dedans.–
C'est moi son mari sur la terre,
Pour gagner du pain aux enfants.

Deux petits.–Alors, sur la plage,
Rien n'est revenu du naufrage?...
–Son garde-pipe et son sabot...

La mère pleure, le dimanche,
Pour repos... Moi: j'ai ma revanche
Quand je serai grand–matelot!–

(*Baie des Trépassés.*)

AU VIEUX ROSCOFF
Berceuse en Nord-Ouest mineur

Trou de flibustiers, vieux nid
À corsaires!–dans la tourmente,
Dors ton bon somme de granit
Sur tes caves que le flot hante...

Ronfle à la mer, ronfle à la brise;
Ta corne dans la brume grise,
Ton pied marin dans les brisans...
–Dors: tu peux fermer ton œil borgne
Ouvert sur le large, et qui lorgne
Les Anglais, depuis trois cents ans.

THE CABIN-BOY

'So, boy, your father's a sailor? . . .'
'A fisherman. Lost a long time before.
Leaving my mother's bed,
He's gone to sleep under the breakers instead . . .

'Ma saves a tomb for him in the cemetery
–But it's empty.–
I'm her husband on this shore,
For the kids keeping the wolf from the door.

'Two little ones.' 'Wasn't anything at all
From the wreck washed up after the squall? . . .'
'One of his clogs and his pipe-holder . . .

'Mother cries for quiescence
On Sundays . . . I'll wreak my vengeance
When I'm grown up–a sailor!'

(*Bay of the Dead.*)

TO OLD ROSCOFF
Lullaby in North-west Minor

A hole for buccaneers, old nest
Of freebooters!–in the tempest,
Sleep your heavy granite slumber
Over your cellars haunted by the combers . . .

Snore with the breeze, snore with the waters;
Through the grey fog your horn high,
Your sea legs in the breakers . . .
–Sleep: you can close your single flashing eye
Open on the open sea, where you've peered
For the English, for three hundred years.

–Dors, vieille coque bien ancrée;
Les margats et les cormorans
Tes grands poètes d'ouragans
Viendront chanter à la marée . . .

–Dors, vieille fille-à-matelots;
Plus ne te soûleront ces flots
Qui te faisaient une ceinture
Dorée, aux nuits rouges de vin,
De sang, de feu!—Dors . . . Sur ton sein
L'or ne fondra plus en friture.

–Où sont les noms de tes amants . . .
–La mer et la gloire étaient folles!–
Noms de lascars! noms de géants!
Crachés des gueules d'espingoles . . .

Où battaient-ils, ces pavillons,
Écharpant ton ciel en haillons! . . .
–Dors au ciel de plomb sur tes dunes . . .
Dors: plus ne viendront ricocher
Les boulets morts, sur ton clocher
Criblé–comme un prunier–de prunes . . .

–Dors: sous les noires cheminées,
Écoute rêver tes enfants,
Mousses de quatre-vingt-dix ans,
Épaves des belles années . . .

. . . .

Il dort ton bon canon de fer,
À plat-ventre aussi dans sa souille,
Grêlé par les lunes d'hyver . . .
Il dort son lourd sommeil de rouille.
–Va: ronfle au vent, vieux ronfleur,
Tiens toujours ta gueule enragée
Braquée à l'Anglais! . . . et chargée
De maigre jonc-marin en fleur.

(*Roscoff.–Décembre.*)

–Sleep, old hull, with a firm painter;
The ember-goose and the cormorant
Your great poets of wild weather
To the tide will descant . . .

–Sleep, sailors' old strumpet;
These waves will no longer make you drunk, as of old
They fashioned you a girdle of gold
With nights by wine made scarlet,
By blood, by fire!–Sleep . . . Against your breasts
Gold will no longer melt in the fry of foamy crests.

–Where are the names of your lovers . . .
–The sea and glory were mad!–
Names of giants! names of Lascars!
From the muzzles of blunderbusses spat . . .

Where have they flailed, these flags,
Tearing your sky in rags! . . .
–Sleep on your dunes under the leaden sky . . .
Sleep: musket balls won't shy
Any longer ricocheting plumb off your belfry
Riddled with grape-shot–like a plum tree . . .

–Sleep: under the black mantelpieces,
Listen to your children's reverie,
Cabin-boys aged ninety,
Waifs of the fine ages . . .

. . . .

Your good iron cannon
Sleeps belly-flopped in its bed of dust,
By the moons of winter hailed on . . .
It sleeps a heavy sleep of rust.
–Come on: snore with the wind, old snorer,
Always keep your violent muzzle pointed
At the English! . . . and loaded
With thin furze in flower.

(*Roscoff.–December.*)

LA FIN

Oh! combien de marins, combien de capitaines
Qui sont partis joyeux pour des courses lointaines
Dans ce morne horizon se sont évanouis! . . .

. . . .

Combien de patrons morts avec leurs équipages!
L'Océan, de leur vie a pris toutes les pages,
Et, d'un souffle, il a tout dispersé sur les flots.
Nul ne saura leur fin dans l'abîme plongée . . .

. . . .

Nul ne saura leurs noms, pas même l'humble pierre,
Dans l'étroit cimetière où l'écho nous répond,
Pas même un saule vert qui s'effeuille à l'automne,
Pas même la chanson plaintive et monotone
D'un aveugle qui chante à l'angle d'un vieux pont.

(V. Hugo.–*Oceano nox*.)

Eh bien, tous ces marins–matelots, capitaines,
Dans leur grand Océan à jamais engloutis . . .
Partis insoucieux pour leurs courses lointaines
Sont morts–absolument comme ils étaient partis.

Allons! c'est leur métier; ils sont morts dans leurs bottes!
Leur *boujaron** au cœur, tout vifs dans leurs capotes . . .
–*Morts* . . . Merci: la *Camarde* a pas le pied marin;
Qu'elle couche avec vous: c'est votre bonne-femme . . .
–Eux, allons donc: Entiers! enlevés par la lame!
                    Ou perdus dans un grain . . .

*Boujaron: ration d'eau-de-vie.

THE END

Oh! how many seafarers, how many captains
Who have weighed anchor joyfully for distant sea
    lanes
Have vanished into this gloomy horizon! ...

. . . .

How many skippers lost with their crews!
The Ocean has taken all their lives' leaves,
And, with one breath of wind, on the waves set
    them loose.
No one will know their end immersed in the deeps ...

. . . .

No one will know their names, not even the
    humble stone,
In the narrow cemetery where echoes answer,
Not even a green willow shedding its leaves in
    October,
Not even the plaintive and monotonous tone
Of a blind man who sings at an old bridge's corner.

             (V. HUGO.—*Oceano nox.*)*

Well, all these seafarers—sailors, captains—men of the sea,
In their great Ocean for ever sucked under ...
Who set carefree for their distant sea lanes
Are dead—as indubitably as they weighed anchor.

So what! it's their job; with their boots on they died!
Their *tots*† at their heart, in their hoods quite jollified ...
—*Dead* ... No thanks: *Madam Death* has no sea-legs;
Let her sleep with you: she's your good lady ...
—As for them, like this: Washed away by the billow! utterly!
          Under a sail the squall pegs ...

* Corbière's epigraph differs in several places from Hugo's text, whether deliberately or by error.
† *Tot:* ration of rum. [T.C.]

Un grain . . . est-ce la mort ça? la basse voilure
Battant à travers l'eau!—Ça se dit *encombrer* . . .
Un coup de mer plombé, puis la haute mâture
Fouettant les flots ras—et ça se dit *sombrer*.

—Sombrer—Sondez ce mot. Votre *mort* est bien pâle
Et pas grand'chose à bord, sous la lourde rafale . . .
Pas grand-chose devant le grand sourire amer
Du matelot qui lutte.—Allons donc, de la place!—
Vieux fantôme éventé, la Mort change de face:
                    La Mer! . . .

Noyés?—Eh allons donc! Les *noyés* sont d'eau douce.
—Coulés! corps et biens! Et, jusqu'au petit mousse,
Le défi dans les yeux, dans les dents le juron!
À l'écume crachant une chique râlée,
Buvant sans hauts-de-cœur *la grand'tasse salée* . . .
           —Comme ils ont bu leur boujaron.—

. . . .

—Pas de fond de six pieds, ni rats de cimetière:
Eux ils vont aux requins! L'âme d'un matelot
Au lieu de suinter dans vos pommes de terre,
                    Respire à chaque flot.

—Voyez à l'horizon se soulever la houle;
           On dirait le ventre amoureux
D'une fille de joie en rut, à moité soûle . . .
           Ils sont là!—La houle a du creux.—

—Écoutez, écoutez la tourmente qui beugle! . . .
C'est leur anniversaire—Il revient bien souvent—
Ô poète, gardez pour vous vos chants d'aveugle;
—Eux: le *De profundis* que leur corne le vent.

. . . Qu'ils roulent infinis dans les espaces vierges! . . .
           Qu'ils roulent verts et nus,
Sans clous et sans sapin, sans couvercle, sans cierges . . .
—Laissez-les donc rouler, *terriens* parvenus!

                    (*À bord.*— 11 février)

FROM *YELLOW LOVES*

117

A squall . . . is that death? the low trimmed sails hammered hard
Across the water!—That's called *floundering* . . .
A blast of the leaden sea, then the mast-yard
Whipping the flattened waves—and that's called *foundering*.

—Foundering—Fathom this word. Your *death* is certainly pale
And nothing much on board, under a heavy gale . . .
Nothing much beside the smile of irony
Of a wrestling sailor.—Come on now, make a space!—
That stale old spectre, Death changes face:
                    The Sea! . . .

Drowned?—Not likely! They're a freshwater bunch, the *drowned*.
—Sunk! with all hands! And, to the little cabin-boy down,
Defiance in their eyes, curses between their teeth!
Spitting to the foam a death-rattle quid of tobacco,
Drinking *the big salt cup* without a retch . . .
          —As their tots of rum have been sent below.—
. . . .

—No cemetery rats, no six foot of depth
For them: they go to the sharks! A sailor's
Soul instead of oozing into your taters,
                    With each tide draws breath.

—Look on the horizon, the surge heavily lists;
          As you might say the loving belly
Of a whore in heat, half pissed . . .
          They're there!—The swell's got a cavity.—

—Listen, listen to the storm bellowing! . . .
It's their anniversary—Very often returning—
Keep your blind man's songs to yourself, O poet;
—For them: the *De profundis* that the winds trumpet.

. . . Let them roll endlessly in the virgin latitudes! . . .
               Let them roll green and nude,
Without nails or coffins, without lids, without tapers . . .
—Let them roll, upstart *landlubbers*!

                         (*On board.*—February 11th)

'Rondels pour après'

RONDEL

Il fait noir, enfant, voleur d'étincelles!
Il n'est plus de nuits, il n'est plus de jours;
Dors . . . en attendant venir toutes celles
Qui disaient: Jamais! Qui disaient: Toujours!

Entends-tu leurs pas? . . . Ils ne sont pas lourds:
Oh! les pieds légers! — l'Amour a des ailes . . .
Il fait noir, enfant, voleur d'étincelles!

Entends-tu leurs voix? . . . Les caveaux sont sourds.
Dors: Il pèse peu, ton faix d'immortelles;
Ils ne viendront pas, tes amis les ours,
Jeter leur pavé sur tes demoiselles . . .
Il fait noir, enfant, voleur d'étincelles!

DO, L'ENFANT DO . . .

Buona vespre! Dors: Ton bout de cierge . . .
On l'a posé là, puis on est parti.
Tu n'auras pas peur seul, pauvre petit? . . .
C'est le chandelier de ton lit d'auberge.

Du fesse-cahier ne crains plus la verge,
Va! . . . De t'éveiller point n'est si hardi.
Buona sera! Dors: Ton bout de cierge . . .

Est mort. — Il n'est plus, ici, de concierge:
Seuls, le vent du nord, le vent du midi
Viendront balancer un fil-de-la-Vierge.
Chut! Pour les pieds-plats, ton sol est maudit.
—Buona notte! Dors: Ton bout de cierge . . .

From 'Rondels for Afterwards'

RONDEL

It's growing dark, child, thief of sparks!
No more nights, no more days;
Sleep . . . waiting for all those who'd remark:
Never! Who'd remark: Always!

Do you hear their step? . . . Quite fey:
Oh! tripping feet! – Love with wings is arrayed . . .
It's growing dark, child, thief of sparks!

Do you hear their voice? . . . Burial vaults are deaf and dark.
Sleep: Your burden of everlasting flowers hardly weighs;
Over here your friends the bears won't stray*
To throw at your butterfly missies their cobbles from the highway . . .
It's growing dark, child, thief of sparks!

ROCK-A-BYE BABY . . .

Buona vespre! *Sleep: Your candle-end* . . .
They put there, then they withdrew.
You won't be afraid alone, poor mite, will you? . . .
It's the candlestick at your inn bed that extends.

Fear no more the prick of the review,
Go! . . . No one's so bold as to arouse you.
Buona sera! *Sleep: Your candle-end* . . .

Is dead. – There's no janitor here any more to attend:
The north and south winds, alone, will come with a tissue
Of finest gossamer to suspend.
Hush! Your ground is accursed, for the dim crew.
– Bunoa notte! *Sleep: Your candle-end* . . .

* Allusion to La Fontaine's fable 'The Bear and the Garden Lover' (VIII, 10).

MIRLITON

Dors d'amour, méchant ferreur de cigales !
Dans le chiendent qui te couvrira
La cigale aussi pour toi chantera,
Joyeuse, avec ses petites cymbales.

La rosée aura des pleurs matinales ;
Et le muguet blanc fait un joli drap . . .
Dors d'amour, méchant ferreur de cigales.

Pleureuses en troupeau passeront les rafales . . .

La Muse camarde ici posera,
Sur ta bouche noire encore elle aura
Ces rimes qui vont aux moelles des pâles . . .
Dors d'amour, méchant ferreur de cigales.

PETIT MORT POUR RIRE

Va vite, léger peigneur de comètes !
Les herbes au vent seront tes cheveux ;
De ton œil béant jailliront les feux
Follets, prisonniers dans les pauvres têtes . . .

Les fleurs de tombeau qu'on nomme Amourettes
Foisonneront plein ton rire terreux . . .
Et les myosotis, ces fleurs d'oubliettes . . .

Ne fais pas le lourd : cercueils de poètes
Pour les croque-morts sont de simples jeux,
Boîte à violon qui sonnent le creux . . .
Ils te croiront mort—Les bourgeois sont bêtes—
Va vite, léger peigneur de comètes !

TIN WHISTLE

Sleep in love, naughty shoeing-smith of cicadas!
In the couch-grass that over you will meet
The cicada will also sing like a treat
For you, with his little cymbals' cadenzas.

With tears of morning the dew will greet;
And lily of the valley makes a pretty sheet . . .
Sleep in love, naughty shoeing-smith of cicadas.

Weeping in a band they'll pass by—the squalls, with sleet . . .

Here the deathly Muse will take her seat,
On your black lips she'll again have these stanzas
Going to the marrow of the effete . . .
Sleep in love, naughty shoeing-smith of cicadas.

LITTLE CORPSE GOOD FOR CRACKS

Go quickly, light comber of comets!
Grass in the wind will be your hair;
From your wide eyes will flare
Will-o'-the-wisps, prisoners of the intellects . . .

The flowers of the grave called wild oats and tares
Your earthy laugh will fully square . . .
And forget-me-nots, those flowers of the dungeon—oubliettes . . .

Make light of it: coffins of poets
For undertakers' mutes are an easy affair,
Violin cases with a hollow racket . . .
They'll think you dead—The bourgeois are bears—
Go quickly, light comber of comets!

Poèmes divers

PARIS DIURNE

Vois aux cieux le grand rond de cuivre rouge luire,
Immense casserole où le Bon Dieu fait cuire
La manne, l'arlequin, l'éternel plat du jour.
C'est trempé de sueur et c'est poivré d'amour.

Les Laridons en cercle attendent près du four,
On entend vaguement la chair rance bruire,
Et les soiffards aussi sont là, tendant leur buire;
Le marmiteux grelotte en attendant son tour.

Tu crois que le soleil frit donc pour tout le monde
Ces gras graillons grouillants qu'un torrent d'or inonde?
Non, le bouillon de chien tombe sur nous du ciel.

Eux sont sous le rayon et nous sous la gouttière
À nous le pot au noir qui froidit sans lumière . . .
Notre substance à nous, c'est notre poche à fiel.

Ma foi j'aime autant ça que d'être dans le miel.

From the Poems Not Included in
Les Amours jaunes

PARIS BY DAY*

Look up in the heavens as the huge copper plate gleams,
The enormous saucepan where the Almighty steams
Manna and leavings, the set meal of the day without let-
Up: it's peppered with love and dripping with sweat.

Near the oven dogged cookhouse urchins wait in a ring,
The sizzle of rancid flesh vaguely jars,
And the drunks are also there, holding out their jars;
One poor devil waiting his turn is shaking.

You think these fatty gobs are thus fried by the sun
Flooded by a golden shower, swarming, for everyone?
No, dog's broth falls from the sky on us.

They're out in the daylight and we're confined to barracks.
For us the cold pot the kettle calls black . . .
Our gall ladled out is our only surplus.

To be sure it's for that, not the honey-pot, I'm covetous.

* The text of this poem is taken from P.-O. Walzer, *Œuvres complètes de Tristan Corbière*, 'Bibliothèque de la Pléiade', Paris, 1970, p. 887. It was written by Corbière on his own copy of *Les Amours jaunes*, which contains other manuscripts, including 'Paris nocturne' (p. 124), and miscellaneous notes. See Walzer's note pp. 1379–82 and Ida Levi, 'New Light on Tristan Corbière', *French Studies*, July 1951, pp. 233–44.

PARIS NOCTURNE
Ce n'est pas une ville, c'est un monde.

–C'est la mer:–calme plat–et la grande marée,
Avec un grondement lointain, s'est retirée.
Le flot va revenir, se roulant dans son bruit–
–Entendez-vous gratter les crabes de la nuit . . .

–C'est le Styx asséché: Le chiffonnier Diogène,
Sa lanterne à la main, s'en vient errer sans gêne.
Le long du ruisseau noir, les poètes pervers
Pêchent; leur crâne creux leur sert de boîte à vers.

–C'est le champ: Pour glaner les impures charpies
S'abat le vol tournant des hideuses harpies.
Le lapin de gouttière, à l'affût des rongeurs,
Fuit les fils de Bondy, nocturnes vendangeurs.

–C'est la mort: La police gît–En haut, l'amour
Fait la sieste en têtant la viande d'un bras lourd,
Où le baiser éteint laisse sa plaque rouge . . .
L'heure est seule–Écoutez: . . . pas un rêve ne bouge

–C'est la vie: Écoutez: la source vive chante
L'éternelle chanson, sur le tête gluante
D'un dieu marin tirant ses membres nus et verts
Sur le lit de la morgue . . . Et les yeux grand'ouverts!

SOUS UN PORTRAIT DE CORBIÈRE
EN COULEURS FAIT PAR LUI ET DATÉ DE 1868

Jeune philosophe en dérive
Revenu sans avoir été,
Cœur de poète mal planté:
Pourquoi voulez-vous que je vive?

PARIS BY NIGHT*
Not a city, but a world.

–It's the sea:–dead calm–and the spring tide,
With a faraway snarl, has gone out.
The tide will come in again, in its clangour rolling wide–
–Do you hear the night crabs scrabble about . . .

–It's the Styx dried up: The rag-picker Diogenes
Goes round with his lantern in his hand, quite at ease.
Along the black gutter, perverse poets
Fish; baiting their lines from their hollow heads.

–It's the fields: Hideous harpies wheel overhead
Swooping to glean filthy lint shreds.
Watching out for rats, an alley cat takes flight
From Bondy Forest's† scavengers, harvesters of night.

–It's death: The police lie low–Love with feet
Up, in siesta upstairs, sucks a heavy arm's meat
Where the extinguished kiss leaves its red disc . . .
The hour is solitary–Listen: . . . not a dream shifts

–It's life: Listen: the spring water is singing
Over a sea god's slimy head the song everlasting,
As he extends his naked green side
On the morgue's bed . . . And his eyes open wide!

ON A PORTRAIT OF CORBIÈRE‡
PAINTED BY HIM AND DATED 1868

Young philosopher drifting,
Without having been there returning,
A poet's heart misplaced:
Why shouldn't I be effaced?

---

* The text of this poem is taken from Walzer, op. cit., p. 888.
† The night-soil dump was at the village of Bondy (Walzer, op. cit., p. 1382).
‡ The text of this poem is taken from the 1891 edition of *Les Amours jaunes*.

L'amour!... je l'ai rêvé, mon cœur au grand ouvert
Bat comme un volet en pantenne
Habité par la froide haleine
Des plus bizarres courants d'air;
Qui voudrait s'y jeter?... pas moi si j'étais ELLE!...
Va te coucher, mon cœur, et ne bats plus de l'aile.

J'aurais voulu souffrir et mourir d'une femme,
M'ouvrir du haut en bas et lui donner en flamme,
Comme un punch, ce cœur-là chaud sous le chaud soleil...

Alors je chanterais (faux, comme de coutume)
Et j'irais me coucher seul dans la trouble brume
Éternité, néant, mort, sommeil, ou réveil.

Ah si j'étais un peu compris! Si par pitié
Une femme pouvait me sourire à moitié,
Je lui dirais: oh viens, ange qui me consoles!...
. . . .
... Et je la conduirais à l'hospice des folles.

On m'a manqué ma vie!... une vie à peu près;
Savez-vous ce que c'est: regardez cette tête.
Dépareillé partout, très bon, plus mauvais, très
Fou, ne me souffrant... Encor si j'étais bête!

La mort... ah oui, je sais: cette femme est bien froide,
Coquette dans la vie; après, sans passion.
Pour coucher avec elle il faut être trop roide...
Et puis, la mort n'est pas, c'est la négation.

Je voudrais être un point épousseté des masses,
Un point mort balayé dans la nuit des espaces,
        ... Et je ne le suis point!

Je voudrais être alors chien de fille publique,
Lécher un peu d'amour qui ne soit pas payé;
Ou déesse à tous crins sur la côte d'Afrique,
Ou fou, mais réussi; fou, mais pas à moitié.

Love! . . . I've dreamed it, my heart wide open
Bangs like a boat's compass at sixes and sevens
That the cold wind frequents
With stranger air currents;
If I were S H E ! . . . I wouldn't want to cast off to this
        unheeding! . . .
Go to bed, heart, and stop flapping your wings.

I'd have liked to suffer for a woman and die for her,
To slit myself from top to tail and on her confer
Flaming, like a punch, this heart here hot under the hot sun . . .

Then I would sing (as usual, off-key)
And I'd go to bed alone in a fog of uncertainty
Awakening, death, sleep, eternity or none.

Ah if I were a little understood! If in pity
A woman could have half-smiled at me,
I would say to her: oh my comforting angel, come! . . .
. . . .
. . . And I would lead her to the women's asylum.

My life's been wrecked! . . . something like a life;
Do you know what this means: look at this head.
Always ill-matched, very good, far worse, madness rife
In me, but not living with myself . . . If I were only dim-witted!

Death . . . ah yes, I know: that woman's very frigid, if
A flirt during life; afterwards, without passion.
To sleep with her you'd have to be really stiff . . .
And besides, death is not, it is negation.

I'd like to be a speck brushed away from the masses,
A point of deadlock swept into the night of spaces,
        . . . And I am not: what's the point!

So I'd like to be a dog whose mistress is a whore,
Licking a bit of love that needn't be paid for;
Or on the African coast, a goddess with flowing mane,
Or insane, but successfully; not half insane.

ÉPITAPHE
POUR
TRISTAN JOACHIM-ÉDOUARD CORBIÈRE,
PHILOSOPHE, ÉPAVE, MORT-NÉ

Mélange adultère de tout:
De la fortune et pas le sou,
De l'énergie et pas de force,
La Liberté, mais une entorse.
Du cœur, du cœur! de l'âme, non—
Des amis, pas un compagnon,
De l'idée et pas une idée,
De l'amour et pas une aimée,
La paresse et pas le repos.
Vertus chez lui furent défauts,
Âme blasée inassouvie.
Mort, mais pas guéri de la vie,
Gâcheur de vie hors de propos
Le corps à sec et la tête ivre,
Espérant, niant l'avenir,
Il mourut en s'attendant vivre
Et vécut s'attendant mourir.

EPITAPH
FOR
TRISTAN JOACHIM-EDWARD CORBIÈRE,
PHILOSOPHER, STRAY, STILL-BORN*

Everything's adulterous medley:
Of fortune and without a penny,
Of energy and without efficacy,
Though bent, Liberty.
Of heart, of heart! of soul, none–
Of friends, but no true one,
Of ideas but no idea,
Of love and no beloved dear,
Lazy without resting.
Virtue in him defaulting,
Blasé soul hankering.
Dead, but not cured of living,
Bungler of life without scope
The head soaked and the body dry,
In denial of the future, hoped,
With an expectation of life he died
And lived expecting to die.

* The text of this poem is taken from the 1891 edition of *Les Amours jaunes*.

Œuvres en prose

CASINO DES TRÉPASSÉS

Un pays,—non, ce sont des côtes brisées de la dure Bretagne: *Penmarc'h, Toul-Infern, Poul-Dahut, Stang-an-Ankou* . . . Des noms barbares hurlés par les rafales, roulés sous les lames sourdes, cassés dans les brisants et perdus en chair de poule sur les marais . . . Des noms qui ont des voix.

Là, sous le ciel neutre, la tourmente est chez elle; le calme est un deuil.

Là, c'est l'étang plombé qui gît sur la cité d'Ys, la Sodome noyée.

Là, c'est la *Baie-des-Trépassés* où, des profondeurs, reviennent les os des naufragés frapper aux portes des cabanes pour quêter un linceul; et le *Raz-de-Sein*, couturé de courants, que *jamais homme n'a passé sans peur ou mal.*

Là naissent et meurent des êtres couleur de roc, patients comme des éternels, rendant par hoquets une langue pauvre, presque éteinte, qui ne sait rire ni pleurer . . .

C'est là que j'invente un casino.

CASINO DES TRÉPASSÉS
(STATION D'HIVERNAGE)
À LA BONNE DESCENTE DES DÉCOURAGEUX
À PIED ET À CHEVAL.

C'est un ancien clocher debout et décorné. Sa flèche est à ses pieds—tombée. Des masures à coups de ruines flanquées en tas contre lui, avec un mouvement ivrogne, à l'abri du flot qui monte et du souffle qui rase.

Ah! c'est que c'est une bonne tour, solide aux cloches comme aux couleuvrines, solide au temps; un vieux nid des templiers, bons travailleurs en Dieu, ceux-là! sacrés piliers de temple et de corps de garde. On sent encore en entrant cette indéfinissable odeur de pierre bénite qui ne s'en va jamais.

L'intérieur est un puits carré, quatre murs nus. À mi-hauteur, une entaille en ogive longue et profonde donne une raie de lumière. La

Prose

CASINO OF THE DEAD

A country,–no, this is the shattered coast of harsh Brittany: *Penmarc'h, Toul-Infern, Poul-Dahut, Stang-an-Ankou* . . . Barbarous names squalled by the squalls, rolled under the deaf rollers, broken among the breakers and lost in goose-flesh across the marshes . . . Names that have voices.

There, under the neutral sky, the tempest is at home; calm is mourning.

There, it's the leaden lake lying on the city of Ys, Sodom drowned.

There, it's the *Bay of the Dead* where bones of the shipwrecked return from the depths to knock at the doors of huts to beg a winding-sheet; and the *Raz-de-Sein*, scored with currents, *that never a man has passed without fear or harm.*

There are born and die beings the colour of rock, condemned like eternal ones, gasping out a poor language, almost extinct, which can't laugh or cry . . .

It's there I imagine a casino.

CASINO OF THE DEAD
(A WINTER RESORT)
A STOPPING-PLACE FOR DISENTHUSIASTS
PEDESTRIANS AND MOUNTED TRAVELLERS.

It's an old belfry standing upright and without its point. Its spire is at its feet–toppled. Under the onslaught of ruin hovels flung in a heap against it with a drunken movement, in the shelter of the rising tide and the levelling wind.

Ah! it just happens to be a good tower, with solid bells and culverins, and standing up to the weather; an old nest of the Knights Templars, good workers in God, those men! holy pillars of the temple and the guard-room. On entering you still feel that indefinable smell of hallowed stone which never goes away.

The interior is a square shaft, with four bare walls. Half-way up, a pointed slit window, long and deep, admits a ray of light. The

brise bourdonne là-haut comme une mouche emprisonnée. De loin
en loin, sur les parois, montent de petits jours noirs : c'est l'escalier
dans l'épaisseur des murailles ; sur les haltes, sont ménagées des
logettes, avec un œil en meurtrière ouvert sur l'horizon. C'est là
que gîteront nos hôtes.

Système cellulaire : douze pieds carrés, murs blanchis à la chaux,
hauteur d'appui en châtaignier d'un beau ton ; autour, des clous-
de-la-Passion pour clouer les vêtements ; une couchette de nonne,
une auge de pierre pour les ablutions, une longue-vue, une espingole
chargée à chevrotines pour les canards ou les *philistins.*–Voilà.

En bas, dans la nef dallée de pierres tombales, la cuisine : cuisine à
tout faire.–On entre à cheval.–Four d'alchimiste ; cheminée grande
comme une chaumine pour coucher les mâtures de navires (car–
Dieu aidant–la grève vaut une forêt en coupe réglée) ; des landiers
d'enfer pour flamber le goëmon.

Sous le manteau, des escabelles pour le bonhomme Homère, le
Docteur Faust, le Curé Rabelais, Jean Bart, saint Antoine, Job le
lépreux et autres anciens vivants ; un trou pour les grillons, s'ils
veulent. Une torche en veille piquée près la crémaillère ; partout des
crampons pour accrocher le sabot aux allumettes, la boîte au sel,
les andouilles, le rameau bénit, les bottes suiffées, un fer à cheval
qui porte bonheur.

Contre le mur culotté, les armes et harnais de chasse, de pêche et
de gueule : canardiers, harpons, filets, vaisselle d'étain, cuivres,
fanaux. À la porte, le billot des exécutions ; au centre, un vrai
dolmen pour la ripaille, entouré de fauteuils roides, charpentés
comme des bois de justice. Aux poutres du plafond, sont hissées des
herses pour les grandes natures mortes. Au coin, dans le clair-
obscur, un coucou droit dans un bon cercueil de chêne, sonnant le
glas des heures. Tout plein le vaste bénitier, une famille de chats
électriques ; dessous, un gras roquet de tourne-broche rognonne, et
clopin-clopant, de ci de là, des canards drôles.

En haut, à une simple élévation de cathédrale, au niveau de la
fenêtre géante, nous ferons l'unique étage, plate-forme en charpente
en manière de *chambre des cloches.* On y montera par l'escalier en
boyau ou par des haubans de vaisseau garnis d'enfléchures avec une
grande hune pour palier.–C'est l'atelier.–*Studio di far niente.*

Le jour est manœuvré à volonté par le rideau d'un théâtre en
faillite. Au milieu, table monumentale jonchée de papiers ; dessous,
des peaux de phoques. Alentour, divans perses. Aux murs, tentures

breeze hums up there like a captive fly. On the inner side of the walls, at long intervals from each other, climb little black openings: it's the staircase in the thickness of the walls; on the steps small cells are contrived, each with a loop-hole, an eye open on to the horizon. It's there that our guests will lodge.

The disposition of each cell: twelve feet square, the walls white-washed, panelled breast-high with chestnut of a good grain; round about, nails-of-the-Passion to hang clothes; a nun's bed, a stone trough for ablutions, a long view, a blunderbuss loaded with buck-shot for ducks or *Philistines*. – There you are.

Below, in the nave paved with tomb-stones, the kitchen: an all-purpose kitchen. – You enter on horseback. – An alchemist's oven; a chimney as big as a small cottage to lodge the masts and spars of ships (for – God willing – the beach is worth a forest properly felled); fire-dogs from hell to singe the seaweed.

Under the mantelpiece, stools for the good fellow Homer, Dr Faust, Parson Rabelais, Jean Bart, Saint Anthony, Job the leper and other living ancients; a hole for the crickets, if they wish. A torch in vigil stuck up near the pot-hook; grappling-irons every-where to hang up the clog used for matches, the box of salt, chitter-lings, the holy palm, boots rubbed with tallow, a horseshoe to bring good luck.

Against the mellowed wall, arms and harnesses for hunting, fishing and eating: screens for duck-shooting, harpoons, nets, pewter, copperware, lanterns. At the door, the block for executions; in the middle, a real *dolmen* for feasting, surrounded by stiff arm-chairs shaped like gallows. To the beams of the ceiling are hoisted harrows and stage-lights for the great still lifes. In the corner, in the chiaroscuro, a cuckoo erect in a good oak coffin, sounding the knell of the hours. Completely filling the huge holy water stoup, a family of electric cats; below, a fat mongrel of a turnspit growls, and in every direction, hobbling about, amusing ducks.

Above, at the mere height of a cathedral, on the level of the giant window, we'll make the only floor above ground level, a timber-work platform in the manner of a *bell-loft*. You climb up there by the narrow staircase or by ships' shrouds trimmed with ratlines with a maintop for a landing. – It's the studio. – *Studio di far niente*.

Daylight is manoeuvred at will by the curtain of a bankrupt theatre. In the middle, a monumental table strewn with papers; below, skins of seals. Round about, Persian divans. On the walls,

d'arlequin; tapisseries, cuirs coloriés, voiles tannées, pavillons, guenilles sordides superbes. Des images d'Épinal collées en lambeaux sur la porte. En face, un poêle russe et la bouilloire à thé. Au fond, un orgue de chapelle pour les musiciens de Barbarie, et des niches pour les vieux saints qu'on ne fête plus. Une grande toile sur châssis pour les peintres déposer leurs ordures. Une chaloupe défoncée pleine de foin nouveau pour les chiens et les poètes. Un lit de camp: des philosophes dessus et deux petits cochons noirs dessous. À côté, un débit de tabacs. Dans l'espace, des hamacs pendus comme toiles d'araignées, parmi des appareils de gymnastique. Au bout d'une chaîne à puits crochée à perte de vue, oscille le lustre, vrai grappin d'abordage forgé par un maréchal-ferrant ivre et vierge.

Plus haut, si haut qu'on peut monter, c'est la galerie extérieure et la plate-forme découverte qui commande là-bas, lavée par les grains, balayée par les trombes, grêlée par les lunes. Un coq rouillé se ronge, empalé sur le paratonnerre.

Des petits jardins engorgent les gargouilles. Aux angles, deux mâchicoulis bayent sur l'abîme et deux clochetons *montrent du doigt le ciel*.

L'un sera gréé en poste de guetteur: mât de télégraphe à grands bras fantastiques et beffroi affolé que les sautes de vent mettront tout seul en branle, dans les nuits de liesse, pour le naufrage.

L'autre, attendant aussi un vent de hasard . . ., attendra.

Là, je veux des petits vitraux obscurs, grillagés, impénétrables dans la barbacane profonde hérissée d'artichauts de fer; une porte de fer à secret, pleine de clous, armée de verrous . . . et grand ouverte.

Je veux l'oubliette aérienne, capitonnée de fleurettes pompadour, encombrée de fleurs en fleurs; un canari empaillé dans une cage dorée, un miroir de Murano plus grand que nature, un sofa Crébillon et un plafond en dôme peint par Mahomet (7ᵉ manière) . . .

C'est pour l'épave qui est en l'air, la flâneuse du rêve, l'ombre grise qui va vite comme les morts de ballade . . . et qui ne vient pas. – Madame Marlbrough, peut-être!

«Anne, ma sœur Anne, ne vois-tu rien venir?–Rien! rien que l'ouragan qui festoie, la girouette qui tournoie, la brume qui noie . . .»

motley hangings; tapestries, stained hides, tawny sails, flags, splendidly dirty rags. Garish Epinal pictures stuck in fragments on the door. Opposite, a Russian stove and the tea-kettle. At the back, a church organ for musicians from Barbary and their monkeys, and niches for the old saints no more held in honour. A big canvas on its stretcher for the painters to deposit their refuse. A launch stove in and filled with fresh hay for dogs and poets. A camp-bed: philosophers on it and two little black pigs underneath. At the side, a tobacconist's shop. In the air, hammocks slung like spiders' webs, among gymnastic apparatus. At the end of a well-chain swinging as far as the eye can see, the chandelier flickers, a true grappling-iron forged by a drunk and virgin farrier.

Higher, as high as it's possible to climb, there's the external gallery and the open platform overlooking below, washed by the squalls, swept by the waterspouts, hailed on by the moons. A rusty cock frets, impaled on the lightning-conductor.

Little gardens choke the gargoyles. In the angles, two machicolations gape into the pit and two pinnacles *point a finger at the sky*.

One will be rigged as a look-out post: a telegraph pole with fantastic great arms and a steeple up the pole that the wind's veering will set going by itself, during nights of revels, for the wreck.

The other, also waiting a wind of chance . . ., will wait.

I want to have there small leaded windows, grilled, impenetrable in the steep barbican bristling with iron spikes; a secret iron gate, studded with nails, reinforced with bolts . . . and wide open.

I want an aerial dungeon, an oubliette, stuffed with flowery Pompadour material, cluttered with flowers in flower; a stuffed canary in a gilded cage, a Murano mirror larger than life, a Crébillon sofa and a domed ceiling painted by Mahomet (7th style) . . .

This is for the waif who's in the air, the loitering woman of dreams, the grey shadow who goes quickly like the dead of ballads . . . and who doesn't come. – Mrs Marlborough, perhaps!

'Anne, my sister Anne, do you see nothing coming? – Nothing! nothing but the hurricane carousing, the weathercock turning, the mist drowning . . .'

CASINO DES TRÉPASSÉS

Oh! la haute vie sauvage que vivra là, messeigneurs, hôtes de céans!

À LA BONNE DESCENTE DES DÉCOURAGEUX.

Nargue de tout!

Oh! *la rude révalescière!* oh! *le grand* à pleins poumons! le cynisme élégant! l'oubli qui cicatrise et le somme qui délie! ...

À nous la libre solitude à plusieurs, chacun portant *quelque chose là,* tous triés d'entre les autres par la lourde brise qui chasse au loin les algues sèches et les coquilles vides.

Ici, nos moyens nous permettent d'être pauvres.

Pas de bonhomme poncif à gâter le paysage, notre mer et notre désert. Frères, voici votre uniforme: chapeau mou, chemise brune en drap de capucin, culottes de toile à voiles, bottes de mer en cuir fauve. Nous sommes beaux, allez!

À vous, chasseurs, les grands sables et les marais; à vous, matelots, la mer jolie et ses poissons qui mangent souvent du pêcheur; voici vos baleinières de cèdre blanc, braves embarcations hissées sous le porche à leurs potences de fer.

Voici nos équipages d'aventure: des *frères-la-côte,* brutes antiques, pilotes comme des marsouins, cuisiniers à tous crins et femmes de chambre ...

Terriens, terrez dans les chaumières. Vous autres, gîtez dans les cellules, nichez dans les aires, perchez dans les haubans!

Pas d'esprit, s'il vous plaît: on est sobre de mots quand on s'est compris une fois.

Toi, fainéant, fais un livre – tout homme a son livre dans le ventre – et l'ennui berceur se penchera sur toi. Peintre ficeleur, dépouille le vieux *chic.* Ô harpiste! écoute et tais-toi. Rimeur vidé, voici venir les heures hantées ...

Humons l'air qui soûle! ... Et toi que es malade de la vie, viens ici cacher ta tête, et repose sur le gazon salé, dans le désabonnement universel.

TRISTAN.
Penmarc'h. – Septembre.

CASINO OF THE DEAD

Oh! the savage high life that will be lived there, my lords, guests of the house!

A STOPPING-PLACE FOR DISENTHUSIASTS.

A fig for everything!

Oh! *the rough restorative soup!* oh! *the sublime* with full lungs! elegant cynicism! oblivion cicatrizing and sleep releasing!

For us the free solitude of several, each carrying *something there*, all sorted out from among the rest by the sultry breeze that hunts dry seaweed and empty shells far and wide.

Here, our means allow us to be poor.

No cliché of a good fellow to spoil the landscape, our sea and our desert. Brothers, here's your uniform: a soft hat, a brown shirt of friar's cloth, breeches of sail canvas, jack-boots of tawny hide. We look fine, don't we!

For you, hunters, the wide sands and marshes; for you, sailors, the pretty sea and its fish which often dine off fisherman; here are your whale-boats of white cedar, fine boats pulled up under the porch by their iron gallows-bitts.

Here are our chance crews; *shore-brothers*, ancient brutes, pilots like porpoises, thorough-going cooks, and maids . . .

Land-lubbers, land up in your cottages. You others, lie in the cells, airily nest in the eyries, perch in the shrouds!

No wit, please: one's sober with words when one's once been understood.

You, idler, make a book—every man's got a book in his belly—and lullabying ennui will bend over you. Parcel-packer of a painter, slough off the old *chic*. O harpist! listen and be quiet. Empty rhymer, here come the haunted hours . . .

Let's breathe in the intoxicating air! . . . And you, so sick of life, come and hide your head here, and rest on the dirty lawn, in universal withdrawal.

TRISTAN.
Penmarc'h.—September.

L'AMÉRICAINE

D'accord, gentlemen-sailors, en France, on n'a pas idée d'un yacht; les cotres anglais sont d'admirables chevaux de course. Et vos goëlettes américaines, jolies comme tout sur la mer jolie! J'ai vu des vieux marins attendris leur prodiguer des noms d'oiseaux! Mais, s'il me fallait, avec ces amours-là sous les pieds, donner dans les brisants, fignoler dans les arêtes, j'aurais peur pour la peinture!

Pour moi, la navigation de plaisance doit être, avant tout, excentrique; une chose défendue aux bourgeois de la mer: sortir quand ils sont forcés de rentrer, chasser dans l'ouragan qui les chasse et battre la lame qui les bat. Braver tranquillement est une des plus grandes voluptés sur terre comme sur mer; et je mets cela bien au-dessus de la satisfaction que vous trouvez à filer plus ou moins de nœuds à l'heure sur vos yachts de plaisance. Sans compter qu'avec mon sabot de misère, par une brise fraîche à démâter, j'aurais sur vous une prodigieuse supériorité de marche et je tiendrais le pari de noyer des clippers encore plus marins que les vôtres.

Mon sabot, c'est un *lougre*, un fin flibustier, brutal à la mer brute, sourd au temps; et, même en calme, avec sa mine de tourmente, il semble toujours faire tête au grain. Ras d'eau, ras de mâture: trois mâts comme des pieux hardiment penchés sur l'arrière. Trois voiles triangulaires tannées, voilà pour courir son bord.

Le poste et la cale prennent la moitié de la coque, l'autre moitié, c'est la chambre, doublée en chêne blanc, nue comme le pont. Un coup de pompe là-dedans et la toilette est faite. Un coup de mer fait aussi bien. Autour sont les soutes qui servent de divans, et ses grands charniers étanchés pour les provisions, les effets et les armes; au milieu, la table à roulis. Pour la nuit, on croche aux barrots de bons cadres de toile douillets et larges comme des lits de noces. Ici, voyez-vous, le vrai confort est la simplicité.

Et mon équipage!

Vous avez, gentlemen-sailors, de superbes marins, des lions de mer au beefsteak, propres comme ma petite sœur, forts comme des demi-dieux, soit.

Moi, j'ai là, jetés sur mon pont, une vingtaine de chenapans bons à rien, bons à tout; triés soigneusement dans les pays où j'ai passé.

THE AMERICAN GIRL

Agreed, gentlemen-sailors,* in France we don't have the least idea of a yacht; the English cutters are wonderful race-horses. And your American schooners, as pretty as anything on the pretty sea! I've seen old sailors fondly lavishing the names of birds on them! But with these fancies underfoot, if I had to breast the breakers, to fiddle among the fish-bones, I'd be nervous about the paintwork!

For me, sailing for pleasure should be, above everything, eccentric; something forbidden to the bourgeois of the sea: going out when they're forced to return, hunting in the hurricane that hunts them and battering the billow that batters them. Quiet defiance is one of the keenest pleasures on seas as well as on land; and I put that far beyond the satisfaction that you have scudding along at more or less knots per hour on your pleasure yachts. Not to mention that in my wretched tub, with a wind brisk enough to dismast it, I'd have a stupendous superiority of speed over you and I'd take on a bet to scuttle clippers far more seaworthy than yours.

My tub is a *lugger*, a first-class privateer, brutal to the brute sea, deaf to the weather; and, even in a calm, with its stormy bearing, it always seems to be standing at bay against a squall. The level of the water, the level of the masts and spars: three masts like stakes tilted riskily on the stern. Three triangular tawny sails, so much for tacking.

The quarters and the hold take up half the hull, the other half is the cabin, sheathed in white oak, bare like the bridge. A turn of the pump in there and the tidying is completed. A wave does just as well. Round about are the store-cupboards serving as couches, and their big water-tight containers for the provisions, belongings and arms; in the middle, the slotted table. For the night, hammocks are hooked to the cross-bar beams: they're as soft and wide as wedding beds. Here, you see, simplicity is true comfort.

And my crew!

You have, gentlemen-sailors,* splendid seamen, beefsteak* sea-dogs, clean like my little sister, strong like demi-gods, so be it.

Flung on my deck there, I have a score of vagabonds, good for nothing, good for anything; carefully selected from the countries that I've visited. All criminals, black at heart, but with their hearts

* English phrases in Corbière's text are asterisked.

Tous gens de sac mais de corde, race scorbutique, assez lâche, mais dure au mal et insouciante du danger par habitude.

Ils se soucient peu de moi et moi d'eux. Ils savent seulement que je les tirerais comme des pingouins, au besoin ou à ma fantaisie. Tout ce qu'ils pouvaient réclamer à la loi c'est le bagne et, galère pour galère, ils préfèrent la mienne.

Quand j'en ai assez, je les change comme du linge sale, en les rendant, s'il me plaît, à leur patrie. C'est ce qu'ils craignent le plus.

J'ai un Maltais, contumace partout, et un Yankee dépendu. – En voilà deux qui manquent de pied à terre. – Deux nègres décrochés d'un garde-manger royal au Gabon. J'ai ensuite un cousin, forçat *in partibus*, dont j'ai un vieux coup de couteau ; je lui ai fait, du reste, avec un rasoir, une croix sur la joue en souvenir ; puis un petit voyou de Paris, un *loustic* qui a une balle de moi dans la mâchoire. Ces deux-là je les garde précieusement en échantillon pour effrayer les autres : ce sont les plus gentils de tous. – Le reste est à l'avenant : douze baleiniers américains pour les deux baleinières ; un bossu qui sert de mousse, de cock, de chien et de porte-bonheur ; un tigre de six mois qui sert de chat.

Dans ce ramas, j'ai pourtant des créatures à moi : quatre Bretons à têtes de taureau, quatre frères, tous les quatre baptisés au berceau du nom de *Fanch'* et n'en voulant pas démordre. Ce sont des hommes en barre, et sur ceux-là, je peux dormir : mon second, le maître d'équipage, le chef de timonerie et le capitaine d'armes.

Pas d'uniforme ; tous gardent leur couleur. Seulement, tous portent au poignet gauche, tatoué à perpétuité, mon chiffre : un T barré.

Quelquefois, pour passer le beau temps, dans un port, je jette à quai cette bordée d'écume rougie. – Tout le monde à terre pour une nuit ! – Ah ! c'est une nuit pour la gendarmerie ! . . . Et on rallie à l'aurore, tous bleus, éreintés, saignants, bienheureux.

———

L'autre jour, pendant un coup d'équinoxe, en bordaillant par le travers de *Douvres*, il me prit idée de laisser porter sur Saint-N . . . Arrivé en vue, la passe était presque impraticable, comme il arrive souvent là, et le navire pas mal désemparé. La jetée était couverte d'un monde avide d'émotions et cette entrée pitoyable fut, pour nous, comme un succès de théâtre.

on their sleeves: a rather slack, scurvy-ridden race, but hardened to misfortune and from habit careless of danger.

They concern themselves little with me, or I with them. They only know that I'd draw and quarter them like auks, at my whim or at a pinch. All they've been able to claim from the law is penal servitude and, galley for galley, they prefer mine.

When I've had enough of them, I change them like dirty linen, by returning them, if I choose, to their native land. That's what they fear most.

I have a Maltese, on the wanted list everywhere, and a Yankee taken down from the gallows.—Neither has anywhere to go.—Also, two Negroes unhooked from a royal meat-safe in the Gabon. Then I have a cousin, a convict *in partibus*, from whom I have an old knife wound; indeed, I've made him a cross on his cheek with a razor as a reminder; also a little street arab from Paris, a *wag* who's got a bullet from me in his jaw. These two I treasure as specimens to frighten the others: they're the nicest of all.—The remainder is of a piece: twelve American whalers for the two whale-boats; a hunchback who serves as cabin-boy, cook, dog and mascot; a tiger of six months which serves as cat.

Nevertheless, among this rabble I do have some loyal creatures: four bull-headed Bretons, four brothers, all four baptized in infancy with the name of *Fanch*' and not wanting to surrender their hold on it. They're men of iron, and I can sleep easy because of them: the first mate, the boatswain, the helmsman and signaller, and the gunner.

No uniform; they all keep their own looks. Only, on his left wrist, tattooed for life, each of them carries my cipher: a barred T.

To while away fine weather in a port, I sometimes discharge this volley of reddened dross on to the quay.—Everybody on shore for a night!—Ah! it's quite a night for the police!... And they return at dawn, black and blue all over, worn out, bleeding, very happy.

———

The other day, during an equinoctial gale, and arsing about on board with *Dover* abeam, it occurred to me to let bear on to Saint-N... Once in sight, the passage was almost impassable, as often happens there, and the ship not a little disabled. The jetty was

J'allai, le soir, au Casino où je trouvai quelques connaissances et tout le *high-life* flottant des yachts de la Manche. (Il y avait eu la veille un match important.) Je fus présenté comme le patron du *Lougre* qui avait intrigué tout le monde. J'exposai, au milieu d'un groupe enthousiaste, ma théorie de navigation de plaisance. Je fus le *champion* du jour. Le grand Chose, un corsaire d'Argenteuil, me pilotait par le bras et je faisais assez mon Zampa de casino.

Une jeune fille nous arrêta brusquement au passage, et, s'adressant à mon pilote:

—Ce gentleman, dit-elle, en me montrant du doigt, voudrait-il se faire présenter à mon père, pour moi?

Je m'inclinai, et la présentation se fit au père, personnage muet du reste; on causa... C'était une Américaine, libre comme l'Amérique, jolie comme vos goëlettes, gentlemen, et blonde, mais blonde!... Le père s'appelait... Au fait que vous importe leur nom.

—Monsieur, me dit-elle, je vous trouve excentrique, vraiment.

—Moi aussi.

—Je trouve que vous ressemblez à votre bateau.

—Il est couvert d'avaries, miss...

—Splendid!... dites-moi, j'oserais vous solliciter de le visiter demain?

—C'est qu'il est bien triste à voir...

—Cela lui sied.

—Eh bien, barque et patron seront très-heureux de votre gracieuse visite, avec monsieur votre père, à l'heure qu'il vous plaira demain...

—L'heure du lunch; mais mon père n'aime pas. Votre ami Chose plutôt?

Cela fut fait le lendemain; l'Américaine se prit d'une grande passion pour *le Lougre*.

—Quel nom a-t-il?

—Un nom de femme, miss.

—Joli?

—Joli.

—Jolie?

—Jolie.

—Je ne le vois pas écrit là?...

—On a passé une couche de peinture noire par dessus.

Elle voulut parler à tous les hommes de l'équipage, et je lui

overflowing with a crowd eager for thrills and this pitiful entry was, for us, like a theatrical success.

In the evening, I went to the Casino, where I found some acquaintances and all the floating *high-life* of the Channel yachts. (The day before there had been an important race.) I was introduced as the skipper of the *Lugger* which had intrigued everybody. In the middle of an enthusiastic group, I expounded my theory of sailing for pleasure. I was the *champion* of the day. Little What's-his-name, a privateer from Argenteuil, piloted me by the arm and I was passably doing my act as Zampa of the casino.

A young girl abruptly stopped us in our tracks, and, speaking to my pilot, said: 'Would this gentleman',* indicating me with her finger, 'like to be introduced to my father, for me?'

I bowed, and introduction was made to the father, a dumb personage moreover; one chatted . . . She was an American, as free as America, as pretty as your schooners, gentlemen,* and blonde, but blonde! . . . The father was called . . . After all, what does their name matter to you.

'Sir,' she said to me, 'I find you eccentric, really.'

'So do I.'

'I think you're like your boat.'

'It's covered with scars, miss . . .'*

'Splendid! . . .* tell me, dare I beg you to allow me to visit it tomorrow?'

'The only thing is that it's a very sorry sight . . .'

'Very fitting.'

'Well, the bark and its skipper will be very pleased to receive your gracious visit, with your respected father, at whatever time suits you tomorrow . . .'

'Lunch-time; but my father doesn't want to. Your friend What's-his-name rather?'

This was accomplished the next day; the American girl conceived a great passion for *The Lugger*.

'What's its name?'

'A woman's name, miss.'*

'Pretty?'

'Pretty.'

'A pretty woman's name?'

'A pretty woman's name.'

'I don't see it written there? . . .'

présentai le chat-tigre qui, tout en *flirtant*, lui enleva d'un coup de griffe un morceau de la main.

—Oh l'amour! dit-elle.

—Miss, vous voilà comme mes gens, tatouée au poignet: vous êtes des nôtres . . .

—Je le veux, en vérité, *my captain!* Et, dans un élan tout marin, elle me fit promettre de l'emmener un peu faire la course, un jour de nuit, par un joli petit temps de sinistres.

J'hésitai . . .

—Vous avez peur, monsieur?

—Mais votre père?

—Content toujours.

On en parla au père, qui dit: *All right!*

Les avaries réparées, je fis donc mettre le lougre en grande rade, l'équipage consigné, en appareillage enfin. Mais un calme implacable. J'allai chaque soir coucher à bord. L'Américaine m'accompagnait à regret jusqu'à la baleinière, me reprochant durement de ne pas savoir commander un peu de tempête pour deux.

Toute la place était au courant; on pariait: Ils iront!—ils n'iront pas!—Et toujours calme plat!—Ma position devenait ridicule.

Enfin, le quatrième matin, belle apparence: une houle sourde, du ressac, des risées et des *haubans au soleil*. Le baromètre sautant à une hauteur stupide.

Je vins à terre:

—Miss, faites votre sac.

Elle faillit me sauter au cou, et courut se mettre en *blue jacket*. Ce n'était pas un travesti de fantaisie, mais bien le patelot et le pantalon d'ordonnance achetés à un matelot en congé et appropriés à la hâte.

Dix heures.—Le baromètre baisse, l'enthousiasme monte. Le vent joue; on fait des paris au déjeuner: Ils iront!—n'iront pas!

Onze heures.—Le thé. Les paris se corsent, la brise aussi. Le sémaphore est à tempête. On chante:

Amis, la ma-tiné-e-est-belle . . .

MIDI.—À bord! . . . . Le vent n'attend pas.—Le père, devant le Casino assemblé, remet solennellement sa fille à mon bon plaisir de gentleman et à ma délicatesse de matelot. Il a parié pour.

—Maintenant, mesdames et messieurs, si quelqu'un désire être des nôtres . . . Personne ne dit mot? . . .

'A coat of black paint has been put over it.'

She wanted to talk to all the members of the crew, and I introduced to her the cat-tiger which, while *flirting*, carried off a piece
of her hand with a scratch of its claw.

'Oh the darling!' she said.

'Miss,* now you are like my folk, tattooed on the wrist: you're
one of us . . .'

'I want that, honestly, *my captain!*'*

And, surging forward quite oceanically, she made me promise to
take her out sailing, on a day like night, during some nice spell of
weather for calamities.

I hesitated . . .

'You're afraid, sir?'

'But your father?'

'He'll be agreeable.'

It was mentioned to the father, who said: '*All right!*'*

The scars repaired, I therefore had the lugger put into the outer
roads, the crew kept in, on the point of getting under sail. But an
implacable calm. Each evening I went to sleep on board. The
American girl accompanied me regretfully to the whale-boat,
harshly reproaching me with not knowing how to order a bit of
storm for two.

All the resort knew what was going on; they had bets on it:
They'll go!–they won't!–And always dead calm!–My position
was becoming ridiculous.

At last, on the fourth morning, a glorious sight: a rumbling
swell, breakers, gusts and *guy-ropes in the sun*. The barometer jumping
to an absurd height.

I came ashore:

'Miss,* pack your bag.'

She nearly flung her arms round my neck, and ran to put on her
blue jacket.* This was not a fantastic fancy-dress, but the proper
regulation coat and trousers bought from a sailor on leave and
cleaned in a hurry.

Ten o'clock.–The barometer falls, the enthusiasm mounts. The
wind frolics; they make bets at breakfast: They'll go!–won't!

Eleven o'clock.–Tea. The bets stiffen, also the wind. The
signal-station registers stormy weather.They sing:

Friends, the morn-ing-is-fine . . .

MIDDAY.–On board! . . . The wind doesn't wait.–In front of

Et nos amis nous accompagnent de leurs paris et de leurs *hurrah!*

L'Américaine saute dans la baleinière, et:

—Avant partout!

La mer brisait déjà dans la passe; il fallait parer chaque lame, et du premier coup, nous étions, malgré nos capotes cirées, traversés jusqu'aux os. Ce jeu dura bien deux heures, avant d'atteindre le mouillage. Il était temps. Le lougre fatiguait abominablement. La chaîne de la maîtresse ancre venait de se casser dans un coup de tangage, en démontant le guindeau. Impossible de ravoir l'autre.

—Attrape à appareiller en double.—Pare trois ris dans la misaine, deux ris dans le taille-vent.—La tourmentin à demi-bâton.—Voilà la toilette.

—Démaille la chaîne et file le bout.—Les ancres au fond, c'est plus simple.

—Hisse, étarque et borde partout.

La lourde brise prend dans la toile avec un bruit de canon, la coque se gîte dans la lame, et nous voilà saillant de l'avant, piquant à quatre quarts dans le lit du vent avec un sillage de huit à neuf nœuds.

Le Casino a disparu dans une *grainasse.*

—Vous êtes toute mouillée, miss.

—Bah! est-ce que la mer mouille!

Un de mes Bretons, Fanch', le plus fin timonier du bord, est à la barre; elle le regardait effrontément.

—Homme beau! lui dit-elle en face.

L'autre ne sourcilla pas.

La brise fusillait maintenant; le navire charroyait trop de toile et donnait de la bande ferme; il fallait se cramponner aux haubans. L'avant *mettait le nez dans la plume* et se relevait à peine. Un paquet de mer nous couvrit de bout-en-bout.

—Vous êtes contente!

—Tout plein!

Fanch', le maître d'équipage, vint à moi:

—Faut-il mollir, patron? Nous encombrons à la douce . . .

—Quoi c'est *mollir*, monsieur?

—Diminuer de voile, miss.

—Alors, je vous prie . . . Non . . . Quoi c'est *encombrer?*

—Ceci.

Et je lui montrai le *beaupré* qui venait de se casser au ras, et le *tourmentin*, emporté au diable, comme un cerf-volant . . .

the assembled Casino, the father solemnly hands over his daughter to my good pleasure as a gentleman and my delicacy as a sailor. He's betted for.

'Now, ladies and gentlemen, if anyone would like to join us . . . Nobody says anything? . . .'

And our friends accompany us with their bets and their *hurrahs!*

The American girl jumps into the whale-boat, and:

'Forward to everywhere!'

The sea was already breaking in the fairway; we had to get ready for each billow, and with the first wave, in spite of our oilskin capes, we were soaked to the skin. This game lasted a good two hours, before the anchorage was reached. It was high time. The lugger was labouring abominably. The cable of the main anchor had just snapped in a particularly violent pitch, breaking the windlass. Impossible to recover the latter.

'Weigh anchor quickly. – Three reefs in the foresail, two reefs in the lug mainsail. – The storm-jib at half-mast. – That's the trim.'

'Unshackle the cable and slip the end. – Anchors to the bottom, it's easier.'

'Hoist, haul taut and all sheets home.'

The heavy wind catches in the sail with the noise of cannon, the hull lists in the billow, and here we are gushing forward, nose-diving at all four points of the compass into the wind's eye with a wake of eight to nine knots.

The Casino has disappeared in a *violent gust*.

'You're all wet, miss.'*

'Bah! so the sea wets you!'

One of my Bretons, Fanch', the shrewdest helmsman on board, was at the helm; she was looking at him shamelessly.

'Handsome man!' she said to his face.

The other didn't flinch.

The wind was cannonading now; the ship was carting too much sail and had a strong list; we had to hold fast to the guys. The bow *was dipping its nose in the foam* and scarcely righting itself. A heavy sea covered us from stem to stern.

'You're happy now!'

'Absolutely!'

Fanch', the boatswain, came to me:

'Should we slacken, skipper? We're floundering nicely . . .'

'What is *to slacken*, sir?'

−*Oh! splendid sport!* fit-elle.

Ni peur, ni étonnement. J'en étais même quelque peu vexé.

−Faut-il mollir, patron?

−La dame ne veut pas, tiens bon.

−*Captain*, j'ai faim.

−Bossu, sers le lunch dans la chambre. Vous, miss, tenez-moi bien pour descendre. Vous allez toujours changer vos vêtements.

Il faut vous dire que j'étais assez vain de mes petits préparatifs: dans la soute aux voiles, toute une petite boutique de lingerie dévalisée en ville et arrimée par le Bossu, ma meilleure camériste. Il m'avait même rapporté triomphalement deux corsets hygiéniques de neuf francs. J'avais préparé moi-même un grand peignoir, pris en Orient, et des bas à coins brodés, souvenir oublié chez moi autrefois . . . bien autrefois.

On avait improvisé au fond du carré un sanctuaire discret, avec un hunier de rechange tendu de haut en bas.

Elle ne fut pas longue à sa toilette! Elle sortit de là gréée de ma vareuse de corvée et d'un pantalon à Fanch', le capitaine d'armes. Et jolie! . . .

Et ça allait toujours, là-haut; on entendait les grosses bottes talonner sur nos têtes. L'Américaine mangeait solidement. La nuit tombait vite. Je pris la carte pour pointer la route. Elle suivait des yeux en fumant une cigarette.

−À présent, *captain*, allons prendre le frais.

−Impossible pour vous, miss, on vient d'amarrer les hommes de quart sur le pont.

−Eh bien! il faut me faire aussi . . .

−Oui, dans votre hamac. Voyez le bel ours qui vous attend-là.

−Oui, superbe peau. Mais je ne veux pas dormir chez un homme; chez mon époux seulement, plus tard. Maintenant, je veux mettre ces grandes bottes qui sont là, et monter avec sur le pont. Allons, aidez-moi.

Il fallut bien! Étendue sur un caisson, elle tendait sa jambe. Heurtée, meurtrie par le roulis, elle m'avait empoigné le cou, et je travaillais de mon mieux. Le gros pantalon ne pouvait entrer dans les tiges; il fallut le couper au-dessus du genou avec mon couteau, qui ne coupait pas. Les damnées bottes montaient toujours; elle se livrait avec une innocence de quartier-maître. Elle riait! . . . je ne riais pas. Quel métier!

−Ne craignez pas, *captain*, je suis un matelot.

'To shorten sail, miss.'*

'Well, I beg you . . . No . . . What is *to flounder*?'

'This.'

And I showed her the *bowsprit* which had just broken nearly level with the water, and the *storm-jib*, gone to the devil, like a kite . . .

'*Oh! splendid sport!*'* she said.

Neither fear, nor astonishment. That rather annoyed me.

'Should we slacken, skipper?'

'The lady doesn't want to, avast.'

'*Captain*,* I'm hungry.'

'Hunchback, serve lunch in the cabin. You, miss,* hold on to me tight to go below. You're going to change your clothes all the same.'

I should tell you that I was rather vain about my little preparations: in the sails' store, a veritable little shop of lingerie lifted in the town and stowed by the Hunchback, my best maid. He'd even brought me back triumphantly two hygenic corsets at nine francs. I'd got ready myself a big dressing-gown, acquired in the East, and some stockings with embroidered segments, a memento forgotten at home of old . . . very much of old.

At the farther end of the mess-room a discreet sanctuary had been improvised, with a spare topsail hung from top to bottom.

She was not long dressing! She emerged from there rigged out in my sailor's jersey and a pair of trousers belonging to Fanch', the gunner. And pretty! . . .

And things still went well, on deck; the heavy boots could be heard stumping up and down on our heads. The American girl ate solidly. Night was falling quickly. I took the map to pick out the course. She watched intently, smoking a cigarette.

'Now, *captain*,* we'll go and take the air.'

'Impossible for you, miss,* they've just lashed the men of the watch to the deck.'

'So what! you must do the same to me . . .'

'Yes, in your hammock. You see the handsome bear waiting for you there.'

'Yes, a splendid skin. But I don't want to sleep in a man's home; only at home with my husband, later. At the moment I want to put on those big boots over there, and go up on deck in them. Come on, help me.'

Help was certainly needed! Stretched out on a locker, she held out her leg. Knocked about, bruised by the roll, she'd seized me

Oui, j'étais bien amateloté! Elle m'étranglait, et j'étranglais,
en conscience; le sang me montait à la gorge ... Des scrupules! ...
Allons donc! ... Seuls, au diable ... roulés au hasard dans cette
nuit perdue ... Des scrupules! ... et trois ris dans la misaine! ...
Sombrer pour sombrer ...

    –Je vous fais mal, monsieur?

    –Un peu, miss.

    Ça ne fait rien, les bottes y sont! ... De l'amour? ... Allons
donc! de l'amour à moi? ... Elle est là-haut, mon amoureuse! ...
L'entendez-vous qui hurle après son amant, battant les flancs,
secouant les mâts, écharpant la toile ... On couchera peut-être
ensemble ce soir ... et la petite aussi, alors.

    –Montons, miss.

    Elle ne pouvait tenir debout, vous pensez. Je la fis saisir par deux
hommes et placer près de moi, amarrée.

    –Tenez-moi bien!

    Et je lui passai mon bras comme une ceinture.

    La tourmente était dans son plein. Nuit aveugle, une pluie
cinglée, pas de ciel. Le pont noyé, la carène geignant lamentablement, et les cris des poulies, les craquements ... Sur l'avant,
quelqu'un chante: c'est la voix du Bossu; elle nous arrive sanglotée,
par lambeaux ...

Adieu, la belle, je m'en vas;
Adieu, la belle, je m'en vas ...

Et les sifflements des rafales et le ronflement des manœuvres, le
claquement des voiles ...

Puisque mon bâtiment s'en va ...

    –Ouvre l'œil au bossoir!

    –Ouvre l'œil ...

    On ne s'entendait pas; nous avions la respiration coupée.

round the neck, and I was exerting myself as much as I could. The
thick trousers wouldn't slip inside the leg of the boot; I had to cut
them above the knee with my knife, which did not cut. The damned
boots were still going on up; she surrendered herself to this with the
innocence of a leading seaman. She was laughing! ... I wasn't
laughing. What a life!

'Don't be afraid, *captain*,* I'm a sailor.'

Yes, I was well-paired, for my share of the ship's work! She was
choking me, and I choked, in all conscience; the blood rose in my
throat ... Scruples! ... Come on then! ... Alone, the devil take
it ... rolled about at random in this abandoned night ... Scruples!
... and three reefs in the foresail! ... To sink in order to sink ...

'Am I hurting you, sir?'

'A little, miss.'*

That doesn't matter, the boots are on! ... Love? ... Come on
then! love for me? ... She's up there, my sweetheart! ... Do you
hear her howling after her lover, battering the sides, shaking the
masts, slashing the sails ... We'll sleep together this evening
perhaps ... and the little one also, in that case.

'Let's go up, miss.'*

She couldn't stand upright, as you can imagine. I had her taken
hold of by two men and put near me, belayed.

'Hold on to me tight!'

And I gave her my arm like a life-belt.

The storm was at its height. Blind night, the rain lashing, no sky.
The deck flooded, the bottom moaning woefully, and the shrieks of
the blocks, the creaks ... In the bows, someone sings: it's the voice
of the Hunchback; it reaches us sobbing, in shreds ...

> *Farewell, my beauty, I'm going away;*
> *Farewell, my beauty, I'm going away ...*

And the hiss of the squalls and the roar of the rigging, the clapping
of the sails ...

> *Since my ship is going away ...*

'Get the cat-head open!'

'Get the cat-head ...'

They didn't hear; we were winded.

Puisque mon bâtiment s'en va,
Je m'en vas faire un tour à Nantes,
Puisque la loi me le commande . . .

–Ouvre l'œil au bossoir! . . .
Rien. Les hommes de bossoir, amarrés à leur poste, se sont
endormis sous les coups de la mer, accablés. On les fait revenir à
coup de garcettes.
–Un quart de rhum au monde.
L'Américaine, collée contre moi, ne bougeait pas.
–Moi aussi, murmura-t-elle, un quart de rhum?
–Oh! . . .
–En vérité!
Elle but dans mon *quart.*
–Fanch', fais sonder aux pompes . . .
–Deux pieds d'eau, patron.
–Bon!
À ce moment, nous vîmes, ou plutôt nous sentîmes passer une
forme noire, monstrueuse. Tout le navire eut comme un frisson.
L'Américaine fit:
–Ah! . . .
Elle m'avait serré jusqu'au sang.
–Connu! . . . grogna le timonier.
–Vous dites «Connu!» vous, l'homme?
–Pardié! . . . *le Voltigeur hollandais.*
–Quoi c'est ça, *captain?*
–Le vaisseau-fantôme, miss.
–Il n'y a pas de meilleur baromètre, ajouta Fanch'.
–C'est signe de quoi, l'homme?
–Un trou dans l'eau, mademoiselle.
–*Aoh! very charming! very very! . . . Charming! . . .*
Ah! ça . . . est-ce qu'elle serait bête? . . .
Nous étions mangés par la mer. Je tenais toujours l'Américaine,
qui se laissait aller sur mon épaule endolorie; j'entendais, contre
mon oreille, ses dents, comme des pierres de meule, broyant un
biscuit de ration. Ses cheveux mouillés fouettaient ma joue en feu;
j'en avais plein la bouche, et je les mordais; ils étaient tout salés
de poudrain, et je buvais . . . Ce poison, l'odeur de femme, m'em-
plissait les narines. Plus rien . . . L'abîme, c'était ses yeux; la
tempête, c'était son haleine. La lampe d'habitacle jetait par instant

Since my ship is going away,
I'll make a trip to Nantes,
Since the law commands me to . . .

'Get the cat-head open! . . .'
No effect. The men at the cat-head, belayed to their post, have fallen asleep under the sea's onslaught, overcome. They're made to come to with a rope-end.
'A quarter of rum for everyone.'
Close against me, the American girl didn't stir.
'For me too,' she murmured, 'a quarter of rum?'
'Oh! . . .'
'Honestly!'
She drank out of my *quarter.*
'Fanch', take a sounding with the pumps . . .'
'Two feet of water, skipper.'
'Good!'
At that moment, we saw, or rather felt a monstrous black shape going by. The whole ship seemed to shiver. The American girl said:
'Ah! . . .'
She had me in an iron grip.
'Identified! . . .' growled the helmsman.
'You say "Identified!" you, man?'
'By Jove! . . . *The Flying Dutchman.*'
'What's that, *captain?*'*
'The phantom ship, miss.'*
'There's no better barometer,' added Fanch'.
'What's it a sign of, man?'
'A hole in the water, miss.'
'*Aoh! very charming! very very! . . . Charming! . . .*'*
Ah! that . . . could she be stupid? . . .
We were being buffeted by the sea. I was still holding the American girl, who was giving way on my aching shoulder; I heard, against my ear her teeth, like mill-stones, grinding a biscuit from the rations. Her wet hair was whipping my cheek into a blaze; I had a mouthful of it, and I chewed it; it was quite briny with spindrift, and I drank . . . This poison, the female smell, was filling my nostrils. Nothing more . . . The chasm was her eyes; the storm, her breath. Off and on, the binnacle lamp threw a trembling beam over us, everything else seemed of the other world. I felt a kind of breath of

sur nous un éclair tremblotant, tout le reste me semblait de l'autre monde. Je sentis passer en moi comme un souffle de beauté, et je mis sur sa bouche un baiser léger, bien léger . . .

Elle dormait, parbleu.

—Quoi! fit-elle en sursaut.

—Rien: le taille-vent enlevé.

Ç'avait été comme un coup de fouet sur nous, puis un frou-frou de soie là-haut.

—Le taille-vent enlevé! . . . Barre dessous toute! . . .

Le timonier tomba sur nous comme une masse.

—Tu es soûl!

Il était mort; l'écoute, en partant, l'avait cinglé. C'était fini de rire. Je sautai sur la barre avec le maître. Heureusement le navire tenait bien la cape sous sa misaine seule.—Tiens bon toujours.

—Miss, il faut descendre dans la chambre.

—Non.

—Je suis le maître.

—Je suis libre.

—Je vais vous faire coucher par le Bossu.

—Oh! . . .

Elle était indignée.

—Hô, Bossu, ici.

—Vous êtes un lâche, Monsieur!

Et elle descendit sans vouloir se laisser aider.

Il était cinq heures du matin. Cette dernière saute de vent était l'agonie de la tourmente qui tomba à plat comme tuée. Le jour tardait, seulement la nuit devenait grise et plus épaisse.—De la brume, il ne manquait plus que ça!—Cela ne manqua pas; et du calme, ce calme atroce qui succède aux grandes crises. Le navire, ne sentant plus sa voilure ni sa barre, roulait bord sur bord à tout arracher, souffrant dans toutes ses coutures et faisant de l'eau comme un panier. Les voiles et les agrès flasques battaient lourdement sur les mâts secoués.

Nous étions jolis! Sur le pont, les deux baleinières aplaties et crevées, les bastingages rasés. Les hommes, rendus, couchés en vache comme des cadavres, heurtant partout au roulis; l'autre aussi, le mort, parmi les autres, la moitié de la tête enlevée, et promenant ses petites flaques d'eau rosée.

—Fanch'! faisons-nous de l'eau toujours?

—Joliment, patron.

beauty run through me, and I set on her lips a light kiss, very light . . .

She was sleeping, by Jove.

'What!' she said, starting.

'Nothing: the lug mainsail's gone.'

That had been like a whip lash on us, then a rustling of silk up above.

'The lug mainsail gone! . . . Helm gone under! . . .'

The helmsman fell on us like a log.

'You're tipsy!'

He was dead; as it came away, the main sheet had lashed him. That was the end of the joke. I jumped towards the helm with the boatswain. Fortunately the ship was holding the try-sail well beneath its single foremast.—Never say die.

'Miss,* you must go below to the cabin.'

'No.'

'I'm the skipper.'

'I'm free.'

'I'll have you put to bed by the Hunchback.'

'Oh! . . .'

She was indignant.

'Hi, Hunchback, here.'

'You're a coward, sir!'

And she went below, unwilling to allow herself to be helped.

It was 5 a.m. This last sudden veering of the wind was the agony of the storm; it fell flat, as if killed. Day was slow in coming, the night was merely becoming grey and thicker.—Fog, it only needed that!—We had all we needed now; and calm, this atrocious calm following great crises. The ship, not answering to the helm or the set of its sails any more, was rolling gunwale under fit to tear out everything, straining in all its sutures and taking in water like a basket. The sails and the slack rigging were beating clumsily on the shaking masts.

We were in a fine way! On the deck, the two whale-boats flattened and split, the bulwarks cut down. Sleeping like cattle, the exhausted men as if corpses, banging about in the roll; the other man too, the dead one, among the others, half his head carried off, and sending out little puddles of pale pink water.

'Fanch'! are we still taking in water?'

'Nicely, skipper.'

'Get the pumps rigged.'

–Fais gréer les pompes.
Et alors ce bruit monotone et sinistre . . .
–Attrape à laver le pont! Un quart d'eau-de-vie au monde!
Personne ne bougea.
–Attends un peu, dit Fanch', je vas te prendre la mesure d'une robe de chambre avec une trique. Hop les amoureux!
On commença la toilette: dégager le pont, réparer le gréement et enverguer des voiles de rechange.
Je descendis rendre visite à ma passagère. Elle était couchée, tout habillée, dans un cadre, avec le tigre-chat qui me montra les dents. Elle avait pris un petit air de galérien tout à fait angélique.
–Monsieur, me dit-elle, où sommes-nous?
–Dans la brume.
–Pour retourner, j'espère?
–Nous attendons; pas de brise et pas de vue.
–Ah!
Ce *Ah* était d'une insolence! . . .
–Voulez-vous déjeuner, miss?
–Merci, je veux m'en aller.
–Soit: débarquez. Libre à vous.
J'étais énervé à la fin.
–Monsieur, assez, je vous prie; je vous dis, je veux être à terre.
–Et moi donc!
Je remontai sur le pont, mécontent et quelque peu inquiet, ne pouvant reconnaître notre position, et le navire ne gouvernant pas. Je voyais seulement, au compas affolé, que nous étions drossés par un courant. La mer hachée et affreusement dure. Tout souffrait à bord.
L'Américaine ne donna pas signe de vie. Un novice était chargé de son service; elle avait outrageusement renvoyé le pauvre Bossu, ma plus fine soubrette pourtant . . . J'évitai d'aller la voir; je lui en voulais de n'avoir pas trouvé un bon mouvement dans tout cela. Intrépide et bête . . . et trop jolie pour elle, cette Yankee. C'était de la beauté perdue.
Vers midi, dans une éclaircie, nous aperçûmes la silhouette démesurée d'un cotre; il était presque sur nous et nous héla:
–Ship, ohé?
–Hô?
–A pilot?
–Yes. Accoste.

And then this monotonous and sinister noise . . .

'Get down to washing the deck! A quarter of brandy for every-one!'

Nobody moved.

'Wait a moment,' said Fanch', 'I'll measure you for a dressing-gown with a cudgel. That'll make you comfortable, you softies!'

The tidying was begun: clearing the deck, repairing the rigging and bending the spare sails to the yards.

I went below to pay a visit to my passenger. She was lying down, fully dressed, in a hammock, with the tiger-cat which showed me its teeth. She looked rather like a perfectly angelic galley-slave.

'Sir,' she said to me, 'where are we?'

'In the fog.'

'Going back, I hope?'

'We're waiting; no wind and no visibility.'

'Ah!'

This *Ah* was insolent! . . .

'Would you like breakfast, miss?'*

'No thanks, I want to leave.'

'Granted: disembark. It's up to you.'

At last I was irritated.

'Sir, that's enough, please; I'm telling you, I want to be on land.'

'And so do I!'

I went back up on deck, displeased and a little worried, not being able to identify our position, and the ship not answering to the helm. I saw from the distracted compass only that we were drifting with a current. A rough sea, churning horribly. Everything on board was suffering.

The American girl didn't give any sign of life. An apprentice was detailed to look after her; she'd insultingly dismissed the poor Hunchback, my most refined maid nevertheless . . . I avoided going to see her; I bore her a grudge for not having got any pleasure out of all that. Intrepid and stupid . . . and too pretty for her own good, this Yankee. It was beauty wasted.

Towards midday, in a fine interval, we saw the enormous silhouette of a cutter; it was almost on us and hailed us:

'Ship* ahoy?'

'Ahoy?'

'A pilot?'*

'Yes.* Come aboard.'

−French?
− Oui. Et vous?
− Guernsey. Pour où, vous?
− Saint-N . . .
− Combien?
− Dites.
− Quinze livres.
− Non.
− Good night!
− Dix livres.
− All right.

Cinq minutes après, le pilote accosta dans son *youyou* et sauta à bord.

− Good morning, captain. Navire de guerre?
− Aventurier.
− Connaissez-vous votre position?
− Non.
− Il était temps. Heureusement la brise se fait. Nous allons pouvoir orienter.
− Un grog, pilote?
− Hein, captain, je parie que, dans ce moment, je vous fais plus de plaisir qu'une belle fille?

L'animal, il ne savait pas dire si vrai avec sa bonne grosse figure en jambon d'York.

Enfin, sur le soir, la brise se leva, une brise carabinée. Nous pûmes prendre connaissance des feux et faire route en forçant de toile. Le lendemain matin, nous attrapions Saint-N . . . et nos bouées d'ancres.

J'avais oublié l'Américaine. Elle me fit demander de la mettre de suite à terre avec le pilote. Je demandai la permission de l'accompagner; elle me fit répondre que *j'étais le maître.*

C'était l'heure du bain sur la plage. Nous avions été signalés. On nous entoura; on avait eu des inquiétudes, etc . . . Le père sembla ne pas avoir remarqué nos deux jours de retard. Il me remercia solennellement, avec une nuance de bénédiction, et, me prenant la main, il cherchait celle de sa fille. Elle était montée chez elle.

Je me retirai aussi. Ce bonhomme avait déjà presque l'air de vouloir me traiter de Turc à More, de beau-père à gendre!

Voilà pourquoi, au soleil couchant, on put voir le lougre à voiles noires appareiller silencieusement et se perdre dans l'ombre comme

'French?'*
'Yes. And you?'
'Guernsey. Where are you making for?'
'Saint-N . . .'
'How much?'
'You say.'
'Fifteen pounds.'
'No.'
'Good night!'*
'Ten pounds.'
'All right.'*

Five minutes later, the pilot came alongside in his dinghy and leapt on board.

'Good morning, captain.* Man-of-war?'
'Adventurer.'
'Do you know your position?'
'No.'
'Just in time. Fortunately the wind's getting up. We'll be able to put you right.'

'Some grog, pilot?'

'Hey, captain,* I bet I give you more pleasure at this moment than a beautiful girl?'

The animal, he didn't know he spoke so truly with his good large face of York ham.

At last, towards evening, the wind got up, a stiff wind. We were able to distinguish the signal lights and make course, crowding on sail. The next morning, we reached Saint-N . . . and our anchor buoys.

I'd forgotten the American girl. Someone asked me on her behalf to put her ashore at once with the pilot. I asked permission to go with her; the answer came back that *I was the skipper*.

On the beach it was bathing-time. We'd been sighted. They surrounded us; they'd been worried, etc. . . . The father didn't appear to have noticed we were two days late. He thanked me solemnly, with a hint of blessing, and, taking my hand, he sought his daughter's. She'd gone home.

I also withdrew. The good fellow already almost seemed anxious to treat me haughtily, as father-in-law to son-in-law!

So that was why, at sunset, the lugger with black sails could be seen weighing anchor silently and disappearing into shadow like the

le *Voltigeur Hollandais*. Un véritable enlèvement ! je m'enlevais moi-même . . .

. . . Et dans l'effort de la lutte, – vous pensez si je me défendais ! – je m'éveillai . . .

Car tout ceci n'était qu'un rêve, un abominable cauchemar.

TRIST.

Flying Dutchman. A real carrying off! I was carried away myself . . .
. . . And in the heat of the struggle, – you can imagine how well I
was defending myself! – I awoke . . .

For all this was only a dream, an abominable nightmare.

TRIST.

Deux lettres à Édouard Corbière

Dimanche le 26 juin 1859.

Mon cher papa,

Puisque j'en ai le temps nous allons causer un peu longuement. Je te remercie bien des *Négriers* que tu m'as envoyés pour donner au proviseur, au censeur et aux autres, car je pense que ça ne pourra que les disposer en ma faveur. J'ai remis tout à l'heure au censeur le livre que tu lui adressais et il m'a dit de te bien remercier de sa part, ensuite j'ai été au cabinet du proviseur mais il était fermé, du reste je lui remettrai demain *le Négrier* en question. Tu fais du bruit au Lycée et tu y as de la réputation malgré la peine que se donne M. Piquot pour te faire regarder comme un auteur semblable à Éleouet, et quand tes livres sont arrivés plusieurs m'ont dit qu'ils les connaissaient et d'autres croyant qu'ils étaient à moi ne faisaient que me demander si je le leur prêterais. Hier j'ai lu dans un livre intitulé *la Duchesse Anne, ou Campagnes à bord d'une corvette*, un passage que m'a montré un de mes camarades. Voici ce qu'il y avait: «C'était un vieux loup de mer que Petit, et sa vie, racontée par un *Corbière*, serait une véritable odyssée.» J'ai bien regretté que ce livre ne fût pas à moi car j'en aurais déchiré ce paragraphe pour te l'envoyer dans ma lettre. J'ai reçu mon paquet en très bon état, et je vais écrire un petit mot à maman pour la remercier. Nous revenons de la procession tout en sueur et couverts de poussière, c'est ça une corvée! *Le Négrier* que tu m'as envoyé pour M. Armand, j'irai le lui porter chez lui jeudi prochain, avec Monsieur Bazin, et je donnerai demain le sien à mon professeur en allant prendre ma répétition. J'ai eu en version une bien mauvaise place à laquelle j'étais loin de m'attendre. J'ai été le 11ᵉ, Monsieur Le Vacher a été second, mais n'aie pas peur, il me gagne pour maintenant, mais quand j'aurai fait ces trois mois et que je serai en troisième, tu verras comme je te l'enfoncerai, car maintenant tout ce que je cherche c'est d'être capable de passer mon examen, mais l'année prochaine ce sera un plaisir de voir comme j'enfoncerai Le Vacher. Du reste, je ne pense pas que cette année il ait des prix, mais il aura plusieurs

Two Letters to Édouard Corbière

Sunday June 26th, 1859.*

Dear Papa,

Since I've got the time we're going to have quite a long talk. Thank you very much for the *Slave-ships* which you sent me to give the head master, the head usher and others, for I think that can only make them well-disposed towards me. A little while ago I handed over to the head usher the book that you put his name on and he said to thank you warmly on his behalf, then I went to the head master's study but it was closed, anyway I'll deliver *The Slave-ship* in question to him tomorrow. You are much talked about at School and you have a reputation here despite the trouble Mr Piquot takes to have you considered a writer like Éleouet, and when your books arrived several people said to me that they knew them and others believing they belonged to me kept on asking if I'd lend them to them. Yesterday I read in a book entitled *The Duchess Anne, or Cruising on Board a Sloop of War*, a passage that one of my friends showed me. This is what it said: 'Petit was an old sea-dog, and his life, told by a *Corbière*, would be a real odyssey.' I was very sorry that this book didn't belong to me for then I'd have torn out this paragraph to send you in my letter. I received my parcel in very good condition, and I'm going to write a note to Mamma to thank her. We always come back from the procession† sweating and covered in dust, what a grind it is! I'm going to take *The Slave-ship* that you sent for Mr Armand to his house next Thursday, with Mr Bazin, and I'll give my teacher his tomorrow when I go for my private lesson. I've had a very bad mark in translation which I was far from expecting. I was 11th, Mr Le Vacher was second, but never fear, he defeats me for the moment, but when I've completed these three months and am in the third form, you'll see how I shall beat him for you, for all I want now is to be able to pass my exam, but next year it will be a pleasure to see how I'll beat Le Vacher. Besides, I don't think he'll get any prizes this year, but he will have several accessits,‡ whose number I shall appreciably diminish next

---

* This letter was first published by H. Matarasso, 'Lettres à son père', *Les Lettres nouvelles*, 19 (September 1954), pp. 406–8.

† The procession for Corpus Christi; the festival is referred to below.

‡ *proxime accessit.*

accessits, dont l'année prochaine je diminuerai sensiblement le nombre. Je me donne de la peine pour mes compositions mais tu comprends que je les travaillerais encore bien plus, si j'avais l'espoir, en étant toujours le premier, d'obtenir quelque chose, mais cela est impossible car il faudrait pour que je raccroche un ou deux accessits que j'aie été et sois toujours premier et, de plus, que ceux qui ont obtenu la place de premier depuis le commencement de l'année fussent les derniers, ce qui n'est pas possible. Je vais bien pour mes répétitions et je commence à savoir un peu mieux le grec, mais je trouve que je ne le comprends pas plus qu'auparavant. Enfin il faut espérer que ça viendra. Hier et aujourd'hui il y avait de l'orage dans le temps et il faisait très chaud, et moi à la procession, j'étais exposé au soleil, avec un gros pantalon de drap, un gilet très épais et doublé en ouate, et une tunique d'une épaisseur que tu ne pourras te figurer que quand tu la verras aux vacances. Il y a des lycées où l'on a des uniformes d'été, il devrait bien y en avoir ici. Je prends toujours mes leçons d'armes et j'aurai mes fleurets et mes masques à la fin de cette semaine. Mes fleurets coûtent 3 francs chacun, je ne sais pas encore le prix de mes masques ni de mes gants. Nous n'allons pas encore à la mer et cependant nous avons tous bien envie d'aller nous baigner, et nous ne prendrons pas de bain avant quinze jours. Ne trouves-tu pas que les vacances approchent ? Moi je les trouve à très peu de distance, mais chaque jour me paraît un siècle. Le mois de juillet va être pour moi le plus embêtant, car je vais être obligé de faire deux fois par semaine des compositions de prix, sans aucune espérance, pas même d'un accessit, enfin voilà ce que c'est, l'année prochaine il faut espérer que ce ne sera pas comme ça, car si je n'ai pas de prix, tu peux être sûr que j'aurai au moins deux accessits, et je passerai sur le dos à Vacher pour les thèmes et les versions. Il me coulera cependant en grec, vers, et arithmétique. Que veux-tu chacun a son faible. Aujourd'hui je suis bien triste de n'être pas à la fête-Dieu de Morlaix et ce qui me fait le plus de peine c'est de penser que je ne la verrai que dans quatre ou cinq ans. Je regrette bien aussi les quatre ou cinq foires hautes qui se passeront sans moi et ce qui me fait encore bisquer c'est que, quand j'aurai fini mes classes, je ne serai plus en âge d'avoir des parts de foire, mais c'est là ce que je regrette encore le moins. Mais j'oublie que j'ai une version grecque à faire, et j'espérais pouvoir t'écrire une longue lettre, lorsque cette maudite procession est venue employer le temps pendant lequel j'aurai pu me repasser le plaisir de t'écrire une lettre

year. I take trouble with my papers but you do understand I'd work at them still harder, if I had any hope, in being always first, of getting something, but that's impossible for it would be necessary for me to pick up one or two accessits for me to have been and still be first and, moreover, for those who have got the first place since the beginning of the year to be last, which isn't possible. I go regularly for my private lessons and I begin to know Greek a bit better, but I find that I don't understand it any more than previously. However it's to be hoped this will come. Yesterday and today the weather has been thundery and very hot, and I was in the procession, exposed to the sun, with coarse cloth trousers, a very thick waistcoat lined with wadding, and a tunic of a thickness you'll be able to conceive of only when you see it in the holidays. There are some high schools where they have a summer uniform, we ought to have that here. I still have fencing lessons and I'll have my foils and face-guards at the end of this week. My foils cost three francs each, I don't yet know the price of my face-guards or gloves. We still haven't been to the sea and yet we all want to go and have a bathe, and we shan't for a fortnight. Don't you think the holidays draw near? I think they're only a little while away, but each day seems a century. July will be most tiresome for me, for I'll be obliged to do papers for prizes twice a week, without any hope, not even of an accessit, however there it is, it's to be hoped that next year it won't be like this, for if I don't have any prizes, you can be sure I'll have at least two accessits, and I'll beat Vacher standing on my head in proses and translations. However he'll swamp me in Greek, verses, and arithmetic. Well, well, everyone has his weakness. Today I'm very sad not to be at Corpus Christi day in Morlaix and what upsets me most is thinking that I'll see it only in four or five years' time. I also very much miss the four or five important fairs that will take place without me and another thing that gets me is that, when I've finished school, I'll no longer be the right age to take part in a fair, but that's what I'm least sorry about. But I forget that I have a Greek translation to do, and I was hoping to be able to write you a long letter when this accursed procession came to take up the time during which I'd have been able to think over the pleasure of writing you a letter which could be worth something, but here I can only expect trials and tribulations. However I'm going to write a few lines to Mamma to thank her for her excellent cherries and to ask her to thank my maid for the cake which I thought very good.

qui puisse compter, mais ici je n'ai à attendre que des contrariétés. Je vais cependant écrire quelques lignes à maman pour la remercier de ses excellentes cerises et la charger de remercier ma bonne du gâteau que j'ai trouvé bien bon. Adieu mon cher papa, embrasse bien pour moi Lucie, Edmond, maman, ma bonne, fais mes amitiés à Françoise et embrasse bon-papa pour moi.

Je t'embrasse aussi de tout mon cœur
  ton fils qui t'aime bien

ÉDOUARD.

Ce mercredi soir 4 juillet 1860, 34 jours avant.

Je relis aujourd'hui ma lettre, je ne sais pas pourquoi car je ne le fais jamais, et je remarque que mon style laisse un peu à désirer. Mais je m'en fiche et vous aussi.

Cher papa,

Embêtement sur embêtement! embêtement aux pieds, embêtement à la tête. Primo, fiasco pour la composition des prix en Version Latine. 2° Connaissance et entrevue excessivement fâcheuse avec le nouveau censeur. 3° Victoire décisive de mon pion. 4° Plus d'espoir. Passons à de plus amples détails. Tu sais, la fameuse composition de version Latine sur laquelle je comptais tant. Ce pauvre chouette prix, tout mon espoir, qui aurait embelli la pompe de mon entrée triomphale dans mon Launay, ce prix, la gloire de la famille et de la branche Corbière en particulier, ce prix qui aurait illustré encore notre nom dans 34 jours, eh bien bonsoir, zut le voilà raflé, raflé, raflé net sans espérance, sans compensation. Au moins un accessit, diras-tu, encore moins, pas la queue d'un dernier accessit. Oh! sacrédié, c'est ça qui m'assomme. Enfin je n'avais qu'à bien faire ma composition et j'avais le premier prix, eh bien j'en bâcle une pire que si j'avais eu une peur de tous les diables d'avoir une bonne et décisive place. Ah! mon Dieu! comme je n'ai pas de chance. Quatre contresens dont une phrase oubliée, c'est toujours ce qui m'arrive. Il est extrêmement rare et presque sans exemple que je n'oublie pas quelque chose. Et enfin cependant j'ai du plomb dans la tête, et j'ai

Good-bye dear Papa, give my love to Lucy, Edmund, Mamma, my maid, remember me kindly to Frances and love to Grandpa.
With love from
    your son who loves you very much

EDWARD.

This Wednesday evening July 4th, 1860, 34 days before.*

I re-read my letter today, I don't know why because I never do this, and I note that my style leaves something to be desired. But I couldn't care less and nor could you.

Dear Papa,

One nuisance after another! from top to tail. Primo, a fiasco in the paper for prizes in Latin Translation. 2nd Acquaintance and excessively troublesome interview with the new head usher. 3rd My usher's decisive victory. 4th Good-bye to hope. Let's fill in with some detail. You know, this famous paper of Latin translation on which I was counting so much. This nice little prize, all my hopes, which would have embellished the ceremony of my triumphal entry into my Launay, this prize, the glory of the family and of the Corbière branch in particular, this prize which would have again given lustre to our name in 34 days, ah well good-night, dash it! there it was carried off, carried off outright without hope, without compensation. At least an accessit, you'll say, not even that, not the tail of a last accessit. Oh! damn, that's what stuns me. I only had to do my paper well and I had first prize, well I made a worse mess of it than if I'd been afraid of all the devils in having a good and decisive place. Ah! God! how I'm unlucky. Four mistranslations with one sentence forgotten, that always happens to me. It's extremely rare and almost without precedent for me not to forget something. And in fact however I'm not scatter-brained, and besides I've improved a

* This letter was first published, incomplete, by H. Matarasso, 'Lettres à son père', *Les Lettres nouvelles*, 19 (September 1954), pp. 432–4.

de plus beaucoup gagné pour l'ordre. Je suis rerentré aujourd'hui même en possession de mon couteau de ma bonnic, et voilà au moins un mois et quelques jours que je l'ai sans l'avoir perdu une seule fois. J'ai toutes mes affaires un peu chiquement arrangées dans ma boîte, va. Mais passons à un autre exercice. J'ai eu une entrevue avec le censeur neuf, entrevue que je me soucie fort peu de renouveler car je tiens un peu plus que pas du tout à mes sorties. L'autre jour, tu sais que le proviseur m'avait flanqué un espèce de suif pour avoir rêvé trop fort au dortoir et pour avoir surtout remercié mon pion de l'épigramme assez gauche qu'il m'avait adressée. Eh bien, cet animal de censeur me fait appeler dans son cabinet et me dit tout simplement : Monsieur Corbière, vous avez remercié ironiquement votre maître d'étude d'une observation piquante à ce que vous prétendez. M. le Proviseur n'a pas jugé à propos de vous punir, mais moi je vous donne une privation de sortie pour commencer – et je suis sorti très peu satisfait de nos premières relations. C'était le 3ᵉ jour qu'il était ici, et on a trouvé très mauvais de le voir de si bonne heure commencer à punir. C'est un petit monsieur excessivement raide, très plat, tout content de lui et on ne peut plus absolu. Cristi, heureusement que je n'ai plus qu'un mois. Nous étions avant menés assez rudement par le rigide prédécesseur de ce petit individu, mais celui-ci va nous faire aller tambour battant, fichtre ! des privations de sortie à peine arrivé. Que sera-ce donc dans quelque temps ? Nous disions donc : 3° Victoire totale du pion (redevenu féroce) oui, car le proviseur m'a fait promettre sous peine d'un bulletin abominable d'être à l'égard du susdit pion d'une politesse plus que raffinée. J'ai même cru comprendre que, dans certaines occasions, il faudrait me mettre à quatre pattes pour lui parler. Tout ce qu'il y a de sûr, c'est que je vais être bien poli, car puisque je ne suis pas encore allé au cachot, je ne vois pas la nécessité d'y monter à la fin. Quoique ce soit le Baptême du Lycéen et quand on n'a pas passé par là on n'est pas *digne de porter l'uniforme*. Seulement, je fais exception à la règle et je porte honorablement le mien, parce que c'est moi, parce que je m'appelle Édouard Corbière. *Quatrièmement* plus d'espoir de lauriers à la distribution si ce n'est le Concours Général, et le Thème Latin, mais n'en parlons pas car ça me fait penser au prix de Version raté et ça me fait un effet ! . . .

Une petite consolation. Hier soir nous avons été à la baignade, l'eau était excellente, et à peine arrivé je me suis fichu dedans, il fallait voir, j'étais le plus crâne. Et puis j'avais parié deux biscuits

lot in tidiness. Today I was even in possession of my maid's knife, and there that's at least a month and a few days that I've had it without having lost it once. I've got all my things arranged quite smartly in my box, so there. But let's go on to another exercise. I've had an interview with the new head usher, an interview that I worry very little about repeating since going out means more than a little to me. The other day, you know the head master gave me a good talking-to for having dreamed too profoundly in the dormitory and especially for having thanked my usher for the rather uncouth epigram which he'd addressed to me. Well, this animal of a head usher called me to his study and said quite simply: 'Mr Corbière, according to what you maintain, you have ironically thanked the supervisor of your studies for a keen remark. The head master has not thought it proper to punish you, but I'm giving you a gating to begin with,' and I went out not at all pleased with our first exchanges. It was his 3rd day here, and we considered it very bad to see him begin meting out punishment so early on. He's a little man excessively stiff, very dull, very self-satisfied and it's not possible to be more arbitrary. The devil, it's fortunate that I have no more than a month. We were managed roughly enough before by the fellow's strict predecessor, but this one is going to drive us beating a drum, the deuce! gatings when he's hardly arrived. So what will it be like later on? We were talking thus: 3rd Total victory of the usher (turned fierce again) yes, because the head master made me promise under pain of an abominable report to behave with regard to the aforesaid usher with a courtesy more than refined. I even believed I understood that, on certain occasions, I should go on all fours to speak to him. The only thing certain is that I'm going to be very polite, for since I haven't yet gone to the cell, I don't see the necessity of going up at the end. Although this is the Schoolboy's Baptism and when you haven't gone through there you're not *worthy to wear the uniform*. Only, I'm an exception to the rule and I honourably wear mine, because I'm me, because I'm called Edward Corbière. *Fourthly* no hope of laurels at prize-giving unless in the General Competition, and the Latin Prose, but don't let's talk about that because that makes me think of the prize for Translation I missed and that has an effect on me! . . .

A small consolation. Yesterday evening we went to the bathing-place, the water was excellent, and I'd hardly got there when in I plunged, it needed seeing, I was the boldest. And then I'd bet two

de mer que j'irais plus loin que le guidon des grands. C'est à peu près long comme le jardin du Launay, de la maison à la tonnelle neuve où je fais mon feu d'artifice. Eh bien j'ai été, seulement il m'a fallu du temps, et en arrivant j'étais esquinté, j'avais à peine la force de me tenir au manche du drapeau qui était piqué dans la mer et joliment au large. Après être resté me reposer quelque temps, je suis revenu à terre. Mais à peu près à moitié chemin, je me croyais presque à terre et j'étais sûr d'avoir pied, quand en voulant me défatiguer (car j'en avais assez) je fais un plongeon un peu chouette, il y avait encore à peu près trois fois ma hauteur d'eau, mais je suis très bien remonté et même je n'ai pas été jusqu'au fond. J'en ai été quitte pour boire un bon coup d'eau salée—dis ça à maman, elle va être contente. Mais je suis très content de moi, je ne croyais pas savoir si bien nager, et ça de suite en me mettant à l'eau comme si je n'avais fait que ça pendant un an, et voilà 11 mois que je n'avais pas nagé. Tu verras comme je vais bien maintenant, j'irai comme toi, aussi loin à condition que tu me remorques quand je serai fatigué. Le beau temps continue et les courses vont être belles. [. . .]

À propos, sacristi, j'avais oublié de vous dire que ma place de premier (le dernier papier qui n'est pas encore déchiré) va me servir pour m'exempter de la privation de sortie du nouveau censeur, de sorte que je m'en fiche. Après demain nous composons un Thème grec mais je n'ai pas de prétentions, cependant je ferai mon possible, car je ne suis pas fait comme les autres, quelquefois je suis presque dernier en quelque chose et quelquefois premier pour la même chose. En vers latins par exemple.

Mais il est temps que je finisse car les deux pages et demie sont remplies et puis j'ai mes devoirs à faire. J'aurais dû ne vous écrire que quand vous m'auriez écrit en m'envoyant un timbre-poste ou deux, mais je vais tacher d'en emprunter.

Adieu mon bon papa, je t'embrasse bien tendrement.

Ton Édouard qui t'aime de tout son cœur.

Tristan CORBIÈRE.

ship's biscuits I'd go further than the seniors' flag. It's about as long as the garden at Launay, from the house to the new bower where I make my fireworks. Well I did, only it took me some time, and when I got there I was tired out, I scarcely had the strength to hold on fast to the flag-staff which was pitched in the sea and nicely in the offing. After staying there to rest for a time, I returned to land. But about half-way there, almost on land as I thought and sure of being in my depth, when, wanting to refresh myself (because I'd had enough), I made a rather nice dive, there was still about three times my height of water, but I came up very well and I hadn't been to the bottom even. I was well out of it with a good drink of salt water—tell Mamma that, she'll be pleased. But I'm very pleased with myself, I didn't think I knew how to swim so well, and that after going into the water as if I'd done nothing but that for a year, and in fact for eleven months I hadn't been swimming. You'll see how well I swim now, I'll go as far as you, on condition that you tow me when I'm tired. The fine weather continues and the sailing will be good. [. . .]

By the way, good God, I'd forgotten to tell you that my first place (this last paper which hasn't been torn up yet) will serve to exempt me from the new head usher's gating, so that I couldn't care less about that. The day after tomorrow we're to write a Greek Prose but I don't have any expectations, however I'll do my best, for I'm not made like the others, sometimes I'm almost last in something and sometimes first for the same subject. In Latin verse for example.

But it's time for me to finish for two and a half pages are filled and besides I have my preparation to do. I ought to have written to you only after you'd written sending me a stamp or two, but I'll try and borrow some.

Good-bye dearest father, with much love from
    your Edward who loves you with all his heart.
                                         Tristan CORBIÈRE.